Bloodshed
of Eagles

Bloodshed of Eagles

William W. Johnstone
with J. A. Johnstone

PINNACLE BOOKS
Kensington Publishing Corp.
www.kensingtonbooks.com

PINNACLE BOOKS are published by

Kensington Publishing Corp.
119 West 40th Street
New York, NY 10018

PUBLISHER'S NOTE
Following the death of William Johnstone, the Johnstone family is working with a carefully selected writer to organize and complete Mr. Johnstone's outlines and many unfinished manuscripts to create additional novels in all of his series like The Last Gunfighter, Mountain Man, and Eagles, among others. This novel was inspired by Mr. Johnstone's superb storytelling.

All Kensington titles, imprints, and distributed lines are available at special quantity discounts for bulk purchases for sales promotions, premiums, fund-raising, educational, or institutional use. Special book excerpts or customized printings can also be created to fit specific needs. For details, write or phone the office of the Kensington special sales manager: Kensington Publishing Corp., 119 West 40th Street, New York, NY 10018, attn: Special Sales Department; phone: 1-800-221-2647.

PINNACLE BOOKS and the Pinnacle logo are Reg. U.S. Pat. & TM Off.

ISBN-13: 978-0-7860-2006-5
ISBN-10: 0-7860-2006-7

First Printing: August 2009

10 9 8 7 6 5 4 3 2 1

Printed in the United States of America

"If there are no dogs in Heaven,
then when I die I want to go
where they went."

—WILL ROGERS, 1897–1935

In Memory of Charley

Chapter One

June 25, 1927
MacCallister, Colorado

Falcon MacCallister had met Zane Grey two years earlier when the author attended a banquet given by the Governor honoring Falcon as *"A true treasure of the state of Colorado; a man whose exploits and heroic deeds will echo down through the corridors of time."*

At that banquet, Zane Grey asked Falcon if he could interview him, to write a story about him. As nicely as he could, Falcon said no. He could still remember the many awful "dime novels" that had been written about him and other notables back in the days when Falcon was most active. All were highly exaggerated tales of derring-do, and the truth was, had any of the pulp writers of the day stopped to do some research, they would have discovered that Falcon's actual exploits exceeded anything the writers ever portrayed.

It was because of those books that Falcon had turned Zane Grey down. Later, however, as Falcon read some of

Zane Grey's books, he realized that the author was not of the "penny dreadful" ilk. On the contrary, Zane Grey's books rang true with a respect for people and Western life, as well as wonderful descriptions of the beauty of the country. Falcon became an immediate fan of his writing, and that was why, when the author contacted Falcon by telephone three days ago requesting permission to call on him, Falcon agreed.

"Big Grandpa, do you really know Zane Grey?" Falcon's great-granddaughter asked. The young girl was actually named Rosanna, after her great-great-aunt, but everyone called her Rosie. "He's very famous. He's a writer like Ernest Hemingway and F. Scott Fitzgerald."

Falcon looked over at the young girl who had been named after his sister.

"Zane Grey is fine, but aren't you a little young to be reading Hemingway and Fitzgerald?"

"I'm sixteen," the girl insisted. "That's not too young."

Falcon thought back to his own youth, and how many sixteen-year-olds he had known who were on their own, some of whom had fought in the Civil War at that age.

"I guess it's not too young at that, darlin'," Falcon said.

Rosie stepped up to the window and looked outside. "Oh, here comes a car. I'll bet that's him!" she said excitedly.

Falcon walked out onto the front porch of his Colorado home, then stood there as the big green Packard sedan glided in stately fashion around the curved brick driveway. Zane Grey stepped out of the car and smiled up at Falcon.

"Mr. MacCallister, thank you for agreeing to see me," the author said.

"It is my pleasure, Mr. Grey. My first impression of you

was wrong," Falcon replied. "I've read some of your books, and I have enjoyed them very much."

"Well, I thank you," Grey said. "All of my Western heroes are fictional, but praise coming from an authentic Western hero like you is flattering indeed."

"Would you like some coffee? It used to be that when a man visited your camp, you'd offer him coffee from the pot hanging over your fire. There is nothing better than coffee brewed over an open fire, but I'm afraid you are going to have to deal with coffee brewed in an electric pot."

"The price of modern living," Zane Grey replied. He looked back toward the car. "I have someone with me. It's an old friend of yours."

"By all means, invite him in as well," Falcon said.

"It isn't a him, it's a her."

Falcon looked surprised. "And you say she is an old friend of mine?"

"Come, we'll help her out of the car," Zane Grey said.

Falcon followed the author back to the car, then stood to one side as Grey opened the door and stuck his hand in to help his passenger exit.

The small, gray-haired woman stepped out of the car, adjusted her hat, and looked at Falcon.

"Hello, Colonel MacCallister," she said. "It has been a very long time."

"Libbie Custer," Falcon said, gasping in surprise.

"Big Grandpa, I baked some cookies this morning as soon as I learned that Mr. Grey was coming," Rosie said after they all moved inside. "Would you like me to serve them?"

"Mr. Grey, Mrs. Custer, this is my great-granddaughter, Rosanna," Falcon said.

"What a lovely thing you are," Libbie said.

"Thank you," Rosie said, blushing at the compliment.

"Rosanna, is it?"

"Yes, ma'am. Well, that's my real name, but everyone calls me Rosie . . . I'm named after my great-great-aunt. She was a famous actress," Rosanna said.

"Oh, indeed she was," Libbie said. "Autie and I saw her and her brother on stage in New York. And they even came to Ft. Lincoln to perform for us there . . . You look just like her, by the way."

Rosie frowned. "She is very old."

Libbie laughed. "I mean you look just like her when she was very young and very beautiful."

"Oh," Rosie said.

"Some cookies would be nice, darlin'," Falcon said.

"All right Big Grandpa, I'll go get them," Rosie said, starting back to the kitchen.

Falcon, Zane Grey, and Libbie Custer were sitting in the parlor. This was the same house that Falcon's father, Jamie, had lived in—it was the same house where his mother had died, shot down on the front porch. And the room that Falcon was using as a parlor had been used for the same purpose when his parents lived here.

There were some major changes, of course. Instead of candles and kerosene lanterns, the parlor, indeed the entire house, was now illuminated by electricity. Some of the furnishings were the same—a rocking chair and a couple of armchairs, for example. The rug on the hardwood floor was the same also, but the sofa was new, and the record player and radio were also new. A telephone hung on the wall near the door.

"Falcon, Mrs. Custer told me something that I had never heard before," Zane Grey said. "She told me that you were with her husband when he was killed."

"I wasn't with him at the exact time he was killed," Falcon said. "I was with Benteen and Reno when the general was killed."

"Falcon, anyone who had anything at all to do with that last scout has written a book or an article about their experiences—some have done quite well and made a good deal of money out of it. Why haven't I heard this about you before?"

"Because my being there was an accident of sorts," Falcon said. "A lot of good men gave their last full measure of devotion on that day. I've never felt it was right to detract from their honor by interjecting myself."

"And I have respected you for that," Libbie said.

"As you know, it has been fifty-one years today since that terrible event. I wonder, Falcon, would you share the story with me now?" Grey asked.

"So you can write a book about it?" Falcon replied.

"I would love to write about it," Grey said.

Falcon shook his head. "In that case, no. I won't share my story with you."

Zane Grey sighed, then picked up his coffee cup and took a swallow. At that moment, Rosie came back into the room carrying a tray of cookies. She offered them to Libbie first.

"Oh, thank you," Libbie said, smiling at the young girl "Oh, these look simply heavenly. And you baked them yourself?"

"Yes, ma'am."

"You are not only a beautiful young lady, you are also very clever," Libbie said.

Rosie served Grey and her great-grandfather as well; then she withdrew from the room. Zane Grey had not spoken since Falcon told him he would not share his story.

"All right," Grey said. "I will make a deal with you."

"What kind of deal?"

"If you tell me your story, I won't write it."

Falcon chuckled. "Well, if you don't write it, what good will it do for you to hear the story?"

"I am more than a writer, Falcon. I am also a hunter, fisherman, explorer, and even an archaeologist of sorts." Zane Grey laughed. "As well as a dentist and one-time baseball player, though at neither of them did I enjoy much success. But mostly, I am a man with a consuming curiosity. And it is that curiosity that has allowed me to realize what accomplishments I have achieved. So I am appealing to you to please satisfy that curiosity for me. Tell me the story. I swear to you, I will not write it."

Falcon looked over at Libbie.

"It's your call, Mrs. Custer."

Libbie put her cup down. "Falcon," she said. "In the years since my Autie was killed, I have written books and articles, I have lectured, I have granted interviews, and I have answered letters—all designed to tell the truth about what happened. Of late, there have been articles printed which would disparage my husband's good name. You are a man of honor and integrity—anything you might say to add to the story could only help to promote my cause.

"I not only approve of you telling the story, I am asking you to please do so."

"It's been over fifty years," Falcon said. "And I've never

told this story to anyone before. I'm not sure I can do it justice."

"Big Grandpa, I've heard a lot of your stories. You tell wonderful stories," Rosie said. "You can do it justice."

The others laughed at the young girl, who, after having served the cookies, had come back into the room and was now sitting quietly over in the corner.

"There you go, Falcon, validation from an unimpeachable source," Zane Grey said.

"I warn you, it is a long story."

The author laughed. "I'm a novelist, Falcon, I deal in long stories. Please, go ahead."

Falcon finished his coffee, then put the cup down. "The year 1876 was what historians will call an eventful year," he began. "In Philadelphia, they celebrated our country's centennial. Colorado became a state, they invented the telephone, and at a lonely place in Montana, General Custer and two hundred sixty-five brave men were killed.

"But in order to tell my role in all this, I suppose I need to go back six months earlier, and start with an attempted stagecoach robbery."

Chapter Two

Jim Garon was thin, with obsidian eyes and a hawklike nose. He stepped up onto the rise and looked back down the road. The coach was just starting up the long incline and the horses were straining in the harness. He could hear the driver whistling and calling to the team, and he could hear the squeak and rattle of the coach.

"Andy? Poke? You boys ready?" Garon called. "It's comin' up the grade now."

"So what, it'll be five, maybe ten minutes afore it makes it up here," Andy said. Andy Parker came up to stand beside Garon and look back down the hill toward the coach.

"Yeah, well, I want us all to be in position when it gets here," Garon said. "The coach will stop as soon as it reaches the top, in order to give the horses a blow and let the passengers get out and walk around."

"How much money is the stage carryin', do you think?" Poke Waggoner asked, coming up to join the other two.

"Poke, you've asked that question a dozen times," Garon said. "I don't know how much it's carryin'. Let me ask you a question. How much money are you carryin' right now?"

"I ain't got much more'n a dollar," Poke said.

"Well, there you go. I'm pretty sure the coach is carryin' more than a dollar," Garon said.

Andy laughed.

The driver's whistle sounded much louder now, and looking back, Garon was surprised to see how far up the hill the coach had come.

"I thought you said it was goin' to take ten minutes or so," Garon said.

"I figured it would," Andy replied.

"Well, it didn't. So I suggest we get back out of the way now and just wait."

There were six passengers in the coach: a mother and two children, one of which was a babe in arms, the other a rather rambunctious four-year-old; a doctor who was gray-haired and overweight; a lawyer who was impressed with his own importance; and Falcon MacCallister.

Falcon was riding next to the window, and as the stage made a turn on one of the cutbacks, he saw a couple of men at the top of the long rise. He would not have paid that much attention to them, except for the fact that they were obviously trying to stay out of sight.

Falcon opened the door.

"Look here, what are you doing?" the lawyer asked.

"I'm going up top," Falcon replied without any further explanation.

The driver was whistling and calling to his team, and the shotgun guard was rolling a cigarette, so neither of them noticed Falcon as he reached the top of the coach, then came up behind them.

"There are some men up ahead," Falcon said.

Because they didn't know he was there, both were startled and they jumped. The guard spilled all the tobacco from his roll.

"Damn, Falcon don't do that!" the shotgun guard said. "Look at all that terbacky you made me lose."

"Sorry, Ben, I just thought I would warn you," Falcon said.

"What do you mean there are some men up ahead? Arnie Sessions, the driver, asked. "How many? What do they want?

"I saw at least two," Falcon replied. "And since they were trying to stay out of sight, I expect that whatever they want is not good."

"You got 'ny ideas?" Sessions asked.

"Yes. When we make the next cutback, stop and let your passengers out. You'll be out of sight then, so they won't see what we are doing and won't get suspicious. Then, when we get up there, we'll be ready for them."

"Sounds like a good idee," Sessions said. "There's a second scattergun down here at my feet. You want it?"

"No, keep it ready for yourself. I prefer the pistol."

When the coach reached the next cutback, it stopped, and Falcon jumped down, then opened the door.

"Folks, we need you to all get out here," he said.

"What? Why, this is preposterous!" the lawyer said. "Why should we get out?"

"Because there are some men up at the top of this grade, and I have a hunch they aren't there just to wave at us as we go by," Falcon said. "I believe you will be safer if you wait down here."

"You are going to put us out just on some hunch? Well, sir, I shall need more than that before I am put afoot."

"Mr. MacCallister is right," the driver called down. "If there's nothing to it, I'll come back for you. But if them fellas up there have somthin' planned for us, well, I'd feel just a heap better iffen none of you was in the line of fire, so to speak. Especially with the little ones."

"I think the driver is right," the doctor said.

"I think this is unconscionable," the lawyer said. "And if you force us to leave this coach, I guarantee you, the stagecoach company shall hear of it."

"Mr. Gilmore, I know you are an important lawyer and all," Ben Carney said. "But we're doin' this for your own good."

"That's all right, Mr. Carney. Mr. Gilmore can stay in the coach with us, if he wishes," Falcon said to the shot-gun guard. "After all, there may be shooting, and if there is we could well use another gun."

"What do you mean there may be shooting?" Gilmore asked. "What are you talking about? I'm not going to get into any shooting battle," the lawyer said.

"No, I think Mr. MacCallister is right. You can stay in the coach, Mr. Gilmore. The more guns we have, the better our chances will be," Sessions said.

The lawyer climbed out of the stage. "No, now that I think of it, I believe someone should stay here and keep an eye on the woman and children," Gilmore said.

"Good idea," Falcon said.

With all the passengers disembarked, the driver started his team again and the coach resumed its long pull up the grade. Falcon sat on top of the coach just behind Sessions and Carney, but just before the coach reached the top, he touched the driver on the shoulder.

"I'm going to jump down here," he said. "I'll see you at the top."

"Right," Sessions said. "Ben, you do have that thing loaded, don't you?"

"Loaded and ready to go," Carney replied, shifting the shotgun.

The horses strained in their harness as they pulled the coach up the last one hundred yards.

"Andy, Poke, get ready!" Garon called out. "The coach is just about here, no more than another minute or so!"

As the coach reached the top of the grade, the three road agents jumped out with their guns drawn.

"Hold it right there!" Garon called, pointing his pistol at the driver and guard. "Driver, are you carrying an express box?"

"Nothin' here but a mailbag," Sessions replied.

"I don't believe you. If you ain't carryin' a strongbox, why do you have a shotgun guard ridin' with you?"

"It's just somethin' the company makes us do," the driver said. "But there ain't no strongbox, and if you don't believe it, you can climb up here and see for yourself," the driver replied.

"All right, throw the mailbag down. And you folks inside the coach, come out!" Garon shouted. "I want all the passengers outside now. Come on, let's see what you have."

"There ain't no passengers," Sessions said. He had not yet thrown down the mailbag.

"What do you mean, there ain't no passengers? This is

a stagecoach, ain't it? How can you have a stagecoach without havin' any passengers?"

"Drop your guns!" Falcon shouted, suddenly appearing on the road behind Garon, Andy, and Poke.

"What the hell?" Andy shouted. He and Poke whirled around and fired at Falcon. Even as the two bullets fried the air by his ears, Falcon returned fire and both men went down.

"No!" Garon shouted, throwing his pistol down and putting his hands in the air. "No, I give up, I give up! Don't shoot!"

With the gun in his hand still smoking, Falcon kept Garon covered as he moved over to check on the two men he had shot. Both were dead.

"Them was my pards you killed, mister," Garon said, angrily.

"I didn't have much choice in the matter," Falcon replied. "It was either kill them, or let them kill me. And I wasn't ready to let them do that."

"What's your name?" Garon asked.

"The name is MacCallister. Falcon MacCallister."

"Falcon MacCallister. I'm going to remember that name," Garon said. "Yes, sir, I'm going to remember it for a long time."

September 10, 1875
Pagosa Springs, Colorado Territory

"Here you go, Mr. MacCallister, fried ham, fried potatoes, a mess of fried okra, and some pan-fried cornbread," the overweight waitress said as she put the plate in front of Falcon.

"Thank you, Mrs. Conners," Falcon said. "It looks delicious."

"How do you think the trial is going?" Sessions asked. Arnie Sessions, Ben Carney, and Falcon had all testified for the prosecution.

"Hell, there ain't no question about it," Carney said. "We got the son of a bitch dead to rights."

"I learned a long time ago never to second-guess a jury," Falcon said.

"Yeah, and wouldn't you know Gilmore would be defending him," Sessions said.

The trial they were talking about was the trial for Jim Garon. All three had testified this morning, and Falcon was still giving testimony when the court recessed for lunch.

"Well, everyone is entitled to a defense," Falcon said, and he used a piece of the fried cornbread to corral some of the fried okra.

"The trial is resuming!" someone called from the front door of the restaurant.

Falcon, Sessions, and Carney got up from the table, as did several other diners, all of whom had been in the gallery.

Outside, several of the town's citizens were streaming back toward the schoolhouse where the trial was actually being held, the town having no courthouse.

"Hear ye, hear ye, hear ye! This court is now in session, the honorable T.J. Hawkins presiding. All rise."

There was a scrape of chairs across the floor as everyone stood for the arrival of the judge. Judge Hawkins was a large, bald-headed man with a full, sweeping mustache.

He took his seat behind what would normally be the teacher's desk.

"Be seated," he said.

Again, there was a scrape of chairs across the floor as the gallery took its seat.

The judge looked over at the bailiff. "Bailiff, show the jury in if you would, please," he said.

The bailiff stuck his head out the door. "The judge has called the jury back in!" he shouted.

A moment later twelve men "good and true" came back into the classroom to take their seats. Not until they were seated did the judge speak again.

"Mr. Gilmore," the judge said to the defense attorney. "Just before the recess, Mr. MacCallister had testified for the prosecution. Do you now wish to cross-examine?"

"I do, Your Honor," Gilmore said, standing up from the defense table.

"The court calls Falcon MacCallister," the bailiff intoned, and Falcon walked up to the witness chair, which was sitting right next to the teacher's desk, which was being used as the judge's bench.

"Mr. MacCallister, I remind you that you are still under oath," Judge Hawkins said.

"Yes, Your Honor," Falcon replied.

"Mr. MacCallister, before the events we are trying here took place, did you, or did you not, make all of the passengers leave the stage?" Gilmore asked.

"I did."

"And I was one of the passengers who left the stage. Is that right?"

"That is correct."

"Why did you do that?"

"I thought it might be safer for the passengers," Falcon replied.

"Did you? Or did you think it might be better not to have any witnesses to what you were about to do?"

"I thought it would be safer for the passengers," Falcon repeated.

"During your testimony, I believe you said that after you forced everyone to leave the coach, you later left the coach yourself and came up behind the defendant and the two who were with him. Is that right?" Gilmore said.

"That is right."

"You shot two of them, did you not?"

"After they shot at me."

"So you say," Gilmore said sarcastically.

"Objection, Your Honor, the driver and the shotgun guard both testified to the same thing," Joe Kincaid, the prosecutor, said.

"Sustained. Jury will disregard defense attorney's last remark," the judge said.

"Mr. MacCallister, did Mr. Garon shoot at you?"

"No, he did not."

"Did he make any threatening act toward you?"

"He was threatening the driver and—"

"Your Honor, please instruct the witness to answer the questions I ask."

"Witness will respond to specific questions asked," Judge Hawkins ruled.

"Mr. MacCallister, I ask you again. Did Mr. Garon make any threatening move toward you?"

"He did not."

"No further questions, Your Honor."

"Redirect, Mr. Kincaid?" the judge asked.

Without standing, Kincaid asked, "Did Jim Garon make any threatening moves toward the driver or the guard?"

"Yes, he did," Falcon replied.

"And your initial response, even before the two deceased fired at you, was to prevent them from shooting at the driver, the guard, or both?"

"It was."

"Thank you. No further questions, Your Honor."

"The witness may step down."

Gilmore called Garon to the witness stand. Garon was sworn in; then Gilmore approached him.

"Mr. Garon, on the first of this month, did you, Andy Parker, and Poke Waggoner confront the Pagosa Springs coach on the Pagosa Springs road?"

"Yeah, we did," Garon replied.

"Was it your intention to rob the coach?"

"No, we wasn't goin' to rob it."

"What was your intention?"

"We was needin' a ride, that's all."

"But there was gunplay, was there not?"

"Yeah, well, this MacCallister fella come up behind us with his gun drawn, and the next thing you know, he shot and killed Andy and Poke."

"Did Andy and Poke shoot at MacCallister?"

"Yeah, but what I think they done was shoot back at him. Only, not bein' professional gunmen like MacCallister is—"

"Objection, Your Honor, to the defendant referring to Falcon MacCallister as a professional gunfighter," Kincaid called.

"Your Honor, may I respond?" Gilmore said. He returned to the defendant's desk and picked up three paperbound novels. "I hold in my hand the book *Falcon MacCallister at Shoot Out Canyon.* Also, *Falcon MacCallister, Gunfighter for Justice,* and finally, *Falcon MacCallister and the Fast Draw Kid.* All three of these books refer to Falcon MacCallister as a professional gunman."

"They are novels, Your Honor," Kincaid said.

"But they are all about Falcon MacCallister, who is a real person."

"Objection overruled," Judge Hawkins said. "Reference to Mr. MacCallister as a professional gunfighter may stand."

"You may continue with your statement, Mr. Garon."

"I lost my place," Garon said.

"Would the court reporter please read back Mr. Garon's last words?" Gilmore asked.

Clearing his throat, the court reporter began to read. "Mr. Kincaid: 'Did Andy and Poke shoot at MacCallister?'

"Mr. Garon: 'Yeah, but what I think they done was shoot back at him. Only, not being professional gunmen like MacCallister is—'" The reporter looked up. "That is as far as he got before the objection."

"Would you please finish your statement, Mr. Garon?"

"Yeah, I was goin' to say that not being professional gunmen, when they shot back at MacCallister they missed. MacCallister didn't miss, and he killed Mr. Parker an Mr. Waggoner," Garon said.

"Thank you, no further questions."

Despite Kincaid's best efforts, he was unable to break Garon's insistence that he, Parker, and Waggoner had only intended to flag down the coach in order to ask for a ride.

Closing arguments for both attorneys did little more than reiterate the arguments they had already presented.

After that, the jury was dismissed so they could return with a verdict.

Deliberation took less than half an hour, then the jury returned.

"Gentlemen of the jury, have you selected a foreman?" Judge Hawkins asked.

"We have, Your Honor," someone said.

"And who is the foreman?"

"I am, Your Honor."

"And you would be?"

"My name is Harris, Your Honor. Clete Harris."

"Mr. Harris, has the jury reached a verdict?"

"We have, Your Honor."

"Publish the verdict, please."

"Your Honor, on the felony count of attempted robbery, we find the defendant, Jim Garon, not guilty."

"What?" Ben Carney shouted out loud. "There's no way that son of a bitch isn't guilty!"

The shotgun guard wasn't the only one to react in such a way. Several others shouted out in protest as well, including Arnie Sessions.

"This ain't right!" the coach driver said.

Judge Hawkins banged his gavel on the desk, and had to do it over and over, shouting, "Order in the court! Order in the court." It took several calls before order was restored. The judge looked back over at the jury foreman. "I must say, Mr. Harris, I find your verdict astounding."

"There is more, Your Honor," Harris said.

"All right, let me hear what else you have to say.

"We have lowered the charge of attempted robbery to

the misdemeanor count of interfering with the transit of a public stagecoach. And on that charge and specification, we find the defendant guilty."

"Misdemeanor?" Judge Hawkins questioned. "You have taken it upon yourself to lower the charge to a misdemeanor?"

"We were led to understand that if we could not find the defendant guilty on the felony charge, that we could lower the charge to a misdemeanor," Harris said.

"Yes, it is within your authority to do so," Judge Hawkins agreed.

"Very good, Your Honor, because that is exactly what we have done. Since the defendant did not discharge his weapon during the incident, and those who did discharge their weapon are now dead, the jury can find no cause for a felony charge."

"You do realize, don't you, that the maximum punishment I can assess for the misdemeanor charge is one hundred and eighty days?"

"Yes, Your Honor."

Judge Hawkins let out a long audible sigh, then ran his hand across the top of his bald head.

"Very well, Mr. Foreman, you may sit down. Sheriff, if you would, please, bring the defendant before the bench."

The sheriff walked over to the defendant's table and signaled for Garon to stand. He then walked with him to appear before the bench.

"James A. Garon, in all my years on the bench, I have never seen a greater miscarriage of justice than what I have witnessed here on this day. You are obviously guilty of attempted stagecoach robbery and, because two of your fellow perpetrators were killed in the failed attempt, you could also be charged with murder.

"However, a jury of your peers has tried the case, and has found you not guilty of any felony charge. They have found you guilty of the misdemeanor charge of impeding the progress of a public coach, so now it is incumbent upon me to sentence you.

"Normally, for misdemeanors, I would assess a sentence equal to time served, or, I would levy a fine. In your case, however, I intend to give you the maximum penalty the law will allow. To my great disappointment and bitter frustration, I can only sentence you to six months in jail. And that, sir, is exactly what I am going to do.

"I hereby sentence you to be incarcerated in the Colorado Territorial Prison in Cañon City, Colorado Territory, for a period of not less than one hundred and eighty days. Sheriff, put this miserable specimen of humanity in irons and transport his carcass, under maximum guard, to the territorial prison."

"Yes, Your Honor," the sheriff replied.

Judge Hawkins turned to the jurors. "The decision you twelve men made today is beyond comprehension. I cannot reverse it. However, I intend to have your names placed on record, and I shall direct the clerk of this court to strike each and every one of you from the jury pool. You are a disgrace to the system."

Judge Hawkins picked up his gavel and brought it down sharply. "The jury is dismissed, and this court is adjourned."

Chapter Three

When the gates of the territorial prison opened to allow Jim Garon to leave, he was met by Clete Harris. Harris brought an extra horse with him.

"The first thing I want to do is get me a beer," Garon said as he swung into the saddle. "I ain't had me no beer in six months—ever since I come to prison."

"There's a saloon no more than a mile from here," Harris said. "I'll buy you a beer, and we can talk."

Clete Harris paid the bartender of the Double Eagle Saloon for two mugs of beer, then carried the beer over to a table where Jim Garon was sitting.

"You could'a knocked me over with a feather when I looked up and seen that my old pard was foreman of the jury," Garon said as he took his first drink. It wasn't just a swallow; it was several Adam's apple-bobbing gulps that took half the mug before he set it down.

"Ahh," he said, wiping some of the foam away from his

mustache. "You don't know how much you miss somethin' like that till you are in a place where you can't have none of it."

"I thought you might want a beer," Harris said.

"I ain't seen you since when? Since we pulled that job together down in Texas, I reckon. Where you been keepin' yourself?"

"Around," Harris said.

"Yes, sir, well, I tell you what, Harris, that was one lucky break I got having you as the jury foreman," Garon said.

"Luck didn't have nothin' to do with it," Harris replied. "I bribed my way onto the jury, and bribed a couple of the jurors to elect me foreman. Then I talked them all into changin' it from a felony to a misdemeanor."

"Why didn't you just get it dropped altogether? I mean, I still had to serve six months in that hellhole. You got 'ny idea what it's like in that place?"

"You should appreciate that I was able to get the charge knocked down at all. Had you been found guilty as charged, you wouldn't get out this side of twenty years."

"Yeah, well, don't get me wrong, I do appreciate it and all," Garon said, "but it does get me curious as to why you done it."

"What do you mean, you are curious? We are pards, ain't we?" Harris replied.

"Yea, I reckon we are," Garon took another swallow of his beer, and again wiped the foam away from his mustache. "But still, I can't help but ask why did you do it?"

"Do I really need a reason to help out a friend?"

"I guess not. I just wonder why, that's all."

"All right, I'll tell you why I done it. I done it 'cause I have a job for you to do."

"What kind of a job?"

"You might say it's a job as a salesman."

Garon shook his head. "No, sir," he said. "I'm glad you got me off with the jury and all, but there ain't no way in hell I'm goin' to be a drummer, then get all dressed up and go around from town to town sellin' goods, makin' a few pennies on ever'thing you sell. Huh, uh, that ain't for me."

Harris laughed.

"What's so funny?"

"Thinkin' of you all dressed up," Harris said.

"Yeah, well, then, you can see why I ain't all too excited about it."

"Don't get yourself all in a bind over it. That ain't exactly the kind of selling I'm talking about," Harris said. "And it won't be a few pennies, it'll be more like makin' ten to twenty dollars on ever'thing you sell."

"What could you possibly sell that would pay that much money?"

"Rifles," Harris answered.

"Rifles pay that much?"

"Sure they do," Harris said. "If you are willing to go where you need to go to find the right customers"

"And where would these customers be?"

"In Montana."

"Montana?"

Harris lifted his mug and smiled before taking a swallow. "We're going to sell rifles to the Indians," he said. "For twenty dollars apiece."

"Are you crazy? I don't cotton to doin' business with Injuns in the first place, but even if I did, why would we sell them rifles for twenty dollars apiece when they are going to cost us that much or more?"

"I already got the rifles," Harris said. "And they didn't cost me nothin'."

"Really? Where did you get them?"

"Let's just say I have a contact in the Colorado Home Guard. These rifles were supposed to be shipped to the armory in Denver, but a simple rerouting of the shipping order caused them to go to a warehouse in Rapid City, in care of Harris Farm Implements. They're waiting there for me now. All we have to do is pick them up and deliver them to Cut Nose."

"Who is Cut Nose?"

"He is a subchief for the Oglala Sioux. The Sioux are off the reservation now, and they need rifles for hunting and such."

"Hunting? Do you really think they will use them for hunting? If they are off the reservation, you know what they will use those rifles for," Garon said.

"Do you care? As long as we get our money?"

Garon was quiet for a moment; then he shook his head. "No," he said. "As long as we get our money, I don't care."

March 22, 1876
The Governor's Office, Denver, Colorado Territory

Governor John Long Routt stood at the window of his office watching the snow come down. Although it was cold outside, the office of the territorial governor was toasty warm, kept that way by a wood-burning stove that snapped and popped as it pushed heat out into the room.

"Will this accursed winter ever end?" the governor asked.

"I think we'll have an early spring," Falcon said.

"I certainly hope so," the governor responded. He

turned away from the window to study the tall, muscular man who was sitting on the other side of the room on a leather sofa that was against the wall. A rack of deer antlers hung from the wall just above the sofa.

"I hope you are right," the governor said. He came back across the room and sat in a chair across from Falcon. "Now, where were we?"

"I was saying no," Falcon replied.

The governor chuckled. "I'll give you this, Falcon. You are not a man who wastes words. But I wish you would reconsider. I'm offering you a state commission of lieutenant colonel. Why won't you take it?" the governor asked.

"I did my time in the military, Governor," Falcon MacCallister replied. He smiled. "And, seeing as you served as a captain in the Illinois infantry, I suppose that, from your point of view, I was on the wrong side."

The governor waved his hand, dismissing Falcon's response. "That's all ancient history," he said. "We are one country now, and from what I know of you, there is no more loyal or dedicated man in the entire territory."

"I'm not the military type," Falcon replied.

"Falcon, please, just hear me out," Governor Routt said. "You know what Chivington did to the peaceful Cheyenne at Sand Creek, don't you?"

"Yes, I know what happened," Falcon said. "Chivington's men fired rifles, pistols, and cannon loaded with canister. White Antelope held up a white flag, calling out in English that they were peaceful, but it made no difference. Several women took refuge in a cave, and sent out a six-year-old girl with a white flag. She was killed on the spot. Then the women were dragged out of the cave, killed, and scalped. Babies had their brains bashed out against rocks, a pregnant woman was killed, and her unborn baby cut from her womb." Falcon was quiet for a moment.

"That pregnant woman was my sister-in-law, Governor. So, yes, I do know what happened at Sand Creek."

The pregnant woman Falcon spoke of had been the sister of Falcon's wife, Marie Gentle Breeze. Like her sister, Marie was now dead as well, killed, not by white men, but by renegade Cheyenne.

"I have always considered Sand Creek a great tragedy," Governor Routt said. "And now, knowing your connection to it, it is even more so. But that makes it all the more imperative that we have someone of your standing serve in such a position. This year, Colorado will become a state. That is the fulfillment of the dreams and hopes of everyone in Colorado. Our territorial Home Guard will become a state militia, recognized as such by the United States Department of War. I do not want to take a chance on another Chivington. That's why I'm asking you to take command."

"Why don't you ask one of my brothers?" Falcon asked.

Governor Routt chuckled self-consciously. "Well, now you force me to confess that I did ask your brother first."

"Wise choice," Falcon said. "I take it he turned you down."

"He suggested that I ask you."

"He suggested that, did he?"

"Yes. He said he thought you would make a fine commandant, and I agree with him. Falcon, I'm appealing, not to your vanity, but to your honor and sense of duty. It is only until the first of August. On that date, Colorado will be admitted to the union as the thirty-eighth state. Then, if you wish, you can resign. I cannot force you to serve as commandant of the Colorado Home Guard, I can only ask, but that I do, with all sincerity."

Falcon was silent for a moment; then he smiled. "John, has anyone ever suggested that you should be in politics? You can be quite persuasive."

The governor laughed out loud. "You think so? Hmm, maybe I should try it." The governor got serious. "Is that a yes, Falcon?"

Falcon nodded. "It is a yes."

"I thank you, Colonel," the governor said. "In fact, all of Colorado thanks you."

April 7, 1876
On the Big Knife in Dakota Territory

Clete Harris and Jim Garon waited alongside the river. Their horses and five pack mules were tied to low limbs from a cottonwood tree.

Harris was chewing on the end of a twig, and Garon was tossing rocks into the water.

"How long we goin' to wait?" Garon asked.

"As long as it takes," Harris answered.

"Yeah, well, I don't particular want to be out here after it gets dark."

Harris chuckled. "Scared, are you?"

"I ain't scared now—but would be, if we was still out here after dark. And you would be, too, if you had any sense."

"Injuns don't attack at night. Ain't you ever heard that?"

"I've heard it," Garon replied. "I don't know as I'm willin' to put that much faith in it. Especially if it's my hide."

"Yeah, well, don't worry. I don't reckon we're goin' to have to wait much longer."

"How do you know?"

Harris pointed. "They's some dust comin' up out there, and I figure that, more'n likely, it's Cut Nose and his boys, comin' to trade."

At that moment one of the pack mules pulled away from its ground hobble and moved down to the edge of the water.

"Keep an eye on that mule," Harris ordered. "Don't let him go wandering off. He's carryin' twenty rifles, and at twenty dollars apiece, that's four hundred dollars I don't intend to lose."

"That mule ain't goin' nowhere," Garon replied. "He's just thirsty, that's all."

"Yeah, well, go get him and bring him back," Harris said.

Garon walked down to the edge of the river and stood there for a moment until the mule had drunk its fill. Then he led the animal back up to the others, tying him off just as several Indians rode up.

"Well, Cut Nose, you made it, I see," Harris said.

"You have guns?"

Harris chuckled. "You ain't much for the small talk, are you? Yeah, I have guns."

"Let me see guns."

Harris walked over to the pack mule, opened the canvas pouch, pulled out one of the lever-action rifles, and handed it to Cut Nose.

Cut Nose jacked the lever down and back up, then lifted the rifle to his shoulder. He sighted down the barrel and pulled the trigger. The hammer fell on an empty chamber.

"Does gun work?" he asked.

"Hell, yes, it works. Why would you ask that?"

"Some white men have sold guns which do not work.

They take out—" He put his finger down in the chamber to show what he meant.

"Don't worry, the firing pins are still there," Harris said. He handed Cut Nose a single bullet, and the Indian put it in the chamber. Once again, he cocked the rifle, aimed, and pulled the trigger. This time he was rewarded with a loud bang as the weapon fired.

"Hoolah!" he shouted, thrusting the rifle high over head.

"You like?" Harris asked.

"I buy. I buy all you have." He pointed toward the pack mules.

"I have one hundred rifles," Harris said. "At twenty dollars a rifle, that's two thousand dollars. Just like we said."

"I have white man's gold," Cut Nose said. He nodded to one of the other Indians, who handed a cloth bag to Harris. Looking inside, Harris saw several gold double-eagle twenty-dollar pieces. Quickly, he counted one hundred of them.

"All right, Cut Nose, the rifles are yours," Harris said.

The Indians began emptying the packs until they had taken all the rifles.

"Can you get more guns?" Cut Nose asked.

"I don't know, it isn't easy."

"I need many, many guns," Cut Nose said.

One of the other Indians said something, and Cut Nose nodded.

"I want gun that shoots many times," Cut Nose said.

"These are all repeating rifles, every one of them," Harris said. "They all shoot many times."

"No. Big gun, many barrels, shoot very fast, many times." Cut Nose made the motion of turning a crank.

"Damn!" Harris said. "A Gatling gun? Are you talking about a Gatling gun?"

"Yes."

"I don't know, Cut Nose. Something like that is going to be very hard to get. And if I can get it, I would have to charge you a lot of money."

"Many Indians are coming together at the place of Greasy Grass," Cut Nose said. "We have left the place, the reservation, where the white men say we must stay. The long knives do not like that we have left and soon, I think, they will come to tell us we must go back. But we will not go back. When they come, we will fight them. Gun that shoots many times very fast will give us much medicine. I think the Long Knives will not be able to make us go back to the place where they say we must stay."

"Yeah, a Gatling gun will give you a lot of medicine all right," Harris said.

"You get for me?" Cut Nose asked.

"You have more money?"

"We have much money," Cut Nose said.

Smiling, Harris nodded. "Yeah," he said. "I'll get a Gatling gun for you."

April 10, 1876
Ft. Junction, Colorado Territory

"If you don't mind my saying so, Colonel, you cut quite a fine figure in army blue," Major Adrian Brisbane said. Brisbane was Falcon's executive officer.

"The last uniform I wore was gray," Falcon answered.

"Well, I wouldn't worry about it, Colonel. Eventually, everyone sees the error of their ways," Brisbane, who had served in the Union Army, replied with a laugh.

"I don't denounce my service with the Confederacy, Major," Falcon replied. "Nor do I hold any animosity for those who served for the North. My brother wore blue."

"There were good men in blue and gray," Brisbane said. "I just thank God that the madness is over."

Falcon picked up some papers that were on the desk and glanced through them.

"What is this about missing rifles?" Falcon asked. "Do we have weapons missing from our arsenal?"

"Well, if you mean have we had rifles disappear from our armory, the answer is no," Brisbane replied. "But they are missing, in that they were supposedly shipped to us, but have never arrived."

"What have you done to locate them?"

"We've telegraphed messages back to Jefferson Barracks in St. Louis, asking for an accounting of them. According to Jefferson Barracks, the rifles were sent out in early January. We also have a report that they passed through Ft. Leavenworth, but we have not been able to track them beyond that."

There was a knock on the door and when Falcon looked up, he saw the Regimental Sergeant Major.

Falcon had asked Sean O'Leary to act as his sergeant major. O'Leary, who was old enough to be Falcon's father, was one of the first to settle in MacCallister Valley in 1845, having come to America from Ireland to escape the Great Potato Famine.

"Yes, Sergeant Major O'Leary, what is it?" Falcon asked.

"Sure an' the mail just come in, Colonel, m' lad," the sergeant major said. "And there is a letter for you from himself the governor."

"Thanks," Falcon said, taking the proffered envelope. Inside, there were two pages. The first page was from the governor.

Office of Governor
Territory of Colorado

April 5, 1876

Lt. Col. Falcon MacCallister
Colorado Home Guard Cmnd'g

Colonel, enclosed is a letter from Sec'y of War Taft. Please respond accordingly.

John Routt
Governor

Falcon put that letter aside, then looked at the second page.

United States Department of War
Washington, D.C.

March 30, 1875

Governor John Routt

Dear Governor Routt:
In order that the Colorado Home Guard receives due recognition and validation from the Department of War, it is requested that the commanding officer present himself to this office soonest.
Once he reports to me I will, after a short interview and with the constitutional authority

vested in my by my office, enter his commission into
the rolls of U.S. Army officers.

Alphonso Taft
Secretary of War

"Well, it would appear that I am to go Washington," Falcon said after he read the letter.

"Aye, laddie, and it's your train tickets I have in m' office now," O'Leary said. "'I've taken the liberty of sendin' you to New York first so you can be visitin' with your brother and sister. From there you'll be goin' to Washington, D.C., to be meetin' with all the highfalutin muckety-mucks there. Falcon, m' boy, I hope this meets with your approval."

"Sergeant Major, you don't call a lieutenant colonel by his first name. And it's for certain that you don't call him 'laddie,'" Major Brisbane said.

"Aye, Major, 'n 'tis right you are," O'Leary said. "But I've known the colonel here since he was but a wee lad, and by his first name I've called him all these years. Sure 'n 'tis hard for an old man to be for changin' his habits now."

"You are fighting a losing battle, Adrian," Falcon said with a chuckle. Then to O'Leary: "You already have my train tickets? You work fast, Sean."

"Aye, after I read the letter, I saw no need to tarry," O'Leary said.

"You read the letter? It was addressed to me, wasn't it?"

"If I brought you everything that was addressed to you now, lad—uh, 'tis Colonel I'm meanin' to say—sure 'n you'd have no time to do anything but read," O'Leary said, feeling no sense of guilt over having read Falcon's mail.

"Taft is Secretary of War?" Brisbane asked after reading the letter. "What happened to Belknap?"

"He got caught up in some scandal and resigned a couple of weeks ago," Falcon said.

"Beggin' your pardon, Colonel, m' lad, but I've taken the liberty of having your horse saddled," O'Leary said. "Your train leaves from Denver in two days, and you're going to have to get started if you are to make it in time."

"Brisbane, take command," Falcon said.

"Yes, sir," Brisbane replied, saluting Falcon.

Falcon chuckled, then looked over at Sergeant Major O'Leary. "That is, if this old horse thief will allow it."

"Now, Colonel, m' boyo, you've known me for a long, long time. I ask you now, have I ever stolen a horse unless it was an absolutely needful thing for me to do?"

Falcon laughed, then left the headquarters building. He saw a private standing out front, holding the reins to Hell, his horse. Instead of the normal saddle blanket, Hell was now boasting a blue blanket, outlined in gold. An oak leaf denoted Falcon's rank.

"Well now, Hell, aren't you all gussied up?" Falcon said as he approached the horse. The private handed Falcon the reins, then snapped a sharp salute.

Falcon returned the salute, then mounted his horse and started the two-day ride to Denver. As he passed through the gate, both guards brought their rifles up in present arms.

Falcon smiled as he returned the salute. Major Brisbane had been a West Point graduate, and Falcon had to give him credit. Very quickly, his executive officer had taught a bunch of farmers, ranchers, and town clerks how to dress, salute, and stand at attention. Falcon had no idea how effective they would be if actually called upon to fight, but at least they looked like soldiers.

As soon as he cleared the gate, he urged Hell into an easy but ground-eating lope. He would back off after he was out of sight of the fort, but the truth was, Hell could easily maintain this gait for an hour.

April 15, 1876
Denver, Colorado Territory

"Five hundred dollars," Harris said as he slid a brown envelope across the table in the Lucky Strike Saloon. "Your share."

"I take it everything went all right," Potter said. He put his hand on the envelope and drew it over to him, but didn't look inside.

"It went very well," Harris said. "But now I need something else from you."

Potter held out his hand. "I took a big chance on setting up the rifles for you," he said. "Everyone from the governor down is trying to find the damn things. If they ever find out I misdirected the shipment, I'll be dead meat."

"How are they going to find out, as long as you are handling all the inquiries?" Harris asked.

"So far, they haven't caught on."

"If you are smart, nobody will ever catch on. And you can pick up another seven hundred dollars real easy."

"Another seven hundred dollars, you say?"

"Seven hundred dollars, and it'll be the easiest money you ever made," Harris said.

Potter drummed his fingers on the table for a moment before he replied. "What do I have to do?"

"I need a couple of Gatling guns."

"What?" Potter said so loud that several other saloon patrons glanced over in curiosity.

"You want to stand up on the table and make a speech, do you?" Harris asked sarcastically.

"No," Potter said, lowering his voice. "But you just asked for the impossible."

"I ain't askin' you to do it for free," Harris said. "I told you, there's seven hundred dollars in it for you. And all you have to do is locate them for me."

"Well, that ain't goin' to be all that easy to do," Potter said. "We don't have any Gatling guns assigned to us."

"Ain't you in position to order some?"

"Maybe," Potter admitted. "But there's no way I can misdirect the shipment again—not after what happened with the rifles. If we ordered Gatling guns and they never showed up, they'd turn heaven and hell upside down to locate them."

"All you have to do is get the guns shipped to you," Harris said. "Then give me the particulars and I'll take care of the rest."

Potter stroked his chin.

"Seven hundred dollars, you say?"

"Seven hundred dollars," Harris repeated.

Potter nodded. "All right, I'll get it all set up. But that's all I can do. The rest will be up to you."

Harris laughed, then reached across to put his hand on Potter's shoulder.

"Don't worry, cousin," he said. "You just give me the particulars, and I'll take care of everything."

Chapter Four

April 24, 1876
New York

From the *New York Standard*

Amusements

Audiences have delighted in the Edward E. Rice production of Evangeline, performed on the stage of the magnificent Niblo's Garden, located at Broadway and Prince.

Of particular delight to the audience is the skillful manipulation of mechanical devices representing a spouting whale and a dancing cow. Andrew and Rosanna MacCallister call upon their skills as both musical and dramatic performers to make the play the most popular in New York.

Falcon had utilized his time in New York to visit his brother and sister and to attend, as their guest, tonight's performance. He was seated in a private box, looking at the show bill when there was a light knock on the door.

"Yes?" he said.

The door opened and one of the theater ushers stepped inside. "Excuse me, Mr. MacCallister, but your brother asked me to give you this note." He handed a folded piece of paper to Falcon.

Falcon,
  My dear brother, I ask you to please accept as a guest in your box the person of General Custer. The gallant general has been kind enough to invite Rosanna and me to a command performance at Ft. Lincoln. And, as you know, both Rosanna and I will take any opportunity to visit the West.

                              Andrew

After reading the note, Falcon looked up at the usher. "Is General Custer nearby?"

"Yes, sir, he is waiting just outside," the usher said.

"Please, show him in."

Falcon had expected to see Custer in uniform, but Custer was wearing mufti.

"Mr. MacCallister," Custer said, extending his hand. "I thank you, sir, for your hospitality."

"I welcome the company, General," Falcon replied.

As they were now within a minute of the rise of the curtain, the volume of the music increased abruptly—martial, insistent, strident, and loud. It soared above all conversation, seizing attention and making conversation in the audience completely impossible.

The curtain rose, and the audience applauded.

* * *

Both Falcon and Custer were invited backstage after the final curtain. Falcon had been backstage before, so the controlled pandemonium was not new to him—actors and actresses scurrying about, still in costume and greasepaint, props being moved about, sets being struck, musicians putting their instruments away, etc.

Falcon's brother and sister, Andrew and Rosanna, were sitting at dressing tables, looking into the mirrors as they removed their make up. The first time Falcon had ever seen his brother in makeup, to include rouge and lipstick, it had given him a queasy feeling. It was still relatively jarring to him, but he had learned to accept it as a part of their trade.

Falcon was amused at Custer's reaction to it all. He was taking it all in with great enthusiasm.

"I've always thought that, if I were not a soldier, I would be an actor," he said. "We have often done amateur dramatic performances at the forts where I have been posted, and people tell me that I am quite talented."

Andrew laughed. "You are a general. Who is going to tell you any different?"

Falcon laughed as well, and was pleased to see that even Custer found the reply amusing.

"Touché, my friend," Custer said. "I will admit that being the commanding officer does give me a certain advantage."

Andrew removed the last of his makeup, then looked up at Falcon and Custer.

"I have a wonderful place in mind for dinner," he said. "I am going to take you both to the Union Club."

"The Union Club?" Custer replied. "Yes, that is a good

place, but isn't it restricted to men only? If we go there, your lovely sister will not be able to join us."

Rosanna was still removing her makeup. "I can't go anyway," she said. "I have a previous engagement."

The Union Club

The Union Club was not only the oldest private club, it was also the most expensive. But expense meant nothing to Andrew because he and Rosanna commanded very high salaries as a result of their stage appearances.

Falcon watched Andrew interact with the maitre d', the waiter, and the buss boys. His manner was easy and friendly, without being patronizing. Andrew was as at home in New York society as Falcon was in the mountains and deserts of the West.

"I always enjoy coming here," Custer said as they waited for their meal.

"Are you a member, General?" Andrew asked.

Custer laughed. "No, I'm afraid the dues are a bit too high for a poor soldier. Although Phil Sheridan is a member, and I've been here with him a few times. I've been here with Grant as well, but I doubt Grant and I will ever socialize again, especially after my recent appearance before the Clymer Committee. We're going after Belknap and Grant's brother, Orville."

"Belknap has already resigned, hasn't he?" Falcon asked.

"Yes, he resigned to avoid being impeached. But that's not going to save him."

"If you don't mind my asking, what was the subject of your testimony?" Andrew asked. At that moment, their meal was delivered. "Ah, thank you, Charles, it looks very good," Andrew said to the waiter.

"Thank you, sir," the waiter replied.

Custer waited until Charles had withdrawn before he spoke.

"It has to do with the sutler trader positions on the army posts," Custer said. "As you know, the on-post traders have a captive audience with the soldiers, so it can be a very lucrative position. Because of that, they have to be appointed by the government. So what has been happening is this; Belknap and Grant will give the appointment to a middleman. That middleman then sells the appointment to the person who will actually operate the trading posts. Then, the middleman kicks money back to Belknap and Orville Grant. At Ft. Lincoln, for example, I know that the trader pays twelve thousand dollars a year for his position."

"When did you testify?" Falcon asked.

"On the twenty-ninth of March, and again on the fourth of April," Custer replied. "I'll be returning to Ft. Lincoln soon. So, Mr. MacCallister, what brings you to New York? Visiting your brother and sister?"

"That is certainly one of the pleasures of my trip," Falcon said. "But I'm going to Washington to meet with the secretary of war to have my commission as lieutenant colonel confirmed."

"You are coming into the army?" Custer asked, surprised by Falcon's announcement.

"Only in a matter of speaking," Falcon said. "I have agreed to serve as commandant of the Colorado Home Guard until statehood."

"Wonderful," Custer said. "In that case, I shall regard you as a brother officer."

"I would not presume to put myself on par with those who are actually serving today," Falcon said. "The army has opened up the West for settlement, guarded rail and stage lines, conducted campaigns against an enemy who is as amorphous as dust, yet as deadly as a rattlesnake. I have nothing but respect for those who go forty miles a day on beans and hay."

Custer laughed out loud, then applauded. "Bravo, Colonel MacCallister, bravo," he said.

As they left the club that night, Custer took a newspaper clipping from his pocket and handed it to Falcon. "You might want to read this," he said. "At your convenience, of course."

"Thank you," Falcon replied.

In his hotel room that night, Falcon turned up the gas lantern to provide enough light to allow him to read the article Custer had given him. The article told of Custer's appearance before the congressional committee.

Dishonesty at the Highest Levels !

PRESIDENT'S BROTHER INVOLVED.

Committee Hears Testimony from Custer.

WASHINGTON, MARCH 29—General G.A. Custer appeared before Congressman Hiester Clymer's committee this morning. The noted Indian fighter is prepossessing in appearance, has regular features with a well-manicured moustache, reddish blond hair, an intelligent expression, and is rather handsome. He was attired in black coat, light pants, red vest, white ruffled shirt, and black cravat.

The general's testimony was given with composure and gentlemanly bearing, without any hesitation whatever. In this respect he contrasted with great advantage to the previous testimony given in a nervous and halting manner by the accused government officials: Belknap and Orville Grant. In his testimony, Custer charged both Belknap and Grant with corruption. "In the frontier swindling business, they have sold their honor for money," Custer said.

"So, what do you think?" Custer asked Falcon the next morning when he joined Falcon, Andrew, and Rosanna for breakfast at Delmonico's restaurant.

"It's an—interesting—article," Falcon said, not sure how Custer wanted him to reply.

"Yes, well, to tell the truth, I wish I had never gotten involved in this nasty business in the first place," Custer said. "I should be back at Ft. Lincoln, preparing my regiment for the scout we have planned. But I was summoned to Washington to give testimony, and I had no choice. And, since I have been released to return to my regiment, I guess it has all worked out well. The important thing is, Belknap has been forced to resign, and the army can only but benefit from that fact."

"General Custer?" someone said, approaching the table. It was a young boy, wearing a blue cap that read WESTERN UNION.

"Yes?" Custer replied.

"Your hotel said I would find you here, sir. I have a telegram for you," the boy said, holding an envelope out toward Custer.

"Thank you," Custer said, giving the boy a coin and retrieving the telegram.

As he read it, his face registered surprise, then frustration.

"Unbelievable," he said, putting the telegram down. "This is simply unbelievable."

"What is it, General?" Andrew asked.

Sighing, Custer picked up the telegram and read aloud.

"In the matter of the hearing against former Secretary Belknap, the United States Senate hereby summons Lt. Col. Brevet Major General Custer to reappear before the Clymer Committee to give additional testimony. Stop."

He put the telegram back down. "This is Belknap's doing, I know it is," he said. "Possibly it is even the president himself." Custer shook his head. "I can't be bothered with this. I have to get back to my regiment. We are going to take to the field soon."

"What are you going to do?" Rosanna asked.

Custer drummed his fingers on the table. "I'm a soldier, which means I will respond to my orders. I'll leave for Washington tomorrow."

"Why, Falcon, that's when you are going, isn't it?" Rosanna asked.

"Yes, it is."

"Perhaps the two of you can travel together," Andrew said.

"Yes, I'm sure we can," Falcon replied.

Custer looked over at Falcon and smiled. "Well, then, the one bright spot is that we will be able to continue our friendship."

Chapter Five

Washington, D.C.

When Falcon met Custer at the train depot the next morning, both men were in uniform. And although they were the same rank, Custer had taken liberties with his uniform. Under his tunic, Custer was wearing a sailor shirt, with wide collars that protruded over the tunic. He was also wearing a bright red scarf held together at the neck with a turquoise and silver ring. The cuffs were trimmed in gold. He was wearing a white Stetson hat with one side pinned up by a pair of crossed sabers, while the other side was decorated with a long red feather.

"What do you think of it?" Custer asked.

"I beg your pardon?"

"My uniform. I see that you have taken an interest in it. What do you think?"

"I'll say this for it, General. It is about the most"—Falcon paused to come up with the right word—"unique uniform I've ever seen."

Custer laughed. "Yes, unique," he said. "That's exactly the way I want people to perceive it. Unique."

Falcon had noticed, for the last several moments, that a young woman had been standing nearby, unabashedly staring at Custer. Finally, as if screwing up her courage, she approached him.

"Are you General Custer?" she asked.

"Yes, madam, I am he," Custer replied a bit grandiloquently.

"Oh, I knew it!" the woman squealed excitedly. "I told my sister that's who you are. I've read all about you, General. It is so exciting to be able to meet you."

Custer took off his hat, made a sweeping bow, then lifted the lady's hand and kissed it.

"Believe me, madam, anytime I get the opportunity to meet a beautiful woman, the pleasure is all mine."

A uniformed official of the railroad stepped up onto a large box, around which was a fixed array of megaphones.

"Attention, attention! The train for Newark, Philadelphia, Baltimore, and Washington, D.C., now boarding on track number nine!"

"That's us," Custer said. "Come, we'll find a comfortable seat."

The two men walked through the door that read TO TRAINS, and stepped out into the huge, covered train shed. Here, at least fifteen trains were gathered, some arriving, some departing, some backed up to the ends of their respective tracks. The sounds of trains in motion, the heavy rolling of steel on steel, and of engines at rest, from the puff of relief valves to the hiss of boiling water, permeated the shed, combining with the shouts and conversations of passengers and railroad workers to create a cacophony that was only slightly below a roar. Steam that was released from the engines drifted through the shed, forming clouds that gathered under just under the roof. As the railroad industry was in transition between fuels, there was a strong, though not unpleasant, smell of burning wood and coal. Finding track number seven, the two men boarded the cars, located a seat, then waited for the train to depart.

"The hardest thing about fighting Indians is in getting them to stand and fight," Custer said. It was noon, and Falcon and Custer were eating their lunch in the dining car. Custer had been very talkative throughout the trip, his conversation extremely self-centered.

"Now, you take the Washita campaign," Custer said. "There have been some in the press who have criticized me for attacking the village in the predawn darkness, but I knew that if I didn't hit them when they were least expecting it, they would all get away. Those who truly understand the art of warfare, and who understand the nature of the Indians, realize that the campaign was a brilliant one."

Custer was not at all inhibited when it came to talking about himself. He told Falcon stories of his exploits during and since the Civil War; he spoke of his writing, and he mentioned that he had been approached to give a series of lectures during the summer for the princely fee of two hundred dollars per lecture.

"I can't accept the offer, though," he said. "As I mentioned earlier, the Seventh Cavalry will be making an expedition this summer, and I shall be riding at its head. I expect it's going to make news."

Throughout the afternoon, as the train proceeded

through Pennsylvania and Maryland, the conversation turned to politics and the upcoming conventions.

"There are some who think I should run for president," Custer said. "And I confess to having given it some thought, but, I have to tell you, Falcon, over this last few weeks, watching how our government operates in Washington, I don't know if I would really want any part of it. No, sir, a horse under me and a regiment behind me is all that I have ever wanted."

After leaving the train in Washington, the two men ate dinner together. Custer had been invited to be a house guest of Ben Holladay. "I'm sure you know of him," Custer said. "He has built stagecoach and railway lines. He is a fascinating man."

"I have heard of him, yes."

"I would be glad to ask him to extend the invitation for you to stay with him as well. I'm sure he would welcome you."

"Thank you, but I have already wired ahead to the Willard," Falcon said. "I'll be staying there."

"I have stayed at the Willard," Custer said. "It is a fine hotel and you will be very comfortable there."

The two men hailed cabs, one going one way, and the other, the opposite. "I'm sure we'll see each other again while we are here," Custer called back to Falcon as his cab drew away.

Falcon smiled. He hoped it wouldn't be too soon. He believed that Custer had more to talk about than anyone he had met.

According to author Nathaniel Hawthorne, the Capitol, White House, and State Department ranked behind the

Willard Hotel as the center of Washington. It had its beginning in 1847 when Henry and Edwin Willard first set up as innkeepers on the corner of 14th Street and Pennsylvania Avenue. In 1853, the brothers purchased the entire row of adjoining houses, uniting them architecturally in a major remodeling. Presidents Taylor, Fillmore, Pierce, Buchanan, Lincoln, and Grant had stayed at the Willard, and it was Grant who coined the term "lobbyist" because so many representatives of special interest groups would camp out in the lobby of the hotel in order to approach Grant with their petition.

In addition to presidents and statesmen, other famous people had stayed at the hotel, including Charles Dickens, Buffalo Bill Cody, and Falcon's father, James Ian MacCallister.

Falcon read about the history of the hotel on a small brochure that lay on the bedside table. He smiled, as he read the part about his father.

Jamie Ian MacCallister, pioneer, trailblazer, scout, and hero of the Alamo made our hotel home while he was in Washington. Songs, articles, books, and plays have been written about this legendary figure.

Chapter Six

"I'm sorry, Mr. MacCallister, Secretary Taft isn't here at the present time. He is attending the Clymer hearings," Taft's clerk said when Falcon presented himself at Taft's office. "He sends his regards, sir, and says that he will meet with you tomorrow."

"Are the hearings closed?" Falcon asked.

"They are actually, but would you like to attend?"

"I think I would, yes," Falcon replied.

The clerk wrote something on a piece of paper, then handed it to Falcon. "Present this at the door," he said.

Office of the Secretary of War

Please admit Falcon MacCallister to the hearings.

For the Secretary,
Jason Mulgrave

Falcon was admitted to the hearing room without question, and when he took his seat, Custer was already testifying.

"General, I know that after your first appearance, we dismissed you so you could return to your regiment. I appreciate your willingness to appear before this committee a second time," Congressman Hiester Clymer said. "And I'm certain that your testimony will be full and truthful."

"It will be, sir," Custer replied.

"Mr. Chairman, let the record show that Colonel Custer did not return voluntarily, but was summoned to reappear," Republican Congressman William Baker of New York said.

"Is that a significant point?" Clymer asked.

"It is, sir," Baker replied. "You spoke of Custer's willingness to appear as if his appearance was voluntary. Nothing could be further from the truth. As I stated, he had left Washington and had to be brought back by summons."

"Congressman, I left Washington because General Sherman had authorized my release," Custer said. "I would point out to you, sir, that I returned immediately upon being summoned. It isn't as if I had been brought here under arrest."

"Though it would have been within the committee's right to force you to return had it been necessary," Baker insisted. "And I'm quite sure you were aware of that."

"Had it been necessary," Custer repeated. "But it wasn't, was it?"

Clymer banged the hammer on the table. "Gentlemen, gentlemen, please. Let us proceed," he said.

Custer reached for a pitcher of water and poured himself a glass as he waited for the first question.

"General, when we spoke in camera, you shared a vignette with me about an incident that happened at Ft. Lincoln," Clymer said. "I wonder if you could share that with the committee."

"Yes, sir, I would be glad to," Custer replied. "Because the post trader was charging soldiers so much money just for the bare necessities, I and some of the officers of the Seventh pooled our resources and bought goods from suppliers in Bismarck. We could get a soldier's needs for almost half of what the post trader charged, and we sold it to the men at cost. But Secretary Belknap sent direct orders prohibiting us from doing that, saying that members of the military could buy only from the post trader."

"Colonel Custer," Baker said, purposely eschewing the use of his brevet rank. "Isn't this order designed to specifically prohibit civilian merchants from taking advantage of the soldier?"

"Meaning it is better for the post sutler to take advantage of the soldier?" Custer responded.

"Mr. Chairman, I request that you inform the witness that he is to show proper respect to the members of this committee, or face contempt of congress charges," Baker said.

"General, you will be respectful at all times, sir," Clymer instructed Custer.

"I beg your pardon, gentlemen of the committee," Custer said. "I meant no disrespect. It was merely my—admittedly awkward—attempt to explain the situation. I apologize."

"Apology accepted," Clymer replied.

Later, the discussion turned to arms, and Custer complained that while his troops were equipped with old, single shot weapons, the Indians were being sold repeating rifles.

"Are you saying, General, that the United States Army is not being supplied with the finest weapons available?" Democrat Congressman Davis of West Virgina asked.

"That is exactly what I'm saying, Congressman," Custer replied.

"May I ask the colonel what is wrong with the weapons your soldiers are carrying?" Baker asked.

It did not escape Falcon's notice that those congressman who were supporting Belknap addressed Custer by his actual rank, lieutenant colonel, whereas those who were supporting Custer's charges addressed him by his brevet rank, general.

"In comparison to the newest, repeating rifles, Congressman Baker, the shortfalls are almost too numerous to mention," Custer said. "But I will tell you the most egregious fault."

Custer took a shell and a bent nail from his pocket and held them up for all to see. "This, gentlemen, is the biggest problem with the Sharps Carbine."

"I don't understand, Colonel," Baker said. "What are you telling us?"

"This is a forty-five-caliber cartridge," Custer said, holding up the shell. "The shell casing is made of copper. At least half the time, after the weapon is fired, the cartridge swells up in the chamber and the ejector, instead of withdrawing the empty casing, merely cuts through the flange, leaving the casing tightly lodged in the chamber." He held up the bent nail. "That leaves the soldier with no alternative, but to use a bent nail to dig the cartridge out." He pantomimed a demonstration, then put the shell and the nail on the table before him. "In the meantime, the Indian, who is armed with a repeater rifle, can get off four or five more shots."

"And you blame Secretary Belknap for that?" Clymer asked.

"I do indeed, sir," Custer said. Then he added, "And I also blame the president's brother, Orville Grant."

At the mention of President Grant's brother's name, there was such an outcry that Clymer had to gavel the meeting back to order.

Once order was restored, Custer continued his testimony, naming names and pointing out specific incidents of corruption.

May 1, 1876
Willard Hotel

The hearings had been going on for two days now, and so far Custer had been unable to arrange a meeting with Secretary of War Taft. He was beginning to think about chucking the whole thing and just going back to Colorado. What difference did it really make whether he had a government commission or not? If the governor didn't like it, he could appoint someone else in his place.

Buying a newspaper, Falcon settled in a comfortable leather chair in the lobby of the hotel and began reading an account of Custer's appearance. Unlike the article Custer had shown Falcon in New York, this newspaper, which was a supporter of President Grant and his administration, was particularly harsh in its appraisal of Custer's latest appearance before congress.

Custer's Testimony

INUENDO AND VILIFICATION.

Shocks Fellow Officers.

Custer, a well-known self-aggrandizer, has gone to great lengths to disparage his fellow officers by means of innuendo, hearsay, and, some believe, perjury. According to Colonel James Forsyth, an aide to General Sherman, "Not a single officer of the army approves Custer's testimony, which is largely made up of frontier gossip and stories."

"Mr. MacCallister?"

Looking up from the paper, Falcon saw a woman who appeared to be in her late twenties or early thirties. She was blond, wearing a dress of dark blue silk and a white hat trimmed with an ostrich feather that was dyed the same shade of blue as her dress. She was, Falcon observed, an exceptionally pretty woman.

"I'm Falcon MacCallister," Falcon said, standing quickly.

"Mr. MacCallister, my name is Lorena Wood," the young woman said. "I'm from Secretary Taft's office. His carriage is outside, and if you would care to accompany me, I'll take you to him."

"Thank you, I'd be glad to," Falcon said.

When they reached the open carriage, the driver started to climb down to help Lorena into the conveyance, but Falcon held up his hand to stop the driver while offering his own assistance to Miss Wood.

Lorena proved to be a delightful companion, pointing out various landmarks and sites as the carriage rolled through the streets of Washington. She also had a good sense of humor, and a rich, throaty laugh.

"Oh, my," the driver said as he drew the team to a stop.

"What is it, Mr. Bailey?" Lorena asked.

"There are two wagons drawn across the road, miss," the driver said "And I have the uncomfortable feeling that they were put there purposely in order to prevent our passage."

"Can you back out?" Lorena asked.

"I intend to try," Bailey said, hauling back on the reins. The horses began to back up, and the carriage started rolling slowly in reverse. Before they had gone very far, three men suddenly appeared from behind the blockading wagons, and they ran up the street toward the carriage, brandishing knives. One of them cut the reins to the team, and the horses stopped.

"Stay where you are, driver," one of the men said gruffly. "Missy, you and your boyfriend throw down all the money you have. And you better pray that you have enough to satisfy me."

"What if we choose not to throw down our money?" Falcon asked.

"Mr. MacCallister, please," Lorena said. "I don't know what it's like where you are from, but these are evil and desperate men."

"You better listen to the lady, mister," the spokesman said.

"You haven't answered my question," Falcon said. "Suppose I choose not to give you any money. What do you do then?"

"Then we kill you," the robber said as an evil smile spread across his face.

"You mean you will try," Falcon replied.

"Are you crazy, mister? I have a knife in my hand," the robber said.

"And I have a gun in mine," Falcon said, raising his hand and showing the pistol.

"Ha! A dandy like you with a pistol?" the robber said. He laughed. "I doubt you could hit a bull in the ass with a bass fiddle."

Falcon fired three quick shots, taking the earlobes off all three men. The men yelled out in pain, then slapped their hands to their mangled and bloody earlobes.

"I could have done worse," Falcon said. "But I wanted to keep you healthy enough to move those wagons out of the way."

"What makes you think we're going to move those damn wagons for you?" one of the men asked.

"Because if you don't move those 'damn' wagons"—Falcon emphasized the word "damn" to throw it back in the would-be robber's face—"I will use the next shot the to take the rest of your ear off," Falcon said. "And if that doesn't convince you, I will kill you."

Falcon cocked the pistol and pointed it at the spokesman's chest. "And I really don't want to do that, because then that would leave only two of you to do the work. Think about it. Wouldn't it be easier for three of you to do it than it would be for two of you?"

"No, no, we'll move the wagons," the leader of the outlaws said, realizing not only that Falcon meant business, but that he was the one under the gun. "Come on, men, let's get the wagons out of there so these folks can pass."

As the three would-be robbers moved the wagons, the carriage driver spliced the cut line, then climbed back into the seat. Less than three minutes after they had been stopped, they were under way once more, en route to the office of the Secretary of War.

Once they arrived, Lorena asked Falcon to wait for a moment in the anteroom while she went in to see the secretary. A moment later, Secretary Taft himself came to greet him.

"Well, Mr. MacCallister, Lorena just told me what a hero you are."

"Nothing heroic about it, Mr. Secretary," Falcon replied. "A pistol against knives is just common sense."

The secretary laughed out loud. "A pistol against knives is common sense," he said. "Oh, my, that is a good one. Well, do come in, Mr. MacCallister. Or should I say Colonel MacCallister. I can guarantee you, your commission will be approved."

"Thank you," Falcon said.

When Falcon followed Secretary Taft into his office, he saw Lorena standing by the secretary's desk, smiling at him.

"Miss Wood, if you don't mind, would you act as a witness while I administer the oath?" Taft asked.

"I would be happy to," Lorena replied.

"If you would please, Mr. MacCallister, raise your right hand."

MacCallister responded as directed, then repeated the oath after the secretary.

"I, Falcon MacCallister having been appointed a reserve officer in the Army of the United States, in the grade of lieutenant colonel, do solemnly swear that I will support and defend the Constitution of the United States against all enemies, foreign or domestic, that I will bear true faith and allegiance to the same; that I take this obligation freely, without any mental reservations or purpose of evasion; and that I will well and faithfully discharge the duties of the office upon which I am about to enter. So help me God."

"Congratulations, Colonel," Secretary Taft said, extending his hand.

"Thank you," Falcon said.

"May I offer my own congratulations?" Lorena asked, extending her hand as well.

Chapter Seven

As Falcon and Secretary Taft left the secretary's office, Custer was waiting outside.

"General Custer," Taft said, surprised to see him. "Is there something I can do for you?"

"Mr. Secretary, last Friday, when I spoke with General Sherman, he told me that he asked you to write a letter to the managers of the impeachment trial, requesting that I be released so I can return to my command," Custer said.

Taft cleared his throat. "Uh, yes, he did ask me to write such a letter."

"And did you?"

"I was ordered not to," Taft replied. "I was directed to designate another officer to command the Seventh."

"You were *ordered* not to write the letter? Mr. Secretary, correct me if I am wrong, sir, but the only person who can order you on such matters would be the President of the United States," Custer said.

"You are not wrong, Custer," Taft replied.

"I cannot believe that Grant would endanger the entire campaign for political retaliation," Custer said. "This is unconscionable. Where is General Sherman? I must speak with him."

"The general is in New York," Taft said. "Perhaps if you went directly to the president to plead your case, he would reconsider."

"I have been to see the president," Custer replied, fuming. "For three days I have been to see him, and today he kept me cooling my heels in his office for five hours. Finally Colonel Ingalls happened by and interceded with the president for me, but Grant sent word that he would not receive me."

"I'm sorry," Taft said.

"Yes, well, being sorry doesn't get the job done, does it?" Custer sighed audibly. He looked over at Falcon, who had been standing by in silence for the entire time.

"Falcon," he said, as if just now noticing him. "I'm sorry you had to be privy to this."

"No need to apologize," Falcon replied. "I can understand your frustration."

"When are you going back?"

"I leave on the evening train," Falcon said.

"I'm going back as well," Custer said.

"Are you sure you want to do that, Custer?" Taft asked. "If I understand you, you have not yet made a courtesy call on the president."

"Oh, I've called all right," Custer said. "The president didn't receive me, but I called. In the meantime, General Sherman has approved my departure. So unless you, Mr. Secretary, give me a direct order to remain in Washington, I will leave this very evening."

"I will not order you to stay," Taft said. "But I'm sure

you understand that no authorization of mine can override the president's wishes."

"The president has not specifically ordered me to stay," Custer said . . . Custer looked over at Falcon and smiled. "What route will you take back?"

"Chicago, St. Louis, Kansas City, Denver," Falcon said.

"Good, good, we'll be together as far as Chicago," Custer said.

May 4, 1876
Union Station, Chicago

At Chicago, Falcon and Custer were due to go their separate ways, Falcon to St. Louis and Custer to St. Paul. They were standing on the depot platform when an army captain, in uniform, approached.

"General Custer?" the captain said as he saluted.

Custer returned the salute.

"General Sheridan's compliments, sir, and he asks that I give you this telegram."

Custer looked at the telegram. "This is from Sherman to Sheridan," he said.

"Yes, sir. But as it pertains to you, the general asks that you read it," the captain said.

TO GENERAL SHERIDAN
FROM GENERAL SHERMAN

I AM AT THIS MOMENT ADVISED THAT GENERAL CUSTER
LEFT WASHINGTON FOR ST. PAUL AND FORT ABRAHAM
LINCOLN STOP HE WAS NOT JUSTIFIED IN LEAVING
WITHOUT SEEING THE PRESIDENT AND MYSELF STOP
PLEASE INTERCEPT HIM AND AWAIT FURTHER ORDERS

STOP MEANTIME LET THE EXPEDITION PROCEED
WITHOUT HIM STOP

Custer handed the telegram to Falcon. Falcon felt a little self-conscious in reading it, but since Custer had handed to him, he thought he had no choice.

"Am I under arrest, Captain?" Custer asked.

"Arrest?" the captain replied, surprised by the question. "No, sir, you aren't under arrest."

"So, if I told you that I intend to proceed on to St. Paul to plead my case with General Terry, you have no authorization to stop me?"

"No, sir," the captain said.

Custer took the telegram back from Falcon and handed it to the captain. "Then kindly inform General Sheridan that if he wishes to see me, he can contact me at St. Paul."

"Very good, sir," the captain replied, saluting once more.

As the captain walked away, Custer bowed his head and pinched the bridge of his nose. He was quiet for a long moment, and Falcon avoided looking directly at him because he was sure he could see a sheen of tears in his eyes.

Custer blinked several times, then cleared his throat.

"You were there, Falcon," he said, finally finding his voice. "You saw what happened. What did I do wrong? Can you answer that for me?"

"As far as I could determine, you did nothing wrong," Falcon said.

"I wonder if you would testify to that effect at my court-martial," Custer asked. "I mean, if it actually comes to that."

"I don't think it will come to that," Falcon said. "But yes, if it does, I would be glad to testify on your behalf."

"Board!" the conductor called.

"That's my train," Custer said. He stuck his hand out. "We'll meet again, Falcon," he said. "The best thing about meeting new friends is the opportunity to make them old friends."

June 25, 1927
MacCallister, Colorado

The ringing of the telephone interrupted Falcon's story, and he looked toward the instrument.

"I'll get it, Big Grandpa," Rosie said, walking over to pick up the receiver and hold it to her ear. She leaned toward the wall-mounted box so she could speak into the mouthpiece. "Hello?"

Falcon, Libby, and Zane Grey could hear someone talking through the receiver Rosie held to her ear, but none of the words were audible.

"Yes, I'll tell him," Rosie said. "Good-bye." Rosie hung up the phone, then returned to her seat. "That was Mr. Barkett," she said. "He's finished with the repairs to your saddle."

"Good," Falcon said, nodding.

"Getting back to your story, Falcon, what happened next?"

Falcon chuckled. "To be honest, I never did learn what happened between Custer and General Terry. I just know that as I saw him board that train, I had never seen a more forlorn expression in anyone."

"But somehow he got the orders rescinded, didn't he? I mean, he obviously did join his regiment."

"I can fill in a few blanks here," Libbie said. "That is, if you don't mind my intrusion."

"Oh, for heaven's sake, Libbie, it isn't an intrusion,"

Falcon said. "Where you are concerned, it could never be an intrusion."

"I'm not surprised, Falcon, that you saw a sheen of tears in Autie's eyes," Libbie said. "General Terry, as I'm sure you know, was in command of the Dakota Territory, and as such, that included Ft. Lincoln and the Seventh Cavalry. That made him Autie's commander, so it was perfectly proper for Autie to go see him, as to see Sheridan would have been a violation of protocol by going around his direct commander.

"Some years later, Terry told me that Autie reported to him with tears in his eyes. Autie explained to Terry that everyone in Washington who was in any position of authority had given him permission to leave. But the problem was that he had publicly attacked Grant and his administration, and Grant was not going to let him get away with it. Grant ordered Reno to take command of the Seventh. If Grant had his way, all poor Autie could do was remain at the post and watch his regiment leave.

"Autie begged Terry to help him, and Terry didn't hesitate. After all, Terry had never campaigned against the Indians either, nor had any of his subordinate officers. He wanted Autie to make the expedition, fully as much as Autie wanted to go.

"Between them, they came up with an appeal that finally worked. In it, Autie sent a telegram to President Grant in which he said: 'I appeal to you as a soldier to spare me the humiliation of seeing my regiment march to meet the enemy and I not to share its dangers.'

"Terry added that, while he had no intent to question the president's orders, that if reasons did not forbid it, 'Lieu-

tenant Colonel Custer's services would be very valuable
with his regiment.'

"Somehow that simple, heartfelt message worked, and
President Grant relented. Autie was allowed to proceed directly from St. Paul to Ft. Lincoln, there to prepare the
regiment for the march."

Libbie was quiet for a moment, and Zane Grey leaned
forward, then reached across to her. Gently, he took her
hand. "Libbie, have you ever thought what might have
been? If President Grant had not rescinded his orders, it is
entirely possible the general would still be alive today."

Libbie's eyes misted over and she took a handkerchief
from her purse, dabbed at the corner of her eyes, then
nodded.

"I have thought about that, Mr. Grey, many, many times,"
she said. "But knowing Autie as I did, I know he would
rather have ridden into the history books with glory—than
live, only to die, many years later, in ignominy."

There was a moment of silence; then Libbie looked over
at Falcon. "Please, Mr. MacCallister. Go on with your
story," she said.

"I'll be glad to," Falcon said. He took a swallow of his
coffee before he continued.

"After the general and I separated at Chicago, I went directly to Ft. Junction."

May 6, 1876
Ft. Junction, Colorado Territory

"Falcon, m' lad, all the troops have turned out on the
parade ground. They are wantin' to welcome you back and
pay their respects," Sergeant Major O'Leary said when
Falcon returned to the fort.

"Sergeant Major, may I remind you that Colonel Mac-Callister is a genuine colonel now, his commission ratified by the United States War Department," Brisbane pointed out. "You cannot refer to him as 'Falcon, my lad.'"

"Sure 'n I know that, Major," O'Leary said. "'Tis forgetful I am sometimes, bein' as I'm an old man and can't help but think of the Falcon I knew as a boy many years ago." O'Leary looked at Falcon. "Colonel MacCallister, it's beggin' your pardon I am for not showin' the proper respect."

Falcon did not want to alienate a longtime friend with the appearance of being rank-happy, but neither did he want to undermine Major Brisbane, who was a valued officer, so he said nothing about it!

"I believe you mentioned that the troops have formed on the parade ground?" Falcon said instead.

"Aye, that they are, Colonel, m' lad," O'Leary replied. "Uh, that is, Colonel, sir," he corrected.

Smiling, Falcon picked up his hat and put it on his head. "Well, we can't keep them standing in the sun now, can we? What do you say we go outside and meet the troops?"

"Good idea," Brisbane agreed.

Out on the parade ground, the flag of the United States rippled in the breeze. Although the official flag had only thirty-seven stars, this flag had thirty-eight, in anticipation of Colorado's upcoming statehood.

There were five companies of sixty men each in the Colorado Home Guard, and as Falcon approached, Sergeant Major O'Leary called out loudly. "Regiment!"

The first sergeants of each company gave the supplemental commands, the five voices shouting out the word "Company!" as one.

"Attention!" the sergeant major called, which was the command of execution.

As soon at the regiment was formed, the sergeant major reported to Falcon.

"Sir, Colorado Home Regiment all present and accounted for."

"Thank you, Sergeant Major. Officers post!"

At that command, the company commanders moved into position at the head of the individual companies.

"Pass in review!"

The regimental band began playing as the regiment marched by.

"Eyes, right!" the commanding officer of the first company shouted as the company drew even with Falcon. The company commander snapped his head to the right, and brought his saber up, hilt to his chin, the silver blade sparkling in the sun as it stood at a forty-five-degree angle.

The right guide of each rank continued to stare straight ahead, while all the other soldiers in the rank turned their head and eyes to the right. Falcon returned the salute of the company commander, then repeated it as each subsequent company passed in review.

Later, after the parade was concluded and the soldiers dismissed, Falcon and Brisbane returned to the headquarters building.

"I have to hand it to you, Adrian, you have done wonders with these men," Falcon said.

"I thank you, sir."

"I told Governor Routt that I intend to hold this command only until Colorado is admitted as a state. After that, I will resign, and I will strongly recommend that you be my replacement."

"I appreciate the confidence, Colonel."

"I suppose that will mean that you will have to go to Washington to get your commission confirmed."

"No, sir, that won't be necessary," Brisbane said. "I already hold a federal commission."

The post telegrapher came into the headquarters building then and, seeing the two senior officers in discussion, he stood quietly by, unwilling to interrupt them.

"Hello, Mr. Potter," Falcon said, noticing the civilian. "Do you have something for me?"

"Yes, sir, two telegrams," the telegrapher said. "One from Ft. Lincoln, Dakota Territory, and one from Ft. Leavenworth, Kansas."

"Ft. Lincoln? That must be General Custer." Falcon reached out toward the telegrapher. "I'll read that one first."

FT LINCOLN, DAKOTA TERRITORY

SEVENTH CAVALRY

TO COLORADO HOME GUARD

LT COL FALCON MACCALLISTER COMND'G

COLONEL MACCALLISTER STOP I HAVE BEEN

RETURNED TO ACTIVE DUTY, AND NOW TAKE

PLEASURE IN INVITING YOU TO FT. LINCOLN WHERE ON

THE 12 TH, INSTANT, YOUR BROTHER AND SISTER WILL

GIVE A PERFORMANCE FOR THE POST STOP

G.A. CUSTER

LT COL BREVET MAJOR GENERAL COMND'G

"Major, how would you feel about taking over command again for a while?" Falcon asked after he finished reading the telegram.

"I'm at your command, sir," Brisbane replied.

"Good." He held up the telegram. "General Custer has invited me to Ft. Lincoln to view a performance given by my brother and sister."

"Then, by all means, sir, you must go," Brisbane said.

"It's just that I hate leaving you again so soon after having been gone for so long."

"Believe me, Colonel, I don't mind," Brisbane said.

Falcon nodded. "All right, I will go. Mr. Potter, you said there were two telegrams for me?"

"Yes, sir," the civilian telegrapher said. He handed the second telegram over to Falcon.

FT LEAVENWORTH KANSAS
TO COLORADO HOME GUARD
LT COL FALCON MACCALLISTER COMND'G
SIR THIS IS TO INFORM YOU THAT TWO GATLING GUNS
ARE BEING TRANSFERRED TO YOUR REG'T STOP THE
GUNS ARE BEING SHIPPED BY TRAIN FROM FT WALLACE
KANSAS TO DENVER AND WILL ARRIVE THERE ON THE
9TH INSTANT STOP PLEASE ARRANGE TO HAVE
SOMEONE PICK THEM UP AT THAT LOCATION STOP

CAPT OLIVER LARKIN
SUPPLY OFFICER

"Gatling guns," Falcon mumbled. He showed the telegram to Brisbane. "Did you order Gatling guns?"

"No, sir, I did not."

"Now why on earth would they be sending us Gatling guns?"

"I don't know," Brisbane said. "But evidently, someone thinks that we need them."

"What about the repeating rifles?" Falcon asked. "Any more news on the Henry rifles?"

"I've had Mr. Potter, the telegrapher, look into it," Brisbane said. "Apparently, the rifles have been misdirected."

Falcon looked over at Potter. "Misdirected to where?" he asked.

"I haven't been able to find out," Potter said.

"Well, keep trying," Falcon ordered.

"Yes, sir."

"If we are lucky, the same thing will happen with the Gatling guns. I know I sure don't want the damn things," Falcon said.

"Colonel, we can't just leave them at the railroad depot in Denver," Brisbane said. "I mean, we are having enough trouble trying to find out what happened to the rifles."

"No, I guess you are right about that," Falcon said. He stroked his chin for a moment as he studied the telegram. "They are supposed to get to Denver on the ninth, you say?"

"Yes, sir."

"If I'm going to be in Ft. Lincoln on the twelfth, I'll have to leave today."

"I see no reason why you cannot go to Ft. Lincoln as planned," Brisbane said. "I can see to the retrieval of the guns."

"All right, we will send someone to get them. I mean, you are right, we can't just leave them there. But let's keep this very quiet, shall we?" Falcon said. "Let's pick the detail with great care. And I don't want anyone to know about the guns until we actually have them here."

"Very well, sir, I'll lead the detail myself," Brisbane said.

Falcon shook his head. "No, I don't think you should. Seeing someone of your rank making a supply run would be absolutely sure to raise some suspicions. Send Sergeant Major O'Leary."

"With or without escort?"

"We normally send an escort when we pick up supplies, don't we?"

"Yes, sir, we normally send four men. Two in front and two behind the wagon. Perhaps we should double the escort."

"No, I don't want this to look any different," Falcon replied. "One wagon, driven by O'Leary, and four well-chosen escorts. As far as anyone who sees them is concerned, it will be just another routine supply run."

When Graham Potter, the civilian telegrapher, returned to his office, he saw Willie Crawford sitting at the instrument, sending a message.

"Here, what are you doing?" Potter demanded.

"I was just exchanging greetings with an old pard who is a telegrapher in Denver," Crawford said.

"You know telegraphy?"

"Yes, I was a telegrapher during the war," Crawford said.

"Well, you ain't a telegrapher here," Potter said. "So get."

Potter watched as the private hurried out of his office. He was about to send a message, and he didn't want anyone who could read telegraphy hanging around. Locking the door and pulling the shade, Potter sat down to his instrument and began tapping out a message. He did not notice Crawford standing just outside the door, listening to the taps.

May 6, 1876
Copperdale, Colorado Territory

A bald-headed and nearly toothless piano player sat at a stained upright, pounding away on yellowed and cracked keys. The Copper Penny Saloon was filled with customers, and smoke from dozens of cigars, pipes, and roll-your-own cigarettes gathered in a cloud just below the ceiling.

From a table at one side of the room, a soiled dove's squeal was followed by the loud, coarse laughter of half a dozen men.

Clete Harris, Jim Garon, Jay Bryans, and Ken Richland were sitting on the other side of the room. There were a couple of empty chairs at their table.

Two cowboys approached, each carrying a mug of beer.

"'Evenin', gents," one of the cowboys said. He gestured toward the empty chairs with his beer. "It's pretty crowded in here tonight. Do you mind if me an' my pard join you?"

"Find another place, cowboy," Harris said gruffly. "These chairs is taken."

"But there's nobody—"

"I said find another place," Harris repeated, his voice even harsher.

"Come on, Boone, I don't want to be where we ain't wanted," the other cowboy said.

Harris waited until the cowboys were gone before he continued his conversation with the others.

"There's two of 'em," he said. "And they're worth two thousand dollars each."

"How in the world did you come up with two Gatling guns?" Ken Richland asked.

"I haven't come up with them yet," Harris said. "If I already had the guns, wouldn't need you."

"But you know where to get them, right?"

"Yeah, I know."

"All right, but my question still stands. Where did you find out about them?"

"Same way I came up with one hundred rifles," Harris said. "I have a contact with the Colorado Home Guard."

"Where are the guns now?" Bryans asked. "And how do we get them?"

"They'll be goin' by wagon from Denver to Ft. Junction," Harris said.

"With the whole army guardin' 'em, no doubt," Richland said. "I can't hardly see the army shippin' a couple of Gatlin' guns out without havin' a lot of guards."

"Only four guards," Harris said.

"How do you know?"

"How do I know? I know for same reason I know that they are comin', and even when they are comin'." Harris took a telegram from his pocket and showed it to the others. "Like I said, I have a contact with the Colorado Home Guard. This here telegram is from the telegrapher at Ft. Junction."

"How'd you get it?" Bryans asked.

"He sent it to me."

"Do you trust him?"

"Yeah, I trust him. The telegrapher is my cousin, Graham Potter. He's in for a share," Harris said.

"A whole share?" Richland asked.

"A whole share."

"That ain't no way right," Richland said. "I mean, what with us doin' the work and him gettin' a whole share."

"There wouldn't be nothin' to share at all iffen Potter hadn't arranged to get the guns in the first place," Garon said.

"Garon, you go along with this?" Richland asked.

"Yeah," Garon said. "I go along with it."

"All right, if you don't have no trouble with it, then I don't reckon I do either."

"What about you, Bryans? Do you have a problem with Potter gettin' his share?" Harris asked.

Bryans shook his head. "No," he said. "As long as I get my share, I ain't got no problem with that."

"Good."

"What else has your cousin told us that we can use?" Richland asked.

"There's only goin' to be five men with the shipment, the driver, who is an old man, and four guards. They are treatin' this like an ordinary supply run, figurin' if they do that, it won't raise no suspicions."

"Ha. And it would have worked, too, if it hadn't been for your cousin' lettin' us in on it," Garon said.

"When are the guns bein' shipped?" Bryans asked.

"They get to Denver on the ninth," Harris answered.

"You're sure we can get two thousand dollars apiece?" Richland asked.

"Tell him, Garon," Harris said.

"Cut Nose said he wanted the guns. Clete here told him it was goin' to cost him a lot of money. Cut Nose said he had a lot of money."

"Where do the Injuns get the money?"

"Ha. They've robbed army payrolls, they've attacked wagon trains and took ever'thing, they've killed prospectors and express riders and taken ever'thing. And since they don't spend the money among themselves, over the years, the money just builds up," Harris said.

"All right, sounds good to me."

"There is one little detail that I haven't mentioned," Harris said.

"What is that?"

"The Sioux are up in Montana somewhere. We're goin' to have to go up there and find them in order to deliver the guns to them."

"Yeah," Garon added. "And I've been hearin' that the army is plannin' to get after the Injuns this summer."

"That's right," Harris said. "So that means we're goin' to have to find 'em before the army does. Otherwise, there ain't likely to be anyone left to buy the guns."

"Wait a minute," Richland said. "You plan to give them Gatling guns, knowin' the army is goin' after them?"

"Yeah," Harris said. "That's my plan."

"But, if the Indians have Gatling guns, won't that be helpin' Indians kill white men?"

"You got 'ny kin in the army?" Harris asked.

"No, I don't," Richland said.

"Then don't worry about it. Most of the army is dumb Irish or Germans anyhow."

"Yeah, I guess you're right."

"Damn right I'm right," Harris said. Harris picked up his beer mug and held it out toward the others. "Here's to two thousand dollars."

The four men clicked their mugs together, then drank.

"Damn," Bryans said. "I just figured out what I'm goin' to do with my share of the money."

"What's that?"

"I'm goin' to use it to outfit myself. Then I'm goin' into the Black Hills and get me some of that gold they say is just lyin' around up there."

Chapter Eight

May 8, 1876
Omaha, Nebraska

As the riverboat Far West backed away from its mooring at Omaha, the steam cylinders boomed like cannons, the sound echoing back from both sides of the Missouri River. Scores of people were gathered on the docks to watch the steamboat begin its journey upriver to the town of Bismarck, Dakota Territory. Captain Grant Marsh blew the long, two-tone whistle and it, like the sound of the cannon-like steam cylinders, rolled back across the water, as if answered by another boat.

"Good-bye, Omaha!" someone yelled from the deck of the boat. "By the time I come back through here, I'll be rich as Croesus."

"If you have that much money, you can buy us all a drink!" someone yelled back from the riverbank, and those ashore and those on the boat laughed.

The paddle wheel, which was in reverse, stopped, then started again, this time rolling forward. For a moment, it did nothing but churn up the water; then it caught purchase and the boat started moving upstream, searching for the channel. As it did, one of the deckhands went to the bow of the boat and threw over a line, then, pulling it up, called out loudly: "By the mark, eight!"

The *Far West* was a stern-wheeler, shallow-draft, wooden-hull packet boat powered by three boilers. It was 190 feet long, and could carry two hundred tons and thirty cabin passengers. On this day, though, there must have been at least seventy passengers, many of whom were making the journey on the deck of the steamer.

Falcon, who had a cabin, was standing at the stern watching the wheel turn, frothing up the water and leaving a rolling wake for a long way behind the boat.

"The first thing I'm going to get me," one of the passengers on the boat said loudly, "is a three-piece suit with a diamond stickpin on my vest. And I'm going to get me a cane, too, one of them black shiny canes, with a silver head. Then, I'm going to walk right down Fifth Avenue in New York and tell them coppers what used to pinch me all them times when I was hungry and I'd take no more'n an apple, that they can just kiss my rich backside."

The pronouncement was met with loud laughter from all the other passengers. With very few exceptions, the passengers were all men, all loud and boisterous, and nearly all from Eastern cities and towns. When asked, they would say that they were coming West to make their fortune in gold. Most were clinging to their little treasure of camping and or mining equipment, bought from unscrupulous suppliers who were going to make their own fortune from the fortune seekers.

Several had maps as well, the maps purporting to show

them exactly where to go, and giving such details as: *Good water here, adequate firewood here, wild fruit and good fishing here.* Falcon, who had been all through the Dakota territory, had seen a couple of the maps. They were not only wrong, they were incredibly wrong—drawn not from any exact knowledge, but simply extrapolated—with a lot of imagination—from published maps. They put rivers, creeks, and lakes where there were none, and mountain passes where only sheer rock walls stood.

The men would often retire to a part of the boat where they could find some privacy, then sit there and study their maps, learning every detail so they would be well prepared when they started on their quest. Falcon tried to tell one that a "good water" stream that was on his map didn't exist at all, but the passenger didn't believe him.

"I paid good money for this map, mister, from someone who came out here and made his own fortune," the passenger said. "This here map not only tells me where to find water and such. It also tells me which creek beds are filled with gold."

"Whatever you say, friend," Falcon replied, not wanting to argue with him.

When Falcon MacCallister boarded the boat at Omaha, he was curious as to why there were so many Easterners on board. He asked Captain Grant Marsh about it, and Marsh replied, his answer accompanied by a snort that betrayed his derision for the passengers.

"They are gold hunters," he said. "They are going into the Black Hills to get rich."

"What makes them think they can get rich in the Black Hills?" Falcon asked. "What they are most likely to get is to have their scalps lifted. Don't they know the Black Hills belong to the Sioux? In fact, the Black Hills are sacred to the Sioux."

"That doesn't matter a whit to them," Marsh said. "These men all have the gold fever, and nothing is going to stop them."

"Surely, when they get out there, the army will prevent them from going into Indian territory," Falcon said.

"I don't think even the army can stop them," Marsh said. "And, from reading that fool article in the newspaper, I'm not sure Custer even wants to stop them."

"What newspaper article?"

"Lord, Falcon, you must be the only one in the entire country who hasn't read it," Marsh said. "It was published out here first, but was picked up by newspapers all over America. Now everyone from Bangor to New Orleans, and from Chicago to Atlanta, is coming out here to hunt for gold."

"They say there are nuggets out there the size of pecans," a nearby passenger said, overhearing the conversation between Falcon and Captain Marsh. "And you don't even have to dig for it. It's clinging to the roots—you just pull up a clump of grass and fill your pockets with solid gold."

"It's that easy, is it?" Falcon asked.

"Yes, sir, it's that easy. That's why we're here." The passenger stuck out his hand. "Billings is the name. David J. Billings."

"Falcon MacCallister," Falcon replied, taking Billings's hand.

Normally, Falcon MacCallister got a reaction anytime he gave his name. Sometimes it was awe, sometimes it was fear, and sometimes it was instant hostility. That was because Falcon and his entire family were well known throughout the West. Dime novels had been written about Falcon MacCallister and his skill with the six-gun.

But Billings gave no reaction at all.

"You aren't from around here, are you, Mr. Billings?" Falcon asked, noticing the complete lack of recognition.

"No, sir, I'm from Newport News, Virginia. I'm a deep-water sailor, Mr. MacCallister, and I have been for most of my life. I've sailed from New York to London, and from Hong Kong to Christchurch. But that has all changed now. Now, you might say I'm a gold prospector. Yes, sir, when I saw the newspaper article, I saw my chance to come onto the beach. Why, I've been looking for something like this all my life."

"Hey, Billings," one of the other passengers called.

"Yes, Jenkins, what do you want?"

"Come here, would you? Me and Todaro are thinkin' of formin' us up a little team and goin' together. You want to come in with us?"

"Sure, why not?" Billings replied. "There's gold enough for all of us."

Falcon shook his head as Billings walked over to join the other two men.

"Come up to the wheelhouse with me, would you, Falcon?" Captain Marsh asked. "I've got a copy of a newspaper from Bismarck. This isn't the first article they've run, and I don't reckon it'll be the last. But take a look at it, and you'll see what's driving all these—fortune hunters." He set the words "fortune hunters" apart from the rest of the sentence.

Falcon climbed the ladder behind Marsh, then stepped into wheelhouse. There, the pilot, Dave Campbell, stood behind a huge spoked wheel, steering carefully to keep the boat in the deepest channel of the river. The best view of the river was from the wheelhouse, which was the highest point on the boat and located just aft of the two fluted chimneys. From up there, there was a 360-degree panoramic view of the river as well as the wooded banks along either side. Falcon saw three deer come down to the edge of the river. They stood there for a moment looking at the boat as it passed them by. Then, believing the boat to represent no danger to them, they dipped their heads to drink.

"Ah, here it is," Captain Marsh said, pulling a copy of the newspaper from beneath a stack of charts. "Take a look at this, then tell me what you think."

Gold in the Black Hills !

Great attention is being drawn to the Black Hills. Well timbered, and with a goodly supply of water, the Black Hills are known to be rich with gold, with the nuggets, some as large as walnuts, lying freely upon the ground.

A college geology professor, several mineral experts and scientists, along with men who are skilled in the profession of mining, accompanied the expedition. In the beds of these streams, the expedition reported finding gold in copious amounts. Such a source of gold needs no expensive or dangerous mining for extraction, as it can be easily panned or, in many cases, simply picked up as shining nuggets. It is said that a two-hour stroll along one of these streams could produce enough gold to provide the equivalent of a year's income for the average worker.

"Is there any truth to this story about gold in the Black Hills?" Falcon asked when he finished reading the paper.

"It's been two years since Custer's great expedition into

the Black Hills," Marsh said. "No gold has been brought out yet."

"Has the gold rush been this heavy?" Falcon asked, pointing down to the many prospectors on the deck of the boat.

"No," Marsh said. "A few have gone in—some have gotten themselves killed, and I think that is what has kept the gold rush down so far. The gold hunters are afraid of the Indians, and rightly so. But now, word is out that Custer will be going after the Indians this summer, and I reckon all the gold hunters figure this is the best time for them to go, seein' as they figure on Custer keepin' the Indians busy."

May 9, 1876
Along Buckhorn Creek

Clete Harris, Jay Bryans, Jim Garon, and Ken Richland were waiting behind a rock outcropping that pushed down so close to the creek that here the wagon road actually had to run out into the water for a short distance. If someone intended to waylay a wagon, this was the perfect place for it, not only because the rocks provided concealment, but also because at this point the wagon driver would have his hands full negotiating the stream.

Harris was lying on his stomach looking through a pair of binoculars back down the creek. He had seen the dust fifteen minutes ago, but now he could see the wagon as well.

"Do you see the wagon yet, Harris?" Bryans asked.

"Yeah, I see it."

"Is it carrying the Gatling guns?"

"Yeah, it is."

"How do you know for sure? Are they just out in the open?" Garon asked.

"Sergeant Major O'Leary is driving the wagon," Harris said. "I don't think the sergeant major would be driving if the wagon was carryin' nothin' more than nails and such."

"How much longer?" Richland asked.

"As slow as they're comin', I'd say another ten, maybe fifteen minutes."

"Hey, Harris, how much did you say the Injuns would give us for them guns?"

"Two thousand dollars per gun," Harris said.

"Damn," Bryans said. "They's two of them guns, they's four of us, that's a thousand dollars apiece."

"They's five of us, countin' Potter," Richland said. "That's eight hundred apiece."

"No, it ain't," Harris said, coming back down from the rock. He dusted himself off. "That's seven hundred dollars for each of you, and one thousand two hundred for me."

"That ain't fair," Bryans said.

"You knew the deal coming into it," Harris said. "I'm the one that found out about the guns, and I'm the one that went up into the Dakota Territory to meet with Cut Nose. Now if you don't like the deal, you can just pull out now, and the rest of us will divide up your money."

"No, no, I didn't say nothin' about pullin' out."

"Harris is right, Richland," Bryans said. "We did make the deal with him."

"Yeah, I know. I was just commentin' is all."

"Well, keep your comments to yourself," Harris ordered.

"Hey, Harris, they must be gettin' a little closer," Richland said. "I can hear 'em."

"Ever'one be quiet," Harris ordered.

Harris climbed back up onto the rock and looked back toward the wagon. They had made better time than he thought, and were now just over two hundred yards away. He could hear the squeal of the wagon wheels and the squeak of the harness and doubletree. The wagon was being pulled by a team of six mules, and there were four soldiers riding with it, two in the front and two to the rear. Nobody was on the wagon seat with the driver.

Harris jacked a shell into the chamber of his rifle, then nodded to the others, suggesting they do the same. They did so. Then, with rifles cocked and ready, they moved into position.

"Bryans, you go for the soldier front left," Harris said. "Garon, you take the front one on the right. Richland, you have the back soldier on the right, and I'll take the back one on the left. Wait until they get into the water, and wait until they are even with us. Otherwise, me and Richland won't have a shot."

The others nodded, then waited.

As the wagon drew nearer, the four watched as the driver called the team to a halt.

"What the hell is he doin'?" Richland asked. "What did he stop for?"

"I don't know," Garon said.

"Let's go get 'em," Bryans said, standing up.

"Get down, you fool," Harris hissed. "If you give us away now, we never will get the guns. We have to wait until they get here, then take 'em by surprise."

"What if they don't come?"

"They got no choice," Harris replied. "They can't sit

there forever, and when they start up again, this is the way they have to come."

"Sergeant Major O'Leary, what are we sittin' here for?" one of the soldiers asked.

Still holding the reins, O'Leary raised his hand and scratched his nose as he studied the road ahead.

"Look up there," he said. "What do you see?"

"I don't see nothin' in particular," the soldier said. "Fact is, it looks like the road stops there."

"No, laddie, the road don't stop," O'Leary answered. "Sure 'n I've drove this before, and 'tis always a bit of worryin' I do about here. The road goes out into the creek bed for a bit, then comes back, you see."

"How deep does the water get?"

"'Tis only six to eight inches is all. That is, if you stay in close to the bank."

"So, if the road goes on, why have we stopped?" the soldier repeated.

"Think about it," O'Leary replied. "If you was a brigand, wantin' to do mischief by us—now where do you think would be the best place to be?"

"Right here?" the soldier replied.

"Aye, laddie, right here," O'Leary replied.

"Well, what are we goin' to do, Sergeant Major? We can't just sit here all day."

O'Leary raised the reins and snapped them against the back of the mules. "We're goin' through, laddie, we're goin' through," he said.

The wagon started forward.

The two lead soldiers went into the water first, followed by the wagon, then the two trailing soldiers.

"Hey, what's the name of that town?" one of the soldiers asked.

"What town?" another replied.

"You know what town. The one that is just real close to Ft. Junction. What's the name of it?"

"La Porte."

"They got 'ny women there?"

"Yeah, they got women there. Of course they do. They got women in any town. That is, if you've got any money."

The other soldiers laughed.

"You men, quit your blabberin' about women and the like, an' keep your eyes open," O'Leary called out to them.

"We're lookin', Sergeant Major, we're—uhn!" The solder's remark was cut off in mid-sentence by the sound of rifle fire. The bullet caught him in the chest, and he went down.

"Somebody's shootin' at us!" one of the others shouted, but his warning was unnecessary because by then several guns were firing.

Within a few seconds, all four soldiers were in the water.

O'Leary recognized at once what had happened, and he slapped the reins against the back of the team, urging them to break into a gallop.

Harris and the men with him had not expected the driver to react so quickly and, before they realized it, O'Leary was out of the water and on the road, moving as fast has his team could pull him.

Richland fired at the wagon, but missed. Cocking the lever, he raised the rifle for a second shot.

"No!" Harris cried out, knocking the end of the rifle down. "Don't shoot!"

"What do you mean, don't shoot? What did you do that for?" Richland asked.

"Yeah, he's getting away!" Garon shouted.

"We can't take a chance on killin' one of the mules! We're goin' to need them to pull the wagon," Harris said. "He ain't goin' nowhere. Get mounted. Let's get after him."

By the time the four men were mounted, the wagon was at least two hundred yards ahead of them.

"Hyah! Get up here!" Harris shouted, slapping his reins to both sides of the neck of his horse. He was well mounted, and his horse broke ahead of the other three, closing quickly on the wagon.

Harris rode right up alongside the wagon, then, raising his pistol, he shot the driver from less than ten yards away. The driver fell forward, but he didn't fall from the wagon. The mules pulling the wagon continued at a gallop.

Harris rode up to the lead mule of the team, then reached down and grabbed the harness. Pulling back, he yelled for the team to whoa and, after another twenty or thirty yards, the team did come to a stop. They stood there in their harness, breathing hard and blowing, as Harris's three partners rode up.

"You got him," Bryans said. "I thought for sure there he was goin' to get away."

Harris stared at him, but said nothing. Instead, he rode around to the back of the wagon. Lifting the canvas flap, he looked inside and smiled.

"Come get a gander at this, boys," he said. "Two guns, and two cases of ammunition."

"Hey, Harris, what about the ammunition?" Garon asked.

"What about it?"

"I know you agreed to sell the guns to the Injuns for two thousand dollars apiece. Did you say anything about the ammunition?"

Harris smiled. "Damn, Garon, maybe you ain't as dumb as I thought you was. That's a pretty good idea. We'll charge an additional five hundred dollars for a case of bullets."

"That's goin' to be a total of five thousand dollars," Richland said. "Where are Indians going to get five thousand dollars?"

"From the Black Hills," Harris said.

"What do you mean from the Black Hills?"

"Haven't you heard? There's gold in the Black Hills."

"Indians don't use money."

"They don't use money in their own culture," Harris said. "But they ain't dumb. They know that the white folks value gold above everything else, and they know that they can use it to get whatever they want from us."

"I just hope they want Gatling guns," Bryans said.

Harris smiled. "Oh, they do," he said. "Trust me, they do."

Chapter Nine

When the *Far West* landed in Bismarck, the gold hunters streamed off the boat as if in a race to get out into the Black Hills. Many of them hurried to the livery stable to try to buy a horse. The horses were going at a premium price, but even so, they sold out quickly. There were just too many gold hunters, and not enough horses to go around.

Falcon walked down the gangplank, then was surprised to see Custer standing on the dock.

"General Custer," Falcon said. "I didn't expect to see you here."

Custer took in all the passengers with a wave of his hand. "Would you look at those fools?" he said. "What in the world has gotten into them?"

"Gold fever," Falcon replied.

Custer snorted. "Yeah, that stupid article in the *Tribune*. It was picked up by newspapers all over the country."

"I thought you approved of it," Falcon said. "The article

seemed to indicate that your expedition was the genesis of all this."

"Unfortunately, it was," Custer said. "But the reports we brought back were greatly exaggerated by the newspaper and, with each telling around the country, the reports grow. Some, I think, would have you believe you could just pull up a plant and find gold nuggets, like peanuts, clinging to the roots."

"How many have come here?" Falcon asked.

Custer shook his head. "I don't know. Several hundred, I suppose. Maybe even as many as a thousand. They are just lucky that all the Indians have moved west to follow the spring grass. If they were here, I wouldn't give a plug nickel for the life of any of these gold hunters."

"Can't you do something about it?"

"Do what?" Custer asked.

"I don't know. Stop them from going into the Black Hills, I suppose."

"Even if the government would let me do that, which I don't think they would, I couldn't do it because I don't have the manpower. Within a few days, I'll be leading the Seventh on a march to find the Indians who have left the reservation and bring them back.

"Well, I'm on Vic, and I brought Dandy for you to ride back to the post," Custer said, leading Falcon over to a hitching rail where two horses stood. "You should feel honored. Dandy is Libbie's horse and she doesn't let just anyone ride him."

"I am honored," Falcon said. He patted Dandy on the neck. "Dandy's a fine-looking horse."

"Mr. MacCallister, your luggage, sir," a black steward from the boat said.

"Thanks," Falcon replied, giving the steward a half-dollar.

"Godin," Custer called, waving at a soldier in uniform.

"Yes, General?"

"See that Colonel MacCallister's luggage gets to the post. Put it in the visiting officers' room."

"Yes, sir," Godin replied, picking up the leather grip and walking away with it.

"Your brother and sister get here this afternoon," Custer said as he swung into the saddle. "I am going to send Tom back into town to pick them up. Tonight, Libbie is planning a big dinner, and tomorrow your brother and sister will perform for us."

"I am very much looking forward to the visit," Falcon said. "I'm sure it will be very interesting."

When Falcon reached Ft. Lincoln, Custer took him directly to regimental headquarters to introduce him around. There, Falcon met Custer's brothers; Tom, who was a captain, and Boston, who was a civilian attached to the quartermaster. He also met Autie Reed, Custer's nephew, and Lieutenant James "Jimmi" Calhoun, who was married to Custer's sister, Margaret.

"And these officers are the same as family to me," Custer said, introducing Captains Yates, Moylan, Keogh, and Lieutenant Weir.

"And my adjutant, Lieutenant Cooke."

"Colonel, it is a pleasure meeting you," Tom Custer said.

Falcon glanced toward Custer.

"I told them you were a colonel," Custer said.

"But only in the Colorado Home Guard," Falcon replied.

Custer shook his head. "Not true. You were given the reserve commission of lieutenant colonel when you were in Washington, weren't you?"

"I was."

"Then you have earned the right to be addressed as and given the respect of a lieutenant colonel."

"Colonel MacCallister, would you care to go into Bismarck with me this afternoon to meet your brother and sister?" Tom Custer asked.

"Thank you, Captain, I would appreciate that," Falcon said.

"Uh, Tom, see that Colonel MacCallister is provided with a horse," Custer said. "I don't think Libbie intended to let him ride Dandy indefinitely."

"I'll pick out a good one for you, Colonel," Tom said.

"Thank you, I appreciate that."

"Lieutenant Weir will show you to your quarters," Custer said. "I hope you find them adequate."

"I'm sure they will be more than adequate," Falcon replied.

"This way, Colonel MacCallister," Weir said.

As they walked from post headquarters to the officers' quarters, Falcon looked out over the parade ground, where he saw scores of men at drill.

"Recruits," Weir said dismissively. "We are about to launch the largest Indian campaign this nation has ever seen, and we are doing it with a regiment that is more than sixty-percent recruits. All those men you see out there arrived from Jefferson Barracks no more than two weeks ago. Half of them have never even been on a horse, fewer still have ever fired a weapon, and damn few of them have ever even seen an Indian."

"Your other left foot, trooper. Your *other* left foot!" a sergeant was yelling, the frustration obvious in his voice.

"Sergeant, I don't understand. I've only got one left foot," the trooper replied.

"Well, that ain't the one you stepped out on now, is it?"

"No, sir."

"Don't say sir to me, Trooper. You say sir to officers, not to sergeants. I'm not an officer. I *work* for a living."

The other troopers laughed.

"Who gave you greenhorns permission to laugh?" the sergeant yelled, bringing on instant silence.

"Now, let's try it again," the sergeant said.

Falcon smiled and shook his head as he followed Weir across the parade ground toward the long, low building that was the bachelor officers' quarters. Weir took Falcon into the building, then opened the door to one of the rooms. The room had a bed, a trunk, and a table with a kerosene lantern, pitcher, and basin. Falcon's leather grip was already sitting on the trunk.

"This is the room General Terry uses when he visits the post," Weir said.

"It's very nice," Falcon replied. "And I'm flattered."

"Yes, sir, well, General Custer is taken by you and he always does right by his friends. Enjoy your stay, Colonel."

"Thanks," Falcon said as Weir left.

Falcon checked the lantern and saw that the little kerosene tank was filled, and because the room was a little stuffy, he raised the window slightly. After that, he decided to take a walking tour of the post. When he stepped into the sutler's store a few minutes later, he saw a major and a captain playing billiards. The major had dark hair, a mustache, and dark eyes. The captain, who looked to be about ten to fifteen years older, had white hair and very pale blue eyes.

The captain had a cue in his hand and was bent over the table about to shoot, when he looked up and saw Falcon come in.

The captain took his shot, and there was a clack of balls as the cue ball hit its mark. The target ball rolled into the corner pocket with a clump; then the captain straightened up and looked toward Falcon. "I take it you would be Colonel MacCallister?" he asked.

"I'm Falcon MacCallister," Falcon replied, still not comfortable with being a colonel.

"I'm Captain Fred Benteen, this is Major Marcus Reno. Welcome to Ft. Custer."

"Ft. Custer?"

"Oh, wait, that's right. Custer didn't manage to get the name changed when he was in Washington, did he? I guess they are going to continue to call it Lincoln, though I don't know why. Lincoln was nothing but a wartime president, whereas Custer is—Custer."

"Fred, you'd better watch that kind of talk," Reno said. "You never know when you are going to run into someone who has come under his spell."

"You may be right, Marcus," Benteen replied. He continued his scrutiny of Falcon. "Tell me, Colonel. Are you under the spell of our illustrious leader?" he asked.

"I am not under anyone's spell, Captain," Falcon replied pointedly.

"I see," Benteen said. Although he had made his shot and the game was still in progress, Benteen walked over to return his cue to the rack on the wall. "I think I should probably see how the training is going with my troops. I hope I haven't offended you, Colonel, and I hope your stay is a pleasant one."

"No offense taken," Falcon replied.

"Mr. Smith, I'll be seeing you," Benteen said with a wave toward the sutler as he left. The sutler, who was inventorying his stock, waved back. Benteen closed the door behind him.

"This is just a guess, mind you, but I get the impression Captain Benteen doesn't care much for General Custer," Falcon said after Benteen left.

Reno put his own cue back in the wall rack. "You will find that there are two elements on this post," Reno said. "There are those, like Cooke and Keogh, Moylan, Weir, and a few others, who believe that Custer walks on water. And there are those like Benteen who have an intense dislike for him."

"And where are you in that picture, Major?"

"I am not on either side," Reno replied. "I joined the Seventh Cavalry too recently to have an opinion, other than that of an officer deferring to his superior. I hasten to add, by the way, that though Benteen dislikes Custer, and I believe the feeling is mutual, my observation is that they have always behaved toward each other in a proper military manner."

"That's good to hear," Falcon said. "A person can't control how he feels, but he can control how he acts."

"Would you join me for a drink, Colonel?" Reno asked.

"Sure, I'd be glad to," Falcon replied, turning toward the door at the rear of the room.

"Where are you going?"

"Isn't the bar in the other room?"

"We don't need the bar. I have my own bottle," Reno

said, taking a bottle of whiskey from the pocket of his tunic. Pulling the cork, he wiped the mouth of the bottle with the sleeve of his jacket and handed it to Falcon.

Falcon took the bottle, held it out in salute. "Here's to you," he said . . . Then he took a drink.

Reno took the bottle back, then turned it up, taking a long, deep Adams' apple-bobbing drink.

"How long will you be with us, Colonel?" Reno asked as he was recorking the bottle.

"My brother and sister are coming here to perform for the post," Falcon said. "I'll stay for that, then probably see the regiment off when you go out on your expedition."

"It will be my first encounter with Indians, you know," Reno said.

"No, I didn't know."

"I was in the war, I've been in battle." Reno pulled the cork and took another drink. This time, he did not offer any to Falcon. "But that was against sane and civilized men. I've heard what these savages do, how they will torture a prisoner to death just for the fun of it, and how they will mutilate a body." He took another swallow. "Even their women and children do that, they say."

"Is Major Reno in here?" someone called from the door.

"Yes, Trooper, I am here," Reno called back.

"Major, you said you wanted to be told when the first sergeant had the morning report ready for your signature, sir."

"Yes, thank you," Reno said. He put the whiskey bottle back into his pocket. "Colonel, I hope your stay is a pleasant one," he said as he left.

"Thank you, Major."

Chapter Ten

May 11, 1876
Bismarck, Dakota Territory

Tom Custer brought an ambulance into town to meet the train. The ambulance was selected because it was well sprung and offered, by far, the best ride of any vehicle on the post. Tom and Falcon had ridden in with the ambulance, which was being driven by young Boston Custer.

The train depot was a busy place, filled with entrepreneurs who planned to meet, and do business with, the arriving gold hunters as well as disgruntled gold hunters, who had already given up the quest, and were waiting for a train to take them away.

An itinerant preacher was taking advantage of the gathered crowd and was standing on a box over at the corner of the depot platform, preaching a sermon.

"And yea, verily, I say unto you, seek not the gold of the Black Hills, for if you findeth gold, what have you found? You have found Satan's door to the eternal fires of hell's

damnation, for surely with gold, you will spend it on whiskey and sinful women."

"Hell, yeah, Preacher. Why, if the woman ain't sinful, they ain't no need in me a-wastin' my time with her," someone shouted, and his response drew loud laughter from those who were gathered waiting for the train.

"Here comes the train!" somebody shouted, and those who had gathered around the preacher abandoned him and crowded down to the track to watch the train's arrival.

The train rolled into the station with the bell ringing and steam gushing from the cylinders. It stopped with a squeak of steel on steel and a rattle of connectors, then sat in the station with popping, cooling journals and venting steam.

Falcon watched the passengers get off until he saw Andrew and Rosanna. Smiling, he went toward them, and shook hands with his brother and hugged his sister.

"Hello, Colonel MacCallister. We meet again, I see."

Disengaging from the hug, Falcon turned to see a beautiful young woman smiling at him. It was the same woman he had met in Secretary Taft's office.

"Lorena Wood," he said. "What are you doing here?"

"General Custer invited me, and I thought it might make an interesting trip. And you?"

"I came to watch my brother and sister perform," Falcon said. "Have you met them?"

"Yes, we met on the train," Rosanna said. "I must say, brother, you made quite an impression on her. She was singing your praises until we told her that we were your brother and sister, and we knew all your foibles. "

"But you couldn't dissuade me, could you?" Lorena said. "I told them, Colonel, that you and I met in Washington," Lorena said. "I also told them how courageous and gallant you were when you saved my life."

Falcon cleared his throat. "Hardly that," he said. "All I did was run a few miscreants off."

"Well, you were certainly my hero that day," Lorena said flirtatiously.

"My, my, it looks as if this visit may be more interesting than we anticipated, you think so, sis?" Andrew asked.

"You may be right, Andrew," Rosanna replied.

"Shouldn't we get back to the post?" Falcon asked.

"Why, Colonel MacCallister, I do believe this pretty lady has gotten you all discombobulated," Tom Custer teased.

The dining table in Custer's house was extended to its fullest length that night in order to accommodate all the guests. Libbie managed the seating arrangement, putting Tom Custer with Rosanna, and Falcon with Lorena. Margaret was with Jimmi Calhoun, Libbie was with Custer. Custer's brother Boston and nephew Autie Reed, along with Falcon's brother Andrew, completed the party.

Custer, as was his right as host of the dinner, was regaling his guests by quoting from memory one of his articles for *Galaxy* Magazine.

"Stripped of the beautiful romance with which we have been so long willing to envelop the Indian, transferred from the inviting pages of the novelist to the localities where we are compelled to meet with him—in his native village, on the warpath, and when raiding upon our frontier settlements and lines of travel—the Indian forfeits his claim to the appellation of the noble red man. We see him as he is and, so far as all knowledge goes, as he ever has been, a savage in every sense of the word, one whose cruel and ferocious nature far exceeds that of any wild beast of the desert."

"You see nothing at all noble in the Indian?" Falcon asked.

"I do not, sir."

"And yet you have Indian scouts upon whom you not only depend for information, but often for your very life."

"Yes, my dear sir," Custer said, holding up his finger as if proudly making a point. "But even those Indians, the Cree, the Crow, serve not for any noble purpose, but for the money we pay them, and also, to carry on their ancient enmity with the Sioux."

"Uncle, I am just happy you were reinstated to duty," young Autie Reed said.

"Yes, it would have been disastrous for the Seventh had I not been allowed to return in time to lead the regiment on this upcoming expedition," Custer replied immodestly. "General Terry admitted as much to me. Can you imagine? Grant, that fool in the White House, wanted to put Reno in charge of the Seventh. And while I'll admit that Reno fought well enough during the war, he wouldn't have the slightest idea of what to do should the Seventh be attacked. It is a totally different thing when you are fighting Lo."

"Lo?" Lorena asked. She had a confused look on her face. "Who is Lo?"

"The soldiers call the Indian Lo, my dear," Libbie explained. "It comes from Alexander Pope's *Essay on Man*."

Libbie began to quote the poem:

Lo, the poor Indian! whose untutor'd mind
Sees God in clouds, or hears him in the wind;
His soul proud Science never taught to stray

Far as the solar walk or milky way;
Yet simple nature to his hope has giv'n,
Behind the cloud-topped hill, an humbler heav'n.

The others at the table applauded in appreciation.

"Libbie just learned to recite that poem to aggravate me," Custer said, and again they laughed.

"Uncle, you were explaining why Major Reno would not be up to leading the regiment," Autie Reed said.

"Yes," Custer continued. "The Indians, always mounted on fleet ponies, often charge in single file past your camp. They are magnificent riders and they show that in such a demonstration. They pass by in easy carbine range, but the soldiers, being unaccustomed to firing at such rapidly moving targets, are rarely able to shoot them. The Indians, riding singly, or by twos or threes, would, with war whoops and taunts, dash across the plain in a line parallel to that occupied by the soldiers until, finally, they turn and ride away."

Custer paused to take a bite of his bread, and he used the remaining roll as a pointer.

"And here," he said, "is where an inexperienced officer, like Reno, would make a fatal blunder. For the inexperienced officer would pursue the fleeing Indians. The Indians would make a great show of trying to get away, all the while leading the soldiers well away from the main body to where they could be surrounded and destroyed by the aid of overwhelming numbers of Indians, previously concealed in a ravine until the ambush could be put into play."

"General, you tell that story as if you are speaking from experience," Falcon said.

Custer laughed.

"You are right, Colonel," he said. "You are absolutely

right. As a new officer, engaging the Indians for the first time, I did make just such a mistake."

"As long as you don't make such a mistake again," Libbie said, but there was no smile on her face as she spoke the words.

Custer chuckled quietly. Then he reached over and put his hand on Libbie's. "My dear sunshine," he said. "How flattering it is to have you worry about me after all these years."

"I confess to being a little worried," Libbie replied. "This next scout is a little different from the sightseeing expedition you took into the Black Hills. On this one, you are looking for Indians."

"Libbie, don't you worry about Autie," Tom said. "I'll watch out for him."

"And who is going to watch out for you, Uncle Tom?" Autie Reed asked.

"Sonny, I have two of these," Tom said, pointing to the Medals of Honor that were pinned to his tunic. "I assure you, I am quite capable of looking out for myself, my big brother, my little brother"—he looked at Boston—"and especially my little snot-nosed nephew." He looked at Autie Reed.

"I don't need you to look out for me," Autie Reed said, stung by the suggestion. "I can look out for myself."

"Really? Well, nephew, you were sure looking for me when the bullets started flying over your head," Tom teased.

"Bullets were flying over your head?" Lorena asked.

"Yeah, Tom's bullets," young Autie Reed replied.

"You should have seen him," Tom said. "I was hiding behind a rock when he came riding up. I shot a couple of bullets over his head and he turned and ran."

"Which is exactly what he should have done," Libbie said. "After all, he's just a boy."

"I'm old enough, Aunt Libbie. I wouldn't have been so frightened except I wasn't expecting anything there."

"Which should be a good lesson for you," Custer added, holding up his finger. "Always expect the unexpected."

"Believe me, Uncle, it is a lesson I have learned well," Autie Reed said.

As they were just finishing dinner then, Lorena offered to help with the cleanup.

"Oh, don't be silly, dear," Libbie said. "Mary and the servants will take care of everything. Won't you, Mary?"

"Yes, ma'am, we sure will," the maid answered with a broad smile.

At that moment, there was a knock on the front door and one of the servants answered. A moment later, she came back into the dining room.

"It's the singers, sir," she said.

"Oh, good, good," Custer said. He looked at his dinner guests. "Come, the singers are here. I think you will enjoy this."

"Singers?" Lorena asked.

"My dear, every army post goes to great lengths to make sure it has men who can sing," Libbie said. "And I think we are blessed to have the very best here at Ft. Lincoln."

"Come," Custer said. "Let's step out onto the front porch and listen to them."

The dinner party moved out onto the front porch where, standing on the lawn before them, there were three ranks of smartly uniformed men. The sergeant in charge saluted, and Custer, Tom, and, belatedly, Falcon returned the salute.

The sergeant turned to his men, held his hands up for a moment, then brought them down. The men burst into song:

> *I'll take you home again, Kathleen,*
> *Across the ocean wild and wide*
> *To where your heart has ever been*
> *Since you were first my bonnie bride.*
> *The roses all have left your cheek.*
> *I've watched them fade away and die.*
> *Your voice is sad when e'er you speak*
> *And tears bedim your loving eyes.*
> *Oh! I will take you back, Kathleen,*
> *To where your heart will feel no pain*
> *And when the fields are fresh and green*
> *I'll take you to your home again!*

After the singing, those on the porch applauded.

"Sergeant Cassidy," Custer said. "March the chorus to the sutler. Tell Mr. Smith to charge the first drink to my account."

"We thank the general, sir!" Sergeant Cassidy replied, with a salute. He turned to the chorus. "Detail, right face. Forward, march!"

As the chorus marched away, they began singing.

> *The hours sad I left a maid*
> *A lingering farewell taking*
> *Whose sighs and tears my steps delayed.*
> *I thought her heart was breaking.*
> *In hurried words her name I blest.*
> *I breathed the vows that bind me;*

And to my heart in anguish pressed
The girl I left behind me

Lorena asked again if there wasn't something she could do to help.

"I'm sure you can find something much more pleasant to do," Libbie said. "In fact, if I may suggest such a thing, Colonel MacCallister, why don't you show Lorena around the fort? I'm sure she would enjoy the tour."

"I'd be glad to," Falcon replied. He glanced toward Lorena. "That is, if Miss Wood would be interested."

"Oh, I can't think of a better way to close out a delightful evening," Lorena replied.

"You had better put a wrap on," Libbie said as they started toward the door. "The nights get a little cool, even this late in the spring."

"You might try this," Tom said, taking off his shell jacket, complete with the two medals, and slipping it over Lorena's shoulders.

"Why, thank you, Captain," Lorena replied.

"Captain, would you prefer to walk Miss Wood?" Falcon asked.

"Why, Colonel, is my company so unpleasant that you would deal me off to another?" Lorena asked.

"No, no, of course not," Falcon replied, a little flustered by her response. "I was merely trying to be magnanimous to my host, that's all."

"I appreciate your generous offer, Colonel, but I prefer to approach the young lady on my own," Tom replied with a broad smile.

"Then, by your leave, sir, I shall enjoy the walk," Falcon replied.

They walked down the front steps of the Custer house, then turned to look back at it. Cream colored with brown trim, a wide porch spread all the way across the front of the house, then ran down along the left side. It was a two-story house with dormer windows protruding from the roof of the second story. Five chimneys serviced the stoves inside, so that the house would stay warm in the winter.

"The Custers certainly live in a nice house," Lorena said.

"Yes, that's one of the advantages of being the commanding officer," Falcon replied.

"Do you have a house like that on the post that you command?"

Falcon chuckled. "Not exactly," he said. "My command is a state guard. We have some quarters, but none as nice as these."

As they passed one of the barracks, they heard singing.

"Oh, listen," she said, holding up her hand. "Why, it's beautiful."

"Yes," Falcon replied.

They stayed just outside long enough to hear the song, which was being sung in four-part harmony. Then they moved on through the post, their way lit but dimly by the ambient light spilling through the windows of the barracks and post quarters.

They heard the loud trill of a woman's laughter, then other women joined in. This came from "Soapsuds Row," so named because it was a row of houses occupied by laundresses.

"Most of them are NCO wives," Falcon explained. "And the money they make, combined with their husbands' army pay, gives them a pretty good income."

They walked away from the quarters, and from the stables, until they were in the most remote corner of the post, on the other side of the parade ground, and some distance from any of the buildings. From there, they could see the Missouri River gliding by, the water gleaming a soft silver in the light of a three-quarter moon.

"Halt! Who goes there!" a voice called from the darkness.

Lorena gasped. "Oh, what is that?"

"It's a sentry, walking his post," Falcon answered. Then, louder, he called out, "A friend."

"Advance, friend, and be recognized," the sentry's voice called back.

Taking Lorena's hand, Falcon moved toward the sound of the voice.

"Halt," the sentry called again.

Falcon stopped and waited until the guard appeared from the gloom of darkness.

"Identify yourself," the guard said.

"I am Colonel Falcon MacCallister," Falcon said. "This is Miss Lorena Wood. We are both guests of General Custer."

The guard brought his rifle into the present- arms position.

"The colonel and his lady may pass," the soldier said.

"Thank you, soldier, and good evening," Falcon said, returning the salute.

Falcon and Lorena continued in one direction, while the guard continued in the other, gradually opening the distance between them.

"That was rather exciting," Lorena said. "Seeing the two of you salute each other, like that."

From the middle of the post came the long, mournful sounds of a bugle playing taps. Looking back toward the flagpole, Falcon and Lorena could see a soldier in silhouette.

As they stood there, listening to taps, feeling a gentle breeze blow against them, with a vaulted sky full of diamonds and a gleaming river behind them, Lorena leaned into Falcon. She shivered, and as she did so, Falcon put his arm around her shoulders.

When taps was completed, there was a long moment of silence.

"That is one of the most moving things I have ever heard," Lorena said.

"Yes, taps can be quite impressive," Falcon said. "But that is the last official act of a military day. I had better get you back before the general sends out a search party."

"Oh, I hardly think—" Lorena began, but she was interrupted by a call from the dark.

"Miss Wood? Miss Wood, it's Tom Custer. Are you out there?"

"Yes, Captain Custer, I am here."

"Alone?"

"I'm with her, Tom," Falcon said.

"Oh. All right. The general was just getting a little worried, is all."

"I'll walk her back now," Falcon said.

"No need," Tom replied. "I can walk her back."

"I guess you were right," Lorena said. "General Custer did send a search party after me."

May 12, 1876

The next day, the ballroom was given over for Andrew and Rosanna to give their performance. Every trooper of the Seventh Cavalry, except for those who had special duty or punishment detail, was present. General Custer himself introduced the act.

"Men of the Seventh Cavalry," he said. "As most of you know, I was recently in Washington and New York. While I was in New York, I attended a show in which Andrew and Rosanna MacCallister were the principal players. And as I watched that show, I couldn't help but think of you back here, and I wished that you could have been there to watch these two wonderful actors perform.

"I knew that wasn't possible, though, as we will soon leave for a long scout." He held up his finger. "But if I couldn't take you to them, I could at least bring them to you. So I invited them to Ft. Lincoln and, I am proud to say, they accepted my invitation.

"Troopers, I present to you Andrew and Rosanna Mac-Callister!"

As the makeshift curtain opened, the soldiers applauded, whistled, and cheered. Andrew and Rosanna were standing in the middle of the stage, back to back. Andrew was holding a jug with his thumb. The jug was poised on his shoulder and, before either of them said a word, Andrew took a big drink, then patted the jug and let out a long "ahhhh."

The piano player began playing then, the music bright and lively, the song "Little Brown Jug."

Andrew and Rosanna began singing in duet, but they did much more than sing. They pantomimed, danced, and pranced around, accenting with their movement, the words of the song.

> *Me and my wife live all alone*
> *In a little hut we call our own;*
> *She loves gin and I love rum,*
> *And don't we have a lot of fun?*

Andrew made a big show of drinking more from the jug and when Rosanna reached for it, he jerked it away and turned his back to her. The audience howled in laughter. They continued, singing in two-part harmony.

> *Ha, ha, ha, you and me,*
> *Little brown jug don't I love thee!*
> *Ha, ha, ha, you and me,*
> *Little brown jug don't I love thee!*

Again, Rosanna reached for the jug, and again Andrew turned away from her. But this time, Rosanna reached around to tap him on his shoulder, and when he turned to look, she grabbed the jug away from him and took a drink as the audience laughed.

> *When I go toiling on the farm*
> *I take the little jug under my arm;*
> *Place it under a shady tree*

Andrew held his hands behind Rosanna's head and clapped them loudly. Startled, Rosanna dropped the jug and Andrew caught it. She shamed him by rubbing one finger against the other as the audience again laughed at their antics.

> *Little brown jug 'tis you and me!*

The song concluded to appreciative laughter and applause.

After that, Rosanna left the stage, and Andrew stood there for a moment, looking out at the audience.

"I want to thank all of you for the warm welcome we have received," he said. "And I want to thank General Custer for the invitation. This next song is dedicated to another of the general's guests, and if you will all look over there, you will see that when the writer wrote this song about a woman named Lorena, surely he had to be writing about someone as lovely as this young lady of the same name.

"Ladies and gentlemen, I give you 'Lorena.'"

As Andrew began to sing the song that had gained its popularity during the Civil War, the soldiers in the room lost themselves in the lyrics and melody. It reminded some of home; it reminded others of the time when they were actually fighting the war.

Falcon looked over at Lorena and saw that she, too, was moved by the beautiful music. He smiled. He had personally requested that his brother sing this particular song.

After Andrew finished his song, and the applause was finished, Custer stood.

"Mr. MacCallister, Miss MacCallister, speaking on behalf of all the troops posted here at Ft. Lincoln, I want to thank you for coming to provide us with such a wonderful show. And now, to further show our appreciation, I call upon our own Seventh Cavalry chorus to sing our regimental song for you."

At Custer's announcement, the same soldiers who had entertained at Custer's dinner party stood up from the audience, then formed themselves into a chorus. The chorus leader, Sergeant Cassidy, resplendent now in his dress blue uniform with stripes and accoutrements, stepped in front and lifted his hands. The chorus began to sing.

Let Bacchus's sons be not dismayed,
But join with me each jovial blade;
Come booze and sing, and lend your aid
To help me with the chorus:
Instead of spa we'll drink brown ale,
And pay the reckoning on the nail,
No man for debt shall go to jail
From Garyowen in glory!
No man for debt shall go to jail
From Garryowen in glory!

Chapter Eleven

Falcon was sitting in the waiting room of the Bismarck depot, drinking coffee with his sister, Rosanna. Andrew had gone out onto the depot platform to see about their luggage.

"I appreciate the two of you coming out here to perform for the men," Falcon said. "I know they really enjoyed it."

"Andrew and I enjoyed doing it," Rosanna said. "You know how much we like to come out West."

"When are you going to come back?" Falcon asked.

"I don't know. I suppose when we get another invitation."

"No, I mean when are you coming back to stay."

Rosanna put her hand out to touch Falcon. "Darling, I thought you knew. Andrew and I are never coming back to stay," she said. "Why, New York is our home now."

Falcon nodded. "I thought as much," he said. "But from time to time, the family wonders about you."

"Ha," Rosanna said. "Mama and Papa left on their own while they were still practically children. Believe me, if there is anyone who would understand why Andrew and I have chosen to go our own way, it would be Mama and Papa."

Falcon chuckled. "You've got that right," he said. "But as long as you are out here, you could run down there now, couldn't you? When is the last time you've seen anyone from the family?"

Rosanna smiled. "We've seen you twice in the last two months."

"I mean other than me."

"I don't know. It's been a while," Rosanna admitted.

"Then a visit is due, don't you think?"

"Oh, Falcon, it would be impossible to go down to Mac-Callister now," Rosanna said. "Andrew and I must start rehearsal for a new show soon. In fact, we were barely able to make the time to come out here to do this."

"I understand," Falcon said.

"I didn't want to tell you this, because I didn't want to spoil the surprise, but we are coming out to spend Christmas in the Valley," Rosanna said. "In fact, we have cleared away our schedule so we can spend at least two months there, visiting everyone."

Falcon smiled broadly, and shook his head. "They will like that," he said. "They will like that very much."

"What about you? When are you going to settle down?" Rosanna asked.

"Settle down? What do you mean settle down?"

"I mean get married."

"I did get married."

"Yes, and tragically, she was taken from you. But you are still a young man, Falcon. Somewhere there is a woman for you." Rosanna smiled. "And she may be right here."

"Here?"

"You aren't blind, Falcon. I know you have seen the way Lorena Wood looks at you."

"I've also seen the way she looks at Tom Custer."

"Have you ever thought she might just be trying to make you jealous?"

"Uh, huh," Falcon replied. "Or maybe she is trying to make Tom Custer jealous."

Rosanna laughed out loud. "Well, I never thought about that," she said. "It could be that you are right. I know that she has decided to stay out here with Libbie until the regiment returns."

Andrew came back then. "I've got the luggage all taken care of," he said. "We won't even have to see it again until we reach New York."

In the distance could be heard a train whistle.

"Is that our train?" Rosanna asked.

"It has to be," Andrew said. "There is nothing else due right now."

Rosanna stood up, and Falcon picked up the suitcase that would be going on the train with her. The three then walked out onto the wooden platform and from there, could see the train approaching from the west. A sense of anticipation spread through the others who were also standing out on the platform. Some began weeping at the prospect of telling a loved one good-bye, while others grew excited as they were eagerly awaiting the arrival of loved ones. The daily arrival and departure of the trains kept Bismarck connected, in a real and physical way, with the rest of the world. Nobody ever treated the occasion with indifference.

"When will you be coming back to New York?" Rosanna asked.

"I don't know," Falcon said. "Next time business takes me that way, I suppose."

"You could come just to visit, you know."

"Don't knock it, Rosanna. He's the only one who ever comes as it is," Andrew said.

Rosanna chuckled. "I guess you are right at that," she said. "Sometimes I could almost believe that Falcon is the only brother I have."

"What about me?" Andrew asked, his face screwed up in response to her question. "Don't you count me as your brother?"

"You are my twin," Rosanna said, as if that answered Andrew's question.

"Yeah, I guess I see what you mean," Andrew replied, understanding perfectly Rosanna's convoluted logic.

Falcon chuckled. Sometimes, he believed that Andrew and Rosanna shared not only the same birthday, but the same brain as well.

By now the train had reached the edge of the town and could be seen visibly slowing. A moment later, it rolled into the station, the bell clanging, steam spewing, and glowing sparks falling from the firebox.

Rosanna put her arms around Falcon's neck, then kissed him. "Give everyone my love," she said.

Andrew reached out to shake his brother's hand. "It's been wonderful seeing you," he said. "Do keep in touch, will you, little brother?"

Falcon smiled as he watched them board the train; then he stood on the platform until the train pulled away. It seemed funny for Andrew to call Falcon his little brother, even though he was. It was not only that Falcon was a much larger man than Andrew. His experiences so far exceeded anything Andrew had ever done that he could never think of Andrew as his elder.

June 25, 1927
MacCallister, Colorado

Once more the ringing telephone interrupted Falcon's recitation of the story. Falcon took a swallow of his coffee as Rosie answered the phone.

"Hello?"

Again, those present in the room could hear a tinny voice over the telephone line, but they couldn't understand what the voice was saying.

"Just a minute, I'll ask him," Rosie said. She reached up to put her hand over the mouthpiece of the phone, then turned toward Falcon.

"Big Grandpa, this is Mayor Presnell. He wants to know if the town can count on you as a guest of honor on the reviewing platform for the Fourth of July parade."

Falcon nodded. "I'll be there," he promised.

Rosie relayed the message, then hung up.

"The phone has been busy today," Zane Grey said.

"Yes," Falcon agreed. "Sometimes, I think it was better before we had telephones. Telephones, radio, motion pictures, automobiles, flying machines."

"Aeroplanes," Rosie said with a little laugh.

"What?"

"You said flying machines. They are called aeroplanes," Rosie said.

"Well, whatever they are called, they are aggravating," Falcon replied. He was quiet for a long moment. "It certainly makes one wonder, though, how different things would have been different on Custer's last scout if there had been such a thing as flying"—he paused and looked at his great-granddaughter—"aeroplanes"—he smiled—"and all the other modern contraptions."

"Are you tired, Falcon?" Zane Grey asked. "Do you want to pause for a while to maybe take a nap?"

"No, no, I'm fine," Falcon said. "What about you, Libbie?"

"I'm doing fine," Libbie said. "As you know, I have written about this story, and lectured about it for years. I must confess that I'm enjoying hearing you tell it from your perspective."

"Did your brother and sister get back that Christmas?" Grey asked.

Falcon nodded. "They did," he said.

"What about the lady, Big Grandpa?" Rosie asked.

"What lady?"

"What lady? Big Grandpa, you know what lady," Rosie said. "The one who came all the way out here to see you. Miss Wood. Did she go back to New York with Uncle Andrew and Aunt Rosanna?"

"No," Falcon said. "She stayed at Ft. Lincoln."

"Yes," Libbie said. "When Autie asked if she would like to stay on as our houseguest, to keep me company until the regiment returned from the field, she agreed. In fact, when we made camp out on the Missouri flats, she came out with us. Do you remember that, Falcon?"

"Oh, yes, I remember," Falcon said. "And we knew, even before the regiment left, where Miss Wood's heart was."

"Where?" Rosie asked.

"Rosie, do you want me to tell this story or not?" Falcon asked.

"Oh, yes!" Rosie replied eagerly.

"Then, don't get ahead of me child." Falcon finished his coffee, then went on with his story.

Chapter Twelve

May 14, 1876
Missouri River Flats

All twelve companies of the Seventh Cavalry had made camp alongside the banks of the Missouri River. A cold rain fell upon the tents, which were laid out in precise military order, creating puddles of water and large expanses of mud to turn the flats into a quagmire.

The largest tent of the encampment belonged to the regimental commander. Libbie and Lorena, who had come to watch the regiment depart, were in the tent, listening to the sound of the rain drumming against the canvas.

"Would you like a cup of tea?" Libbie asked. "I think it has brewed now."

"Yes, on a cold, damp day like this, I think a cup of tea would be lovely," Lorena replied.

Libbie picked up the silver teapot.

"Oh, what a beautiful teapot," Lorenea said.

"Yes, isn't it? It was given to Autie by General and Mrs. Sherman," Libbie replied. "We have so many nice things.

Some think it out of place to bring such things into the field, but there have been many times when Autie and I had to live in a tent, much like this one, for months on end. And I always felt that if little things, like this teapot, could give those experiences a little more civility, then why not use them?"

"Oh, I agree. Libbie, I thank you very much for inviting me to come out with you to watch the regiment depart," Lorena said as Libbie poured cups of hot tea for the two of them. "I can't imagine anything more exciting."

"The general and I are pleased to have you as our guest," Libbie replied. She smiled. "But I don't think anyone is as pleased over it as Tom is."

"I have been working for the War Department for more than two years," Lorena said. "Until I came out here, I didn't realize what the soldiers in the field actually go through. I mean, right now, General Custer is somewhere outside in the cold rain when he could be dry and warm in here with us."

Libbie smiled. "Oh, don't you worry about the general, my dear," she said. "Believe me, he is in absolute heaven. He loves the army." Libbie got a wistful look about her. "Sometimes, I even think he loves the army more than he loves me."

"Oh, that's not possible," Lorena said. "I've only been here for a few days, but I have heard the way he talks to you, and about you, and I've seen the way he looks at you. All women should be so lucky." She paused for a moment, then added, "I should be so lucky."

"Maybe someday you will be," Libbie suggested. "I know Tom certainly seems taken with you. Though you may be more interested in Falcon MacCallister."

"Falcon? No, I—I don't think so," Lorena replied. "There is something about him, a deep sadness in his past. I'm not sure what it is, but sometimes, in an unguarded moment, you can look into his eyes and see all the way down to the scars on his soul."

Libbie shivered, then pulled a shawl about her shoulders.

"Are you cold?" Lorena asked.

"Yes. No," Libbie said. "For some strange reason, I am very apprehensive about this scout. More so than any previous scout he has ever made, and what you said just now, about a deep sadness, seemed to resonate with me a little more than such a comment would normally."

"Oh, I'm sorry," Lorena said. "I had no wish to cause you melancholy."

Libbie laughed, then reached over and patted Lorena's hand. "Don't be silly, dear. I'm a soldier's wife. Apprehension and unexplained bouts of melancholy are part of it."

Outside Custer's tent, most of the soldiers were staying in their own tents, out of the rain. The soldiers and civilians who were attached to the supply train had no such luxury, though. They were working with wagons that were sometimes hub-deep in mud, trying to move them to more solid ground.

As Lorena pointed out, Custer had eschewed the relative comfort of his tent so that he could be personally involved in getting the regiment ready for departure. At one point, he had the men tie a rope on front of the wagon, then he pulled, helping to extricate it from a particularly difficult mud hole.

Falcon, who the day before had gone to the railroad depot in Bismarck to see his brother and sister off, had delayed his own departure until after the Seventh left on their scout. He had come to the field with them, and was sharing a tent with Mark Kellogg, who was a reporter for the *Bismarck Tribune* and the *New York Herald*.

Kellogg was sitting at a small field table, writing. "Colonel MacCallister," he said. "What do you think of this?"

Picking up the tablet, Kellogg began to read. *"General George A. Custer, dressed in a dashing suit of buckskin, is prominent everywhere. Here, there, flitting to and fro in his quick eager way, taking in everything connected with his command, as well as generally, with the keen, incisive manner for which he is so well known. The general is full of perfect readiness for the fray with the hostile red devils, and woe to any of the scalp-lifters that come within reach of himself and his brave companions in arms."*

Kellogg looked up from his table with a broad smile, eager for Falcon's response.

"Sounds like you think the Indians will be easy," Falcon said.

"Oh, come on, please, Colonel MacCallister," Kellogg said. "Against General Custer and the mighty Seventh? I've no doubt there will be some difficult times on the march, but as to any actual fighting? The Indians will scarcely give battle, I think."

"Mr. Kellogg?" someone called from outside the tent. "May I come in, sir?"

"Yes, yes, of course, Johnny, come in out of the rain," Kellogg replied.

The person who stepped into the tent was a boy, no

older than fourteen. He was wearing a slicker against the rain, but his face was wet and the hat, which was a billed cap rather than a hat with a brim, had done little to keep his hair from getting soaked.

"Colonel MacCallister, this is Johnny McVey. He works for Western Union," Kellogg said. "What brings you out here, Johnny? Do you have a telegram for me? Or a message from my editor?"

"Neither one, Mr. Kellogg. This is a telegram for Colonel MaCallister."

"I'm Colonel MacCallister," Falcon said.

"You're not in uniform."

"No, I'm not."

"How do I know you are who you say your are? I'm only supposed to give this to Colonel MacCallister."

"I will speak for him, Johnny," Kellogg said. "This is Colonel MacCallister."

"All right," Johnny said. "If you speak for him, Mr. Kellogg." The boy handed the telegram to Falcon. "This is for you," he said.

"Thanks."

Falcon gave the boy half a dollar, and took the telegram.

COLONEL FALCON MACCALLISTER
FT LINCOLN DAKOTA TERRITORY
FROM MAJOR ADRIAN BRISBANE
FT JUNCTION COLORADO TERRITORY

COLONEL IT IS WITH REGRET THAT I INFORM YOU THAT
SERGEANT MAJOR SEAN O'LEARY CORPORAL DARREL
BATES AND PRIVATES DEACON MORGAN AND SMITH
WERE KILLED WHILE ATTEMPTING TO DELIVER GATLING
GUNS TO FORT JUNCTION STOP

IT WASN'T UNTIL AFTER THEY WERE KILLED THAT
PRIVATE WILLIE CRAWFORD REPORTED OVERHEARING
SOME OF A TELEGRAPH MESSAGE SENT BY GRAHAM
POTTER IN WHICH POTTER WAS TALKING ABOUT THE
GUNS STOP I IMMEDIATELY PLACED POTTER UNDER
ARREST AND QUESTIONED HIM STOP

FROM WHAT WE HAVE BEEN ABLE TO GATHER, THE MAN
POTTER DEALT WITH WAS CLETE HARRIS STOP WE
BELIEVE HARRIS IS GOING INTO THE MONTANA
TERRITORY TO SELL THE GATLING GUNS TO INDIANS
AND IS THERE EVEN NOW STOP WE HAVE ALSO
LEARNED THAT THE RIFLES WE BELIEVED LOST IN
TRANSIT WERE IN FACT DELIBERATELY SENT TO A
FALSE LOCATION BY PORTER SO HARRIS COULD
ACQUIRE THEM STOP IT IS BELIEVED THAT HARRIS
SOLD THOSE GUNS TO THE SAME INDIANS THAT
GENERAL CUSTER WILL BE CONDUCTING HIS
EXPEDITION AGAINST STOP

I HOPED TO GET EVEN MORE INFORMATION BUT
SOMEHOW POTTER HAS MANAGED TO ESCAPE STOP

IN THE MEANTIME GOVERNOR ROUTT REQUESTS THAT
YOU EXTEND HIS APOLOGY TO GENERAL CUSTER FOR
ANY PROBLEM THESE REPEATING RIFLES MAY CAUSE
HIM AND HE ASKS YOU TO ATTEMPT TO FIND THE
GATLING GUNS STOP

ADRIAN BRISBANE
MAJ COMND'G OFFICER (ACTING)
COLORADO HOME GUARD

"Damn," Falcon said, when he finished reading the telegram.

"What is it, Colonel? Trouble?" Kellogg asked.

Falcon folded the telegram up and put it in his pocket. "Yeah," he said. "In fact, it could be a lot of trouble. I need to talk to Custer."

Although Custer had been out and around through the company area most of the day, Falcon found him back in his tent. Standing outside and calling, Falcon was invited in by Libbie.

The tent was actually a double Sibley tent, which was twelve feet high and thirty-six feet in diameter. Its large size allowed it to be divided into rooms by use of canvas walls. The tent was also well furnished with folding tables and chairs.

"Colonel MacCallister, how nice of you to call," Libbie said. "Won't you have a cup of hot tea? It will help to push away the gloom of this cold, rainy day."

"Thank you, Mrs. Custer, but I need to speak to the general if he is here."

"Yes, he is here. He is in the back putting on some dry clothes. I'll get him. Lorena, you don't mind entertaining Colonel MacCallister for a few moments, do you?"

"Of course not," Lorena said. "I would be happy to entertain the colonel."

"Lorena," Falcon said after Libbie left them alone together. "I'm sorry that such awful weather is spoiling your adventure."

"Oh, don't be silly, Falcon. Weather like this is part of the adventure," Lorena replied. "Are you sure you wouldn't like some tea?"

Falcon smiled and nodded. "All right," he said. "Perhaps some tea would be nice after all."

Lorena poured a cup of tea and handed it to him.

"Thank you." As Falcon took a swallow of his tea, he looked at Lorena over the edge of his cup. "Am I like the weather?" he asked.

"I beg your pardon?"

"Am I a part of your adventure?"

Lorena laughed, a rich, throaty laugh. "Why, Falcon MacCallister, how clever you are," she said. "Is that what you want to be? A part of my adventure?"

"Colonel MacCallister," Custer said, coming from behind the canvas wall and speaking, thankfully, before Falcon had to answer Lorena's question. "Are you staying dry?"

"I am, yes, thanks to Mr. Kellogg generously sharing his tent with me," Falcon said.

"Libbie said you wanted to see me."

"Yes, I do," Falcon replied. He showed Custer the telegram he had received from Major Brisbane.

Custer read it, then nodded. "Am I to understand that this man, Porter, is responsible for supplying the Sioux with repeating rifles?"

"I'm afraid so, General," Falcon answered.

Custer stroked his mustache as he contemplated the telegram. Finally, with a sigh, he handed the telegram back to Falcon.

"You were right to come to me with this," he said. "What are you going to do now?"

"Well, General, as you can see from the telegram, Governor Routt wants me to find the Gatling guns before they, too, wind up in Indian hands. So that's what I'm going to do. I'm afraid I'm going to have to borrow a horse from you."

"Yes, yes, of course, see the saddler sergeant. Tell him I said to let you pick out any horse you want."

"Thank you, General."

"Do you have any idea where to start looking for these guns?"

"Not exactly."

Custer chuckled. "You aren't going to just go out hither and yon, searching for your Indians like Diogones, carrying his lantern in search of an honest man, are you?"

"Whatever works," Falcon replied with his own chuckle.

"Well, I do have an idea—that is, if you are amenable to it," Custer said.

"At this point, General, I am open to any suggestion."

"You could come on this scout with us," Custer said.

"I don't know," Falcon replied. "I don't know how much looking I would be able to do if I stayed with you."

"Oh, don't get me wrong. You don't have to stay with us," Custer said. "As a matter of fact, I wouldn't want you to. You would be acting as a scout. That way you can break away from us anytime you want, go anywhere you want, but always have a base to which you can return. And you would be able to perform double duty—looking for the Gatling guns while, at the same time, helping us look for the Indians."

"If I agree to do that, General, you will have to know that my first duty will be to find those two guns."

"That's fine," Custer replied. "I, for one, would not want to have those Gatling guns in the hands of the Indians. So—in that respect, you would be serving me, even as you serve yourself."

"All right, General. I'll go along with that," Falcon agreed.

"Good, good, and I have just the scout to work with you."

Falcon held up his hand. "There's no need for that, General. I would not want to take one of your scouts away from his regular duty."

"Believe me, Falcon, if there is any chance that there may be a couple of Gatling guns out there, helping you find them would be a part of his regular duty. I think you will find him very helpful. He used to live with the Indians, he speaks the language, and he knows the area." Custer stuck his head out and called to his messenger. "Trooper!"

"Yes, sir!" the soldier replied.

"Find Isaiah Dorman. Tell him I wish to see him."

"Yes, sir," the trooper said, hurrying off on his errand.

"I think you'll find Dorman an interesting fellow," Custer said. "He has been a mail carrier—no easy job out here where you have to travel hundreds of miles in a trackless wilderness all alone. And he was a guide and interpreter for the builders of the Northern Pacific Railroad. Mr. Dorman also acted as an interpreter for me on a few occasions."

A moment later, the messenger called from outside the tent. "General Custer, I have Dorman here, sir."

"Send him in," Custer called back.

The flap to the tent parted, and Dorman stepped inside. "Gen'rul, you wanted to see me?"

Falcon was surprised to see that Isaiah Dorman was a black man.

"Yes, take Colonel MacCallister to see the saddler sergeant. Tell Fitzsimmons I said he is to make a horse available for the colonel. The colonel has some looking to do, and I want you to go with him. He'll fill you in."

"All right, Gen'rul," Dorman said. He looked over at

Falcon. "You want to come with me, Colonel? We'll get you that horse."

"I like the looks of that horse," Falcon said, pointing to a buckskin.

"Sorry, Colonel, but you can't have that one," Sergeant Fitzsimmons said. "That one don't belong to the cavalry. That there horse is the personal mount of one of the officers."

"Comanche, come here," Dorman called, and the horse, shaking his head, came over to Dorman and began nuzzling him.

"This noble beast belongs to Cap'n Keogh," Dorman explained as he patted the horse on its nose. "He puts so much store in him that he bought him from the army just so's no one else would ever ride him."

Falcon reached up to tug on Comanche's ear. "I don't blame him," Falcon said. "This is a good-looking horse, and you can tell by looking at him that he has spirit."

"That's a good horse over there," Dorman said, pointing to a bay.

"I'll take your word for it," Falcon replied.

"I'll get him saddled for you, Colonel," Sergeant Fitzsimmons said.

May 17, 1876
Ft. Lincoln, Dakota Territory

The sky was overcast and a fog crept up from the river itself, but that didn't alter Custer's plans for a grand departure. With wives, children, and post personnel who were staying behind making up the audience, Custer readied his command for a parade.

The regimental band formed in the middle of the parade ground, just in front of the flagpole. The songs "Garryowen" and "The Girl I Left Behind Me" provided stirring martial music for the occasion. Falcon was given the honor of standing by Custer as the regiment rode by, led for this occasion by Major Reno.

Reno rode by first. A flag bearer rode immediately behind him carrying the blue and gold regimental standard on the same pole as Custer's personal pennant, which was red and blue with crossed white sabers. The twelve companies of the Seventh came after that, the troopers all mounted on matching horses for each company, and riding in columns of fours.

As each company passed in review, the company guidon in front of each company would dip and the company commander would render a salute to Custer, who proudly returned the salute.

"Look at that," Custer said. "I ask you, Falcon, have you ever seen a finer body of men anywhere in the world?"

"It is a fine-looking regiment, General," Falcon replied.

"The world will take note and long remember what we will do on this scout," Custer said. "From this day forward, the Seventh Cavalry will live in fame. I will lead them to glory."

When the last of the regiment paraded by the flagpole, Custer turned to Falcon. "You can wait here for Dorman. I told him to come back for you after the parade."

"All right," Falcon agreed.

"And you, my dear, come ride with me," Custer said to Libbie.

Libbie was wearing a blue shell jacket with a double row of brass buttons, which presented a very military appearance. Custer's horse, Vic, and Libbie's horse, Dandy, were tethered just behind the flagpole, and the two mounted, then raced to the front of the column, where Custer relieved Reno. Libbie rode by his side as Custer then led the regiment by the enlisted barracks, where those soldiers who weren't going for one reason or another stood outside, watching their comrades and shouting encouragement to them.

"Johnny, mind you don't leave your scalp out there, you ain't got all that much hair to begin with!" one of the infantrymen shouted to a friend in the cavalry. Those around him laughed.

Once beyond the enlisted barracks, the column passed by the married NCO quarters, also known as "Soapsuds Row" since so many of the NCOs' wives were laundresses.

"Billy, you'll be comin' back to me now, you hear? You'll be comin' back to me," one woman shouted.

"There's your daddy. Wave to your daddy, boys, wave to your daddy," another woman said, holding one young boy in her arms while a second clung to her skirt.

Finally, they rode past the officers' quarters, where a cluster of wives and children stood together, watching anxiously. Once they were beyond the officers' quarters, Custer led them at left oblique toward the front gate. As he did so, Falcon heard gasps and excited voices from those who were staying behind . At first he didn't know what they were reacting to. Then he saw several of them pointing up.

There, just over the long column of mounted troopers, was a very vivid mirage. In the mist above was a mirror image of the long row of riders so that the Seventh Cavalry was marching, not only on the ground, but in the sky. Some of the wives, seeing their husbands ride off to do battle, shivered in fear, certain they had just seen a sign from heaven.

The band continued to play, the notes bouncing back now from the walls of the nearly empty post. The band director, seeing that the regiment had left, finished the song, then ordered the band to mount and ride quickly to take its place in the ranks.

Falcon saw Isaiah Dorman riding toward him at a fairly rapid trot. "Have you watched all the soldier boys go by, Colonel?" Dorman asked.

"I have."

"Then, if you come with me, we'll get to scoutin'." Dorman was chewing tobacco, and he punctuated his comment with a brown, wet spit. He wiped the back of his hand across his lips.

As the regiment was now moving very slowly to match the pace of the wagons, Falcon and Dorman caught up with them quickly. The scouts were led by Lieutenant Charles Varnum, and he came back to speak with Falcon.

"Colonel, I'm not exactly sure what the protocol is here," Varnum said. "Clearly, you outrank me. But I—"

Falcon interrupted Varnum with a raised hand. "Lieutenant, as you can see, I am not in uniform," he said. "This is your command. You do whatever you planned to do without regard to me. For the most part, I'll just be coming along for the ride. But in fact, I plan to go out on my own quite a bit, to try and locate those two Gatling guns before the Indians get them."

"Yes, sir," Varnum said. "Well, if there is anything I don't want, it is to have Indians with Gatling guns, so please, do whatever you have to do. And, if you need me for anything, just let me know."

"How about letting Isaiah Dorman ride with me?" Falcon asked. "He knows the lingo. If we run into any friendly Indians, he might be able to help me find the guns."

"Right, the general said to make him available to you," Varnum said. "Dorman, you ride with the colonel."

"Whatever you say, Boss," Dorman replied.

As the two men rode away from the rest of the Seventh, Falcon looked back in time to see how Custer had organized his line of march. He'd divided his command into three battalions, taking the center battalion himself, giving the right wing to Major Marcus Reno, a junior major, and the left wing to Captain Frederick Benteen, a senior captain.

"Mr. Dorman," Falcon said. "What do you think of Reno and Benteeen?"

Dorman leaned over and squirted out another quid.

"If you ask me, the gen'rul is just askin' for trouble with them two," Dorman replied.

"What do you mean?"

"If you was to give a boot full of piss to Reno, he wouldn't have sense enough to pour it out," Dorman said. "And if you was to give it to Benteen, why, that evil sum' bitch would more'n likely pour it out on Custer."

Falcon chuckled. If Dorman was that observant, then he was just the kind of man Falcon would need if he was to have any chance of finding the Gatling guns.

May 17, 1876
Little Heart River

Custer and the Seventh Cavalry reached the first crossing of Little Heart River at about two o'clock in the afternoon.

Here, the entire expeditionary force was brought together under General Terry. The force consisted of the Seventh Cavalry, commanded by Custer, with twenty-eight officers and 747 men; two companies of the 17th Infantry and one company of the 6th Infantry, comprising eight officers and 135 men; one platoon of Gatling guns with two officers and thirty-two men; and forty-five scouts. In addition, the wagon train had 114 six-mule teams, thirty-seven two-horse teams, and seventy other vehicles, including ambulances, with eighty-five pack mules, all manned by 179 civilians. Included in that number were Boston and Autie Reed Custer.

Although the expedition was commanded by General Alfred H. Terry, one would scarcely know that to see Custer. Custer was constantly on the move, not only seeing to his own command, but issuing orders to the other commands as well, seeing to the placement of the advance guard, the rear guard, and the flanks.

Once they reached their encampment on the Little Heart River, Custer's orderly, Private John Burkman, erected the double Sibley tent for him as Custer continued to move around the campsite . . . Mary Adams, Custer's cook, began preparing their supper.

Libbie, Maggie Calhoun, and their houseguest, Lorena Wood, had all three accompanied the regiment this far, and they began helping Burkman pitch the tent.

As the regiment settled in for its first night's encampment, Falcon and Dorman started out on their first scout.

They rode out about ten miles, but saw nothing of particular interest until Dorman pointed out an elk.

"If I'm goin' to be ridin' with someone out in Injun territory, I'd like to have me an idee as to how he can shoot,"

Dorman said. "It'll be a good shot if you can bring him down. And a little roast elk is a heap better than skillgilly."

"Roast elk doesn't sound bad," Falcon said, pulling an army carbine from the saddle sleeve. Raising the Sharps, Falcon took aim and fired. Even from there, they could see a little mist of blood erupt from the elk's head.

"Damn," Dorman said, impressed with the shot. "You hit his head plumb center. Colonel, you can ride with me anywhere."

Falcon and Dorman returned to join the regiment just as the Seventh was going into bivouac.

Benteen was standing beside one of the wagons with his shirt off and his gold-colored suspenders down along his sides, hanging in such a way as to make a loop across the gold stripe on his pants. The captain had lather on his face, and he was looking into a mirror that was propped on the side of the wagon. He looked around as Falcon and Dorman returned to the camp.

"Colonel, if you'll excuse me, I'm goin' to look up Bloody Knife," Dorman said.

"Sure, go ahead," said Falcon.

"Did you find anything?" Benteen asked as Dorman moved away.

"No," Falcon replied.

"Uh, huh, I didn't think so," Benteen said, and he reached one hand up to pull his cheek taut, then lifted the razor, returning to the task of shaving. "You aren't likely to find anything as long as you have that nigger with you."

"Oh?" Falcon said. "I don't know why you would say that. Mr. Dorman seems quite capable to me."

"It's not a question of his capability," Benteen said. "It's a question of his loyalty."

"Why would you question his loyalty?"

"He turned Indian out here," Benteen said. "They call him 'Black White Man,' and he is married to a squaw from Inkpaduta's band of the Santee Sioux."

"I thought he had been working for the army for some time now," Falcon said.

Benteen took a towel and wiped the rest of the lather from his face. "Oh, he doesn't mind taking money from us," he said. "But this will be the first time he has ever had to go up against his own."

"What about Bloody Knife? Are you worried about him?"

"No," Benteen said, reaching for his tunic. "Gall killed Bloody Knife's two brothers. Bloody Knife hates the Sioux."

At that moment, a bugle call was sounded and some of the men cheered.

"What is that?" Falcon asked.

"Pay call," Benteen said. "Custer decided to withhold the soldiers' pay until after we left the fort. He was afraid there would be too many hangovers and too many desertions if he paid before we left."

Within minutes after the soldiers were paid, several dozen card games began. The soldiers sat on the ground with an army blanket laid out between them to hold the cards and the money.

Shortly after pay call, Falcon and Dorman were getting ready to go out again when Lieutenant Cooke came up to them. Falcon was adjusting the cinch strap on his saddle.

"Hello, Cooke," Falcon said.

"The general's compliments, sir, and he asks if you would join him and Mrs. Custer, Captain and Mrs. Cal-

houn, Captain Custer and Miss Wood for a picnic lunch.
The ladies will be leaving with the paymaster as soon as
he starts back to Ft. Lincoln."

"Captain Custer and Miss Wood?"

"Yes, sir," Cooke replied. "Uh, Colonel, I wonder if I
might have a word with you, sir," Cooke said.

"Sure, go ahead," he said.

Cooke looked over at Dorman. "Alone, sir."

"I'll just move over there and you two can talk all you
want," Dorman said, leading his horse away.

"What is it?"

"The way you questioned me when I said Captain
Custer and Miss Wood. Did that bother you?"

Falcon chuckled. "No, it didn't bother me. I just found
it rather funny the way you said it in the same way you said
General and Mrs. Custer and Captain and Mrs. Calhoun."

"Yes, sir, I sort of meant to say it that way," Cooke said.
"And that's why I wanted to talk to you alone. Tom—that
is, Captain Custer—wants to know your intentions toward
Miss Wood."

Falcon chuckled. "Couldn't he ask me that question
himself?"

"I reckon he could," Cooke replied. "But when it comes
to women, Tom is sort of shy."

"You don't say? Well, now, that's funny. I never would
have figured Tom for the shy type."

"Well, he's not exactly shy," Cooke replied. "Except
around women. So, what can I tell him, Colonel? About
your intentions toward Miss Wood, I mean."

"I have no intentions toward the young lady, Cooke,"
Falcon replied. "I do think she is a very nice person who

could probably be hurt quite easily. And I wouldn't like to see that happen."

"What do you mean, sir?" Cooke asked.

"You tell Tom Custer what I said. I think he will know exactly what I mean," Falcon replied.

"And as to the general's invitation to lunch? What shall I tell him?" Cooke asked.

"What time?"

"Oh, I expect within the hour, sir," Cooke said.

"All right. Tell the general I will be happy to accept his invitation."

"Very good, sir."

As Cooke walked away, Dorman returned. "You'll enjoy the picnic with the general," he said. "Like as not he'll have some sort of fancy thing from back East. Mrs. Custer sets a lot of store about such things."

"You heard the conversation, did you?"

"I'm a scout, Colonel. A good scout uses his ears as well as his eyes."

"Speaking of scouting, I'd like to go back out again, right after lunch," Falcon said.

"Yes, sir, I'll be ready."

When Falcon walked up to Custer's double Sibley tent, he saw that a large square of canvas had been spread out on the ground in front of the tent. The canvas square was filled with viands of every description. There was a basket of fried chicken, a ham, beans and rice, smoked oysters, tinned peaches, biscuits, butter, and jam. There were also a couple of bottles of wine, but Custer, who was a teetotaler, was drinking lemonade.

The entire party was sitting on the canvas around the food. Mary Adams, Custer's black maid and cook, was standing nearby.

"Falcon, I'm glad you could join us," Custer said. "Pull up a piece of the canvas and have a seat." He augmented his invitation by a wave of his hand.

"I don't mind if I do," Falcon said. "Where are Boston and Autie Reed?" he asked.

"Boston is earning his keep as a member of the trains," Custer said. "He and Autie Reed are with the wagons."

"You must try the beans and rice, Colonel MacCallister," Tom said. "It's Mary's own secret recipe that she made up herself."

"Now, Cap'n Tom, you got no business sayin' somethin' like that," Mary said. "It ain't nothin' of the kind my own recipe. I got this recipe from my mama, and she got it from her mama, which, where she got it, I don't know."

Tom laughed. "Well, wherever you got it, it's good," Tom said.

"Do you keep up with politics, Falcon?" Custer asked as he spread butter on a biscuit.

"I keep up with local politics," Falcon said. "One of my brothers is a sheriff back in Colorado. I always make certain that I'm home to vote for him."

"See there, Tom?" Custer said, looking across the table toward his brother. "Colonel MacCallister supports his brother. Is it too much for me to expect your support?"

"If you run for sheriff, Autie, I will surely support you," Tom replied. "But when you start talking about running for president, you are a little out of my league."

"President?" Falcon asked.

"Maybe," Custer said. He chuckled. "As you know, I have

made it very difficult for Grant and his administration over the last few months. There are some who say that, because of my congressional appearances, the Republican Party has been greatly weakened. And, in a few weeks, the Democrats will be holding a convention in St. Louis to select a candidate for president. On the twenty-seventh of June, to be exact. I'm sure you can agree with me when I say that the timing could not be more fortuitous."

"I'm not sure I follow you, General."

"Don't be dense, man," Custer replied. "I have some supporters who will be at the convention in St. Louis and they will put my name into nomination. When I come away with a big victory over the Sioux, the headlines it generates will ensure that I am selected. That makes the timing of this expedition extremely critical. I must complete the scout before June 27."

"General, I thought the mission of the expedition was to return the Sioux to the reservations."

"It is, Colonel, it is," Custer said. "But tell me, how can an early and successful conclusion to the expedition not be for the good of the mission? I mean, do you see a contradiction there?"

"No," Falcon admitted. "I see no contradiction."

"Well, then," Custer said, holding up his glass of lemonade. "I suggest that we drink a toast to a successful and early conclusion to this noble scout."

"Successful and safe," Libbie added.

"Of course, Sunshine," Custer replied, using his pet name for her. "Successful and safe."

"Hear, hear," Tom Custer and Jimmi Calhoun said, lifting their wineglasses in salute.

Chapter Thirteen

May 17, 1876
Montana Territory

Clete Harris was driving the wagon, and he pulled back on the reins.

"Whoa, mules, whoa," he said. Using his right foot, he set the brake against the wheels to hold the wagon in place.

"What did we stop for?" Bryans asked.

"I need to climb up there and take a look around," Harris said, pointing to the butte just in front of them.

"We goin' to be here long enough to make some coffee?" Bryans asked. "I could sure use me a cup."

"Yeah, go ahead," Harris said. Climbing down from his seat, he walked to the back of the wagon, untied his horse, then swung into the saddle. "I'm goin' to ride up as far as I can, have a look around, then come back. It'll prob'ly be half an hour or longer. Save some coffee for me."

"You got some?" Bryans asked.

"You're goin' to make some anyway, aren't you?" Harris asked.

"Yeah, for me. I ain't got enough coffee to make some for you, too, but if you give me some of yours, I'll make it."

Harris opened his saddlebag and took out a small cloth sack, then tossed it down to Bryans. "You're one selfish son of a bitch, Bryans," he said. "Did anyone ever tell you that?"

Slapping his legs against the side of his horse, Harris followed the trail that led toward the hill. When the trail started up the side of the Rainy Butte, he rode for as long as he could. Then, when the horse started struggling, he dismounted and began walking, pulling the horse along behind him. After a climb of some considerable distance, he found a flat area that stuck out to one side. He walked out to the edge to have a look.

He could see the wagon and the three men who had come with him. From here, the wagon was so small that it looked almost like a child's toy. This vantage point also allowed him to look back along the Heart River.

He could see as far as the Little Powder River, but saw nothing of particular interest to him. That was good. If he was up here to sell Gatling guns to Indians, he didn't need to see anyone poking around.

Harris worked his way back down the side of the mountain. There, he saw that Bryans, Garon, and Richland had already unsaddled their horses and were making camp.

"Did you make coffee for me?" he asked.

"Yeah. It's in the pot."

Harris poured himself a cup of coffee and looked over at the wagon. "I think we could make better time without the wagon."

"How are we going to carry these guns without a

wagon?" Garon asked. "They weigh about fifteen hundred pounds each."

"They're on caissons," Harris said. "We'll just pull them."

"Yeah, I guess that'll work."

"Better get a good night's sleep. We'll leave first thing in the morning."

"Harris, what's the name of this Indian we're goin' to be doin' business with?" Bryans asked.

"His name is Cut Nose."

"Have you ever considered the possibility that Cut Nose might just decide to take these guns, then kill us?"

"I don't think he would do that," Harris replied.

"You don't think he would? You mean he might, but you don't think he would?"

"Let's put it this way," Harris said. "We've done business before, and I figure he will want to do business again in the future. Why would he want to just take the guns and kill us? He'd have to find someone else who is willing to trade with him."

"All right, if you say so," Bryans said.

May 18, 1876
Little Heart River

The trumpeter blew reveille at five a.m. the next morning and, grumbling, the troopers rolled out of their blankets to start the new day. Soon, the smell of bacon and coffee permeated the entire area, and though Falcon was invited to join the officers' mess of the Seventh, he decided to take his breakfast with Isaiah Dorman.

In addition to the bacon, Dorman made griddle cakes, which he shared with Falcon.

"Oh, that's good, Mr. Dorman. That's very good," Falcon

said, taking his first bite. "If you were a pretty woman, I'd have to marry you for being able to cook like that."

Dorman laughed. "Well, if I was a pretty woman, why would I be waistin' my time marryin' up with the likes of you? No, sir, I'd go to New Orleans and work in a fancy house makin' a lot of money."

Falcon laughed as well. "Mr. Dorman, when we go out this time, I'd like to stay out ten to twelve days. You think we can draw rations for that long?"

"I'll take care of it for us," Dorman replied. "But I'd be pleased if you'd drop the mister, and just call me Dorman. I tell you the truth, for a colored man like me, it's hard to get used to bein' called mister."

"I figure every man has the right to be called mister until he does something that changes my mind about him," Falcon replied. "But if you want me to drop the mister, I'll do it."

"Seems a mite friendlier to me is all," Dorman said.

The encampment was busy with drivers hitching up their teams and with soldiers tending to their mounts. Then, just as Falcon and Dorman were finishing breakfast, Custer's orderly, John Burkman, came over to them.

"Sir, the general sent me over to tell you that, in case you wanted to tell them good-bye, the ladies are leaving camp now. They're goin' back to Ft. Lincoln."

"I'd be glad to tell them good-bye." Falcon looked over to where the ladies were getting ready to leave. "Mary isn't going back with them?"

Dorman chuckled. "No, sir, he ain't goin' to be sendin' her back. Mary, why, she'll travel with the gen'rul at least till we get to base camp. The gen'rul, he's a fella that don't like army rations all that much, so he keeps Mary along to cook for him."

"Well, having eaten some of her cooking last night, I can't say as I blame him," Custer said.

"Now you done gone and hurt my feelin's Colonel," Dorman said. "Talkin' that way 'bout Mary after you was tellin' me what a good cook I was this mornin'."

"Here, don't you go getting all jealous on me, Dorman," Falcon said, laughing as he walked over to Custer's tent, where the general, Jimmi Calhoun, and Tom Custer were standing out front to tell the three women good-bye. He stood back, close enough to be there, but far enough back to allow them a little privacy.

"Oh, I have yellow ribbons for all of you to wear until we get back," Custer said. Reaching down into the side pocket of his buckskin jacket, he pulled out three yellow ribbons. One he gave to Jimmi Calhoun, and one he gave to his brother Tom. "We'll pin them on you," he said.

"You do know what it means when a woman wears a cavalryman's yellow ribbon, don't you?" Tom asked.

"No, not exactly," Lorena replied.

"It means you are his girl," Tom explained, pinning the ribbon on her before she could protest.

As Tom pinned the ribbon on Lorena, she glanced over at Falcon with an expression as if to say, *I hope you understand.* Then she turned back to Tom with a smile.

"Good-bye, Colonel," Maggie called over to him.

"Good-bye, Mrs. Calhoun."

"Excuse me a minute, Tom," Lorena said. She walked over to Falcon and extended her hand. "Colonel, it has been delightful meeting you," she said. "I do hope we meet again."

"I'm sure we will," Falcon said.

Lorena glanced back toward Tom. "He is a very good man, you know," she said quietly.

"I'm sure he is."

"He asked me to be here for him when the regiment returns."

"And will you be?"

Lorena nodded. "Yes, I think I will be," she said.

"I'm sure he will appreciate it."

"Colonel, I—"

"You don't have to say anything, Miss Wood," Falcon said, interrupting her. "Like you said, Tom Custer is a good man."

After Lorena walked back to the paymaster's ambulance, Libbie came over to speak to Falcon. She was smiling brightly as she approached.

"Colonel MacCallister, it was so nice of you to come visit us."

"It was nice of you and the general to invite me," Falcon said. "I thoroughly enjoyed my visit."

She glanced back over her shoulder at Tom Custer, who was now helping Lorena into the ambulance.

"Tom seems quite taken with Lorena. He"—she paused for a moment—"needs someone, if you know what I mean. I hope that isn't a problem for you."

"No, of course not. Why should it be a problem?"

"I don't know. I thought the first night that there seemed to be some mutual interest between you and Miss Wood."

"Please, Mrs. Custer, don't worry about it," Falcon said.

The smile left Libbie's face, to be replaced by a look of anxiety. "I told Autie's orderly to look after the general. I would never say anything like this to the general's face but, oh, Colonel MacCallister, of all the engagements Autie was in during the war, of all previous Indian engagements, I have never had such an overwhelming sense of foreboding as I do now."

"Look at the size of this force, Mrs. Custer," Falcon said, taking in the expedition with a sweep of his hand. "John Burkman won't be the only one looking after the general. Everyone here will be looking out for him, and for each other."

"Yes, but you must understand, if there is fighting to be done, Autie always puts himself at the head."

"That's because he is a good soldier," Falcon replied.

"Libbie, come, we must go!" Maggie called.

"I'll be right there," Libbie replied and, as she walked back toward the ambulance where Burkman stood holding her horse, Dandy, Falcon walked back with her. Burkman helped her mount; then Libbie nodded to the ambulance driver. The driver returned her nod, then slapped the reins against the backs of the four-horse team, and the ambulance started forward on its thirteen-mile trip back to the post.

As the ambulance rolled through the encampment carrying the paymaster and Lorena as passengers, and accompanied by Libbie and Maggie on horseback, Falcon stood alongside Custer, who was waving and smiling.

"Libbie couldn't hide it from me," Custer said. "She is nervous about this scout."

"I think that is probably true of the wife of any soldier who is going off to do battle," Falcon suggested, not wanting to give away what he believed Libbie had confided to him in private.

"Yes," Custer said. "But that is the way of it, Falcon. A good soldier must divide his time between two mistresses, his wife and the army. And when he is with one, the other must suffer."

Falcon turned to start back to where he had left Dorman.

"Are you going out this morning?" Custer asked.

"Yes."

"Good luck to you."

"Thanks."

Dorman was waiting patiently.

"Are you ready?" Falcon asked.

"Colonel, it wasn't me that stood here to watch them pretty women leave."

Falcon laughed as well. "You got me on that one, Dorman," he said. "Did you draw the rations?"

"I did."

Falcon swung into the saddle. "All right. Let's go."

May 21, 1876
Montana Territory

Falcon had just started across a small stream when a bullet popped by his head and ricocheted off a large rock outcropping right beside him.

The gunshot was followed by Indian war cries.

"Colonel MacCallister!" Dorman shouted.

Dorman's warning wasn't needed as, ahead of them, just where the creek curved, a dozen Indians came galloping toward them, whooping and brandishing weapons. The weapons, Falcon noticed, were Henry repeating rifles.

Falcon drew his pistol and shot the two Indians in the lead. Seeing two of their number go down, the others stopped, experiencing a moment of confusion and doubt.

"This way!" Dorman called, heading up a small trail that paralleled the stream.

The Indians, thinking Falcon and Dorman were running from them, gathered themselves and resumed the charge.

Dorman darted around a rock, and Falcon was right behind him. Once he had the rock between him and the charging Indians, Falcon pulled his horse to stop, jerking back on the reins so hard that the horse almost went down on its haunches.

"Here," Falcon shouted. "We'll fight from here!"

Falcon jerked the army-issue Sharps from the saddle sheath, then stepped around the rock with the carbine raised to his shoulder. He fired, brought down one Indian, then, using the Sharps as a club, brought down a second. Dorman, having come back in response to Falcon's call, brought down a third, and now, with his pistol in his hand, Falcon killed two more.

In less than one minute, the twelve Indians who'd believed they had a sure thing saw their number decreased by more than half. Only five remained, and they turned and galloped away, leaving their dead behind them.

"Damn!" Dorman said as he stood alongside Falcon, watching the Indians retreat. "You're one hell of an Injun fighter, Falcon. I been at this game for a long time, I don't think I've ever seen anything like that."

Falcon walked over to one of the dead Indians and picked up the rifle the Indian was carrying. It was a Henry, 44-caliber, rim-fire, lever-action, breech-loading rifle. When he looked at the butt of the rifle, he saw branded into it the words COLORADO HOME GUARD.

These were the missing rifles.

"I'll be damn," he said.

"What is it?"

"The Colorado Home Guard is missing one hundred rifles. It looks like we just found a few of them."

"You mean, in addition to the Gatling guns we're lookin' for, there's also a bunch of repeating rifles out there?"

"Yeah."

"That ain't good."

"No, it's not good at all," Falcon said. "Come on, help me pick up the others." Falcon put that rifle aside and for the next minute or so, they wandered through the dead Indians, retrieving rifles.

"Damn," Dorman said as he stood over one of the bodies. "This here is Running Bear."

"You knew him, did you?"

"Yeah, I knew the son of a bitch. This here is Cut Nose's brother."

"I take it you weren't friends."

"No, I don't think you could rightly call us friends. Cut Nose sure set a big store by him, though, seein' as how he mostly raised him after their pappy was killed. He ain't goin' to take too kindly to your killin' 'im."

Falcon chuckled. "Now tell me, Mr. Dorman, do you really think Cut Nose was ready to be friends with me before I killed his brother?"

Dorman laughed out loud. "Now that you mention it, I don't reckon you killin' his brother is goin' to make matters any worse."

"What do you say we get these rifles back to Custer?"

Moon of Making Fat
Sioux encampment

The encampment was temporary only, because the three hundred Indians were on their way to join with others during a time the Sioux called the Moon of Making Fat, at a place called Greasy Grass. Even though it was a temporary settlement, the band of Indians who were following Cut Nose were experienced nomads and they knew how to set up a camp quickly and efficiently.

The nearly one hundred teepees were arranged in concentric circles with each teepee in a precise position within those circles. As far as the occupants of the village were concerned, it didn't matter whether they were going to be in position for one night or thirty nights; they carried on as if every location was permanent. The position wasn't decided by hierarchy, but by precedence, the exact positioning allowing for friends and relatives to be able to locate each other.

The women were busy carving meat into very thin slices and hanging them up to dry, the children were playing games, the old men were sitting in little groups telling stories of old battles and ancient hunts, and the young men were cleaning recently cured game.

Cut Nose was aware of the fact that a large group of soldiers had left various military posts to take to the field, and earlier in the day, he had sent out a dozen warriors to see where they were and if they represented any danger to his band. He was shocked when he saw that only five of the twelve warriors returned. He was dismayed when he saw that one of those who did not return was his brother, Running Bear.

"Where is my brother? Where are the others?" Cut Nose asked.

"Running Bear is dead. The others are dead," One Hawk replied.

"The Long Knives? Did you see the Long Knives?"

"No, we did not see the soldiers. We saw only two. Black White Man and Tall Warrior."

"Only two, but seven are killed? Did you kill the two?"

"No, Cut Nose."

"Did you kill one of the two?"

"No, we did not kill one of the two."

"Ayieee! Seven were killed but not one of the enemy?"

"Cut Nose, never have I seen men fight with such fierceness and bravery," One Hawk said.

"I did not know that Black White Man was a warrior of such skill."

"It was not Black White Man. It was Tall Warrior who fought with such skill. It was Tall Warrior who killed Running Bear."

"Who is this Tall Warrior? I do not know him," Cut Nose said.

"No one has seen him before. We gave him the name because he is very tall and very ferocious. I believe he was born in thunder. That is why we do not know him."

"I will know him," Cut Nose said. Cut Nose pulled his knive, then sliced through one side of his nostril. The cut started bleeding immediately, and profusely. "This wound is my brother, Running Bear," Cut Nose said. "I will keep this wound fresh, until I have killed the one who killed my brother."

"Cut Nose, Crazy Horse comes!" someone called.

Cut nose dismissed One Hawk, then walked out to greet Crazy Horse.

As a young man, Crazy Horse had a vivid dream of a rider in a storm on horseback who wore his hair long and unbraided and had set a small stone in his ear. The warrior also had a yellow lightning bolt symbol on his cheek, and several small red dots of hail decorating his body.

In Crazy Horse's dream, many tried to claim coups on the warrior, but nobody could touch him. People clutched at the rider, but could not hold him. After the storm, a red-backed hawk flew over the rider's head.

When Crazy Horse awakened, he saw, flying over his head, a red-backed hawk, and he knew that it was a symbol for him. Like the warrior in his dream, Crazy Horse wore his hair long and unbraided, and he decorated his face and body with the lightning bolt and dots of hail. He also wore a headdress, adorned with a red hawk feather.

He was so attired now as he swung down from his horse, upon which he had put a red palm print. Crazy Horse and Cut greeted each other.

"Where do you take your band?" Crazy Horse asked.

"I go to join with the others at Greasy Grass."

"Join your band with me. I have many Cheyenne and Oglala."

"I am Lakota," Cut Nose reminded Crazy Horse.

"We have Oglala, Brule, Minneconjou, Cheyenne. We are gathered from everywhere to defeat the white man in battle once and for all. It is in this way that we may forever reclaim our land," Crazy Horse said.

"I will join you," Cut Nose said. "But when I come, I will bring great medicine with me."

"What medicine will you bring, my brother?"

"I will bring gun that shoots many times very fast," Cut Nose said. He made a cranking motion with his hand, then began making popping sounds.

"Geetleen gun?" Crazy Horse asked, not quite sure how to pronounce it.

"Geetleen gun, yes!" Cut Nose agreed enthusiastically. "I will have Geetleen gun."

"With Geetleen gun, you will be a chief that many will look up to," Crazy Horse said. Then, as if noticing it for the first time, Crazy Horse put his finger on Cut Nose's wound.

"How?" he asked.

"It is honor wound for my brother, Running Bear. He was killed by Tall Warrior."

"I do not know Tall Warrior," Crazy Horse said.

"You will not know him, for I will kill him."

"Yes, I can see," Crazy Horse said. "It is right that you must kill him."

Crazy Horse remounted, then looked down at Cut Nose. "When you have Geetleen Gun, you will join me," he said.

"Yes, when I have Gatleen Gun, I will join you," Cut Nose promised.

With the encampment of the Seventh Cavalry

Custer raised one of the rifles Falcon and Dorman brought back to camp—sighted down the barrel, pulled the trigger on an empty chamber, cocked it, and pulled the trigger a second time, still on an empty chamber. Then he lowered the rifle and examined it.

"These rifles do fire faster," he said. "But the Sharps has greater range. The truth is, if the ammunition manufacturers would do something about the cartridge cases, I do believe the Sharps would be a better weapon."

"The Sharps is better for infantry troops, I agree," Falcon said. "But for cavalry, I think the Henry would be better."

Custer sighed. "I think you are right. Unfortunately, the decision is not ours to make." He handed the weapon back to Falcon. "I'm sure you would prefer to keep this, but if you don't mind, I would like to pass the others out to my scouts."

"Of course I don't mind."

"Well, I just ask, because they are your weapons after all. It is clearly marked on the rifle butt."

"Please, General, don't rub it in," Falcon said.

Custer chuckled. "I'm sorry, I meant nothing by it. Anyway, it is the Gatling guns that we are worried about now. No sign of them anywhere?"

"Not yet," Falcon said. "But we will be going out again tomorrow."

Chapter Fourteen

They had been on the scout for four days when they saw several buzzards making circles over one spot.

"You see that?" Dorman asked, pointing to the birds.

"Yeah, I see them."

"There sure are a lot of them. Whatever is dead up there is bigger than a rabbit, or a deer," Dorman said.

The two riders slapped their legs against the sides of their horses to hurry them into a trot, and they closed the distance in just over a minute. They could smell the stench long before they got there. They saw the wagon first; then, as they drew closer, they saw the two dead mules. Wolves had been at the mules and much of the flesh was eaten away, leaving exposed rib cages and entrails . . . There was an arrow protruding from each of the mules, and three other arrows sticking out of the wagon.

"Damn," Dorman said. "That is one powerful stink. What is it, do you suppose? Prospectors?"

"I don't know, I don't see any bodies," Falcon said. "Wait a minute, look at this."

On the canvas of the wagon, not obvious as they had approached, but now clearly visible, were stenciled words:

COLORADO HOME GUARD

"That's the wagon we've been looking for," Falcon said, dismounting and hurrying over to look into the back. "The guns aren't here. But I didn't think they would be."

"Whoever took 'em, it wasn't Injuns," Dorman said. He pointed to the mules. "And as nearly as I can tell, the mules weren't killed in any sort of a fight. It looks like they have been shot through the head. Don't think the Indians would have done that."

"I think you are right. Harris evidently decided he would be better off without the wagon," Falcon said. "These wagons normally take a team of six, they've taken four of the mules with them. Two for each gun."

"It ain't goin' to be hard to follow them," Dorman said. "Pullin' them caissons like they are, why, they might as well be leavin' us maps. Depends on how long a head start they have."

"From the looks, and the smell of the mules, I would say we are about six or seven days behind them," Falcon said.

"Seems about right," Dorman said. "Listen, Falcon, you seen all you need to see here? I got to get away from this stink, else I'm goin' to start pukin'."

"I've seen all I need to see," Falcon agreed.

"Let's get on out of here then."

Falcon nodded, and the two rode away, following the clear trail left by the gun caissons.

It came up a thunderstorm that afternoon, and as Falcon and Dorman rode through the rain, it slashed against them and ran in cold rivulets off the folds and creases of their ponchos. It blew in sheets in front of them, turned the trail into mud, and whipped into the trees and bushes. Wicked forks of lightning were followed immediately by thunder, snapping shrilly at first, then rolling through the valleys, picking up the resonance of the hollows and becoming an echoing boom.

"The rain is washing the trail away," Dorman complained. He had to yell to be heard over the storm.

"True," Falcon called back. "But they were going this way when we lost their trail, and there's really no other way they can go except straight ahead."

It stopped raining around nightfall, and though the moon was in the third quarter, it was a surprisingly bright moon that peeked out from behind a large, fluffy, silver cloud. Mud puddles and rivulets of water reflected the glow, helping to provide enough illumination to allow the two men to proceed without danger of misstep in the dark. They continued on until about ten p.m., then tied down for the night.

May 26, 1876

When Clete Harris awoke that morning, he saw Cut Nose and at least thirty other Indians standing there, looking down at him.

"What the hell?" he shouted in a loud, startled voice. "Garon! Bryans! Richland! Wake up!"

"Damn!" Garon said, waking then to see the array of Indians.

"Bryans, I thought you were keeping guard," Harris said.

"I was," Bryans answered. "But at four, I turned it over to Richland."

"You have Geetleen guns?" Cut Nose asked.

"Gatling guns, yeah, I've got two of them," Harris said.

"I want."

"Well, that's why we come up here, Chief. We brought them to you." He pointed to the two guns. "Do you have any money?"

Cut Nose looked at one of the other Indians, who walked back to his horse, then brought two cloth bags. He emptied the bags onto the blanket Harris had been sleeping on. The contents were a mixture of gold coins and gold nuggets. Even the quickest estimate convinced Harris that there was more money here than he had anticipated. So much that he didn't even bring up the idea of charging more for the ammunition.

"It is not as much money as I wanted, but it will do," he said, not wanting to let on how pleased he really was with the amount. "But we brought the guns here, so they are yours."

"You show how to use," Cut Nose said.

"Yeah, all right," Harris said.

Opening the box on the caisson of one of the guns, he took out an empty magazine, then showed it to Cut Nose.

"This is called a magazine," he said.

Opening one of the cases of ammunition, he took out a handful of bullets and started sticking them down into the magazine.

"Before you can shoot the gun, you have to fill the magazine with bullets. Like this." He demonstrated by pushing several down into the magazine.

"Next, you stick it down in here like this, point at what

you want to shoot"—he aimed the gun at a small bush—
"then turn this crank."

Harris turned the crank rapidly, spinning the six barrels.
As each barrel came under the firing pin, it fired the
rounds in rapid sequence.

The gun roared, fire leaped out from the end of the
barrel, and the small shrub that Harris had selected as a
target, began disintegrating as the stream of heavy fifty-
caliber bullets whipped through the branches.

"Ayeee!" several of the Indians shouted at the demonstration.

"Now you try it," Harris said, holding his hand out
toward the gun and stepping away so Cut Nose could move
behind the gun. Cut Nose stepped behind the gun and
started turning the crank. It began firing, but because Cut
Nose was not bracing it, the gun pivoted about on its caisson wheels, spraying bullets everywhere. Harris and his
men managed to get down. But one Indian and two of the
Indian ponies were hit, and they went down.

Despite the fact that he had shot one of his own, and two
ponies, Cut Nose let out a shout of enthusiasm and excite-
ment. After that, he started dancing around, and the others
joined him.

"Listen to that! That's a Gatling!" Falcon said, slapping
his legs against the side of his horse and urging him forward.

Dorman hurried behind him.

After a short gallop, they were close enough that they
could hear some of the bullets cutting into the trees around
them.

"Whoa, hold it!" Falcon said, reining in his mount. "I don't know what's going on, but we'd better stop here."

Both riders stopped, then led their horses into a little draw where they would be protected from stray bullets. Pulling their carbines from their saddle sheaths, they climbed up the side of the butte to get into position to look down on the other side. Once in position, they saw the two guns, and those who were gathered around them. One of the Indians was pushing shells into the magazine, while one of the white men was showing him how to do it.

"That's Cut Nose," Dorman said quietly, pointing to the Indian. "He's a mean one, all right. If he could get these guns back to the Indians before the gen'rul runs into 'em, why, he could become the top dog among 'em."

"And I recognize two of the white men," Falcon said. "That is Clete Harris, and that is Jim Garon. It's no wonder now that Garon beat the stagecoach robbery charge. Harris was the foreman of the jury. The two men were in cahoots."

Suddenly, an Indian leaped out from behind them and with a yell, charged with his war club erect. Falcon turned just in time to see him and, as the Indian closed on him, Falcon grabbed the Indian by the wrist to keep him from using his war club, then fell on his back, put his feet in the Indian's stomach, and threw him over. The Indian went over the edge of the butte, screaming as he fell, headfirst, over one hundred feet down.

"Harris, up there!" one of the white men shouted, and Cut Nose pushed the magazine into place, then elevated the gun and began shooting.

He could not elevate the gun high enough, and the bullets ricocheted off the stone wall, several feet below Falcon's position.

The others began firing as well, and their shooting had more effect as the bullets whizzed by very close, some of them even kicking up little chips of rock that cut into Falcon's face.

Falcon and Dorman began returning fire, and one of the white men went down as well as two of the Indians.

Cut nose turned and leaped onto one of the mules that were still attached to the Gatling gun and with a yell, started the team running. Seeing him, one of the other Indians jumped on the back of the mules attached to the other gun, but Falcon shot him, and the mules stood their ground.

There was a further exchange of fire; then all the Indians and the whites were gone, the Indians going one way, the whites another.

"Which ones are we going after?" Dorman shouted.

"We have to get that other gun back," Falcon said. "We can't let the regiment go up against them."

Retrieving their horses, Falcon and Dorman rode back down into the flat where they had seen the guns. There were three dead Indians and two dead ponies. The Indians had gotten away with one of the guns, but the other one was still there. There was one white man lying near the gun and he was alive, but barely.

"They left me," the white man said. "The sons of bitches run off and left me."

"Who are you?" Falcon asked.

"The name is Richland. Ken Richland," he said. "You are Falcon MacCallister, ain't you?"

"Yes."

Richland coughed, and blood oozed from the corner of

his mouth. "I thought so. You don't know me, but I've seen you before."

"I recognized Clete Harris and Jim Garon," Falcon said. "Who was the other man?"

"Why should I tell you that?"

"Why not? Like you said, they ran off and left you."

"Yeah," Richland replied, his voice strained with pain. "Yeah, they did, didn't they?"

"The third man. What is his name?"

"His name is Bryans. Jay Bryans."

"Why did you do this, Richland? Why did you put Gatling guns in the hands of the Indians? Don't you know they are going to use them against whites?"

"We did it for money," Richland said. "And we got us a lot of money for them guns. A lot of money."

"It's not doing you a lot of good right now, though, is it?" Falcon asked.

The smile left Richland's face as he realized the truth of what Falcon was saying. Then his face was racked by a spasm of pain. He coughed again, coughing up more blood, then, with a gasp, quit breathing. His eyes remained open, but the stare was sightless.

Standing up, Falcon looked over toward Dorman, and saw that he was squatting by one of the Indians.

"Is he still alive?"

"Not now, he ain't," Dorman replied. "His name was Two Bears."

"Did you know him?"

Dorman nodded. "Yeah, I knew him," he said. "Falcon, we're in a lot of trouble here."

"What do you mean?"

"Accordin' to Two Bears, they's Indians from all over

the nations gatherin' up for this fight. They actually figure on pushin' the white man out of here once and for all."

"How many Indians are we talking about?" Falcon asked.

"They're comin' from six tribes. Miniconjou, Oglala Blackfeet, Hunkpapa, Cheyenne, and Sans Arc," Dorman said. "Maybe as many as twenty thousand of 'em."

"Twenty thousand?"

"If all them tribes get together, there will be that many," Dorman said. "I'm tellin' you the truth. We are goin' to have us one hell of a fight on our hands."

"You're right," Falcon said. "I don't think the general realizes that."

"So, what do you want to do? Try to run down that gun? Or go back and tell the gen'rul what we found out?"

"Look," Falcon said, pointing to a couple of boxes of ammunition. "They got away with one of the guns, but none of the ammunition."

"Don't you think they've got bullets?"

Falcon shook his head. "Not this kind," he answered. "These are special fifty-caliber bullets. The cartridges have to be machine-made to fit these guns, or the gun will jam up. We'll spike this gun and burn the ammunition. Without bullets, I don't think they will be able to do much with the gun they got. We'll go back and warn the general."

A few minutes later, as they were riding away, they heard the ammunition explode. Falcon hadn't recovered the guns, but he had made it so that they weren't going to pose a danger to the cavalry.

Chapter Fifteen

May 27, 1876
The Bighorn Mountains

It was getting dark as Falcon and Dorman followed the path of a swift-running mountain stream. They had been riding in silence for a couple of hours, with the only sound being the scraping of shod hooves on the gravel along the streambed.

Dorman interrupted the silence.

"There's someone down there," he said.

"Where?" Falcon asked.

"Down there, in that ravine." Dorman pointed. "Do you see him?"

"I see something," Falcon said. "Don't know if it's a rider or just an animal. It's too dark to make out."

"We'd best keep our eyes open," Dorman said. "If it's an Injun and we seen him, then that means he sure as hell has seen us."

The two men rode on, maintaining their silence. Dorman

took a bite of his tobacco twist, then held it out in offer to Falcon.

"Never picked up the chewin' habit," Falcon said.

"You're smart. It's a nasty habit," Dorman replied. "Only, when you got a hankerin' for terbaccy, like now, well, a chaw is a lot better'n a smoke. Injuns can smell terbaccy smoke from a mile away."

The moon was but a sliver of silver in an overcast sky, making it very dark, too dark to proceed any further. They moved into some trees, tied off their horses, then stretched out on the ground.

"Benteen tells me you were married to a Sioux," Falcon said.

"Yeah, I was," Dorman said defensively.

"I was married to a Cheyenne."

Dorman raised up on his elbows and looked over at Falcon, though in the darkness, Falcon could barely see him. Dorman chuckled.

"I'll be damn," he said. He chuckled again. "I should of know'd there was somethin' I liked about you. That Injun that I was talkin' to back there? Two Bears? He was my brother-in-law."

"Too bad."

"Yeah, well, I didn't much care for the son of a bitch when I was married to his sister."

"Where are you from, Dorman?"

"If you had asked me that fifteen years ago, I wouldn't have give you a answer. I would'a figured you was tryin' to take me back."

"Take you back?"

"I was borned a slave," Dorman said.

"I wouldn't have taken you back."

"Someone tole me that you was in the Rebel army."

"I was," Falcon said. "My brother was in the Yankee army. But the thing is, neither one of us held with slavery."

"Then how come you fought for the South?"

"There was a lot more to that war than slavery."

"Not for me, there wan't," Dorman said.

"I can understand that."

"My pap was a Jamaica man. My mammy was a slave woman down in Louisiana for the D'Orman family. When I got old enough—around fifteen or so, I reckon—I just up and run off. I kept on a-runnin' and a-dodgin', avoidin' anyone I thought might be a slave catcher, till finally I wound up out here. Some Sioux found me wanderin' around in the Paha Sapa, more dead than alive. They took me back to the village with them, fed me, and brought me back to life so to speak. You can understand why I made friends with them." Dorman chuckled. "They didn't quite know what to make of me. I was the first colored man any of them had ever seen. They called me 'Black White Man.'" Dorman laughed. "Black White Man," he repeated. "But I don't reckon bein' called a white man would have got me into any restaurants back where I come from. Anyhow, I married up with a Sioux woman, stayed with her till she up an' died on me. Then, didn't really feel like stayin' with the Injuns any longer, so I left. I started carryin' mail, choppin' and sellin' wood, until the gen'rul hired me to do some scoutin' for him. Lots of folks don't know this, Falcon, but them soldier boys only get thirteen dollars a month. Do you know how much money I get?"

"I don't have any idea."

I'm getting a hunnert dollars a month. Can you imagine

that? A colored fella like me, gettin' a hunnert dollars a month?"

"That's a lot of money, all right," Falcon agreed.

"Yes, sir, it is. 'Course, the question is, is it enough money to get myself kilt over?"

"Do you think that is likely?" Falcon asked.

"I don't know," Dorman answered. "If I didn't tell you I was a site more fearful 'bout this particular scout than any other'n I been on, I'd be lyin' to you."

"What makes you fearful?"

"Even before we left Ft. Lincoln to come on this scout, I seen me a couple of Injuns that I know," Dorman said. "They say there's a feelin' runnin' amongst the Injuns that somethin' big is goin' to happen. It's like Two Bears told me. They're actually plannin' to run all the white men out of Montana and Dakota territory. I don't mind tellin' you that I don't feel none too particular good about this."

"That's funny," Falcon said. "Libbie Custer has the same feeling."

"When women has feelin's like that, you ought to pay attention to 'em," Dorman said. "Lots of times, women just knows more than men."

"I wouldn't want to argue with that," Falcon said. He yawned. "But are we goin' to talk all night, or get some sleep?"

"I don't know about you, but I'm going to get some sleep," Dorman replied. "And if you answer me this time, you'll be talkin' to yourself."

May 28, 1876

Both men slept well, and both were awake by sunrise the next morning. After a cold breakfast of jerky and water, they saddled up and got under way, riding as alertly as possible. As they approached each knoll, one of them would dismount and hand the reins of his horse to the other, then go up to the top of the knoll to have a look around before riding over it. They had been taking turns doing that all morning, and this time it was Dorman's turn. Dismounting and giving his horse over to Falcon, the scout moved cautiously to the top. There, he got down on his stomach, took off his hat, and rose up to have a quick look over the crest.

Then, suddenly, Dorman spun around and, bending low, ran back to his horse.

"We've got to get out of here, now!" Dorman said. Leaping into the saddle, he turned his horse back down the trail and lashed it into a gallop.

Falcon followed without question, and the two horses raced toward a bluff that was some distance ahead of them. Not until they reached the bluff did they dismount and pull their horses in behind some trees.

"Tie 'em off and come up here and have a look," Dorman said.

Falcon did as Dorman suggested, and no sooner did he reach the top than he saw what had Dorman spooked. There were scores upon scores of Indians, at least one hundred and maybe more. They were now where Falcon and Dorman had been but a few moments earlier, and as the Indians advanced down the side of the knoll, they were scattered out all across the valley, as if they were looking for something.

Suddenly, one of the Indians stopped and stared at the ground. Calling one of the other Indians over, he pointed to the ground, and a few others came over as well. For a moment, they appeared to be talking excitedly among themselves, though they were too far away from Falcon for him to hear.

"They've spotted our trail," Falcon said.

"They have that all right," Dorman replied. "And they are going to be on us like a fly on shit if we don't get out of here."

"Let's go," Falcon said, turning toward his horse.

"Wait," Dorman said. He pointed to a nearby mountain. "Let's go that way."

"You know that way?"

"Yeah, I've hunted there. It will be rough for the horses, but I think we can make it. And even if the Injuns follow us, there are so many of 'em that they can't all come through at the same time, and the ones that have to hold back are goin' to slow the other ones down."

"Good idea," Falcon said.

The two men started out at a trot, taking advantage of the flat ground while they could. By the time they reached the base of the mountain, the Indians had discovered them and, though they were still some distance away, they were coming up hard and fast.

The mountain looked very close, but Falcon had spent his entire life in mountains, and he well understood the illusion of a mountain being much farther away than it appeared to be. Not wanting to overtax the horses, they trotted, galloped, and walked, reaching the actual mountain after about eight miles. But by the time they were actually at the foot of the mountain, the horses were beginning to tire from their long flight.

"If we don't give these horses a blow, we're going to kill them," Falcon said.

"I think you are right," Dorman replied. "All right, we'll let 'em take a break."

The two men dismounted. Falcon took off his hat, poured some water from his canteen into it, then held the hat in front of the horse. The horse began drinking thirstily.

"As I recall, we are some distance away from water right now," Dorman said. "Could be you're goin' to need that water for yourself."

"I'm going to get thirsty, that's for sure," Falcon replied. "But I can take it better than the horse. I can't have him going out on me now."

"Yeah," Dorman said. He took off his own hat. "Yeah, I reckon you would be right about that."

Like Falcon, Dorman gave his horse some water. Then both men unsaddled their mounts and for the next few minutes, allowed the horses to crop the nearby grass.

At the end of half an hour, they put the saddles back on, and had just finished when Falcon saw the Indians closing fast.

"There they are!" he shouted. "We have to get out of here!"

Falcon and Dorman swung into their saddles, just as a volley of shots rang out.

"Quick, into that timber!" Falcon shouted, pointing to a nearby thicket. "It's our only chance!"

The two riders wheeled toward the timber that lay to their left. Falcon's horse was hit by a bullet. It stumbled, and nearly went down, but recovered and continued to run, keeping pace with Dorman's mount despite its wound. There were so many Indians that, even though they were shooting as individuals, it was almost as if they were firing in volley. Fortunately, because they were shooting from horseback, the firing, though intense, was very inaccurate.

Just as they reached the timber, Dorman's horse was also hit, and it was limping badly as it carried Dorman into the woods. Once inside the tree line, Falcon and Dorman hastily dismounted at the edge. There, they drew their long guns and began firing back. Dorman had the Henry Falcon had given him, and so was able to maintain a high rate of fire. But the bullet that had hit Falcon's horse had also shattered the chamber of his own Henry.

Tossing the useless Henry aside, Falcon drew his pistol and took aim at one of the Indians who had come closer. He fired, and the Indian tumbled from his saddle. Although there were only two of them against at least four score Indians and more, Falcon and Dorman's fire was so accurate that, within a few moments, at least ten of the Indians lay dead or dying on the field. The rest of the Indians withdrew from immediate pistol range, but they didn't leave the field of battle. Instead, they just gathered on the other side of the open area, out of range, not only of Falcon's pistols, but of Dorman's rifle.

"Look there, Falcon," Dorman said, pointing. "Ain't that Cut Nose there leadin' 'em?"

"Yeah, that's him all right," Falcon said.

"Next time them heathen bastards come across, let's make particular sure that we kill that son of a bitch," Dorman said. "Him bein' the leader, if we kill him, it might take some of the fight out of the rest of 'em."

"We'll have to get him into range," Falcon said. "If he stays back there and directs the fight, we'll never get a chance at him."

"Oh, I'll get the son of a bitch into range all right," Dorman said.

"How are you going to do that?"

"I'm going to use you as bait," Dorman said.

Falcon chuckled. "I'm not sure I'm all that excited about being used as bait, but I have to admit that I'm interested in seeing how you are going to do that."

"I'm going to speak the words in English first, so you'll know what I'm saying," Dorman said. "Then I'm going to shout them out in Lakota."

"All right, go ahead," Falcon invited.

Dorman nodded, then cupped his hands around his mouth to yell.

"Cut Nose! The white man who killed your brother is here! He is waiting for you!" Dorman shouted. Then he repeated the shout in the guttural Lakota language.

Cut Nose shouted back.

"Black White Man. We fed you when you were hungry. We gave you blankets when you were cold. You married one of our women and your children live with us now. You were our blood brother. Why do you fight with Tall Warrior against us? You have betrayed us. When we catch you, we will show you our anger!"

"Well, it appears you have a name," Dorman said. "You are Tall Warrior."

"I guess I could have a worse name," Falcon replied.

"They think I betrayed them," Dorman said.

"This is just a guess, but I'd say they are pretty mad at you," Falcon said.

Despite the tenseness of the moment, Dorman laughed. "You're right," he said. "But so far ole' Cut Nose ain't mad enough to come out on his own. I guess I'm going to have to try again."

Again, Dorman cupped his hands around his mouth and called out loudly.

"Cut Nose, I speak for Tall Warrior who does not know our tongue! Tall Warrior says that Running Bear died a coward! Tall Warrior, believes you are a coward!"

Again, Dorman translated his challenge into Lakota, and it was answered almost immediately.

"Tall Warrior is the coward. He will not meet me in the test. I will kill Tall Warrior, then we will kill you, White Black Man. We will let the women roast you as if you are a buffalo hump."

"Do you think he really would meet me in a fair fight?" Falcon asked.

Dorman shook his head. "Any other time he might," Dorman said. "But I think if you showed yourself now, they would kill you."

"Tall Warrior says he will not fight a coward," Dorman shouted. "Tall Warrior says to send your women after us. Your women are braver than you are!"

"Ayieee! Tell Tall Warrior it is a good day for him to die. It is a good day for you to die!"

"Well, I think we did it," Dorman said with a chuckle. "Ole' Cut Nose is so mad now that he can barely breathe. I reckon they'll be comin' after us now. When he does, all we got to do is shoot the son of a bitch."

"Good job, Dorman. But wait until he gets into pistol range," Falcon replied. "With both of us shooting, the chances of getting him are a lot better."

"Right," Dorman said, cocking his rifle, then holding it barrel-up as he as waited.

They didn't have to wait long. A moment later, cries and war whoops echoed across the field as the Indians came dashing toward them. Falcon waited, listening to the rolling thunder of the horse hooves and watching the cloud of dust billowing up behind them, as the Indians galloped across the plain, rapidly closing the distance between them.

"Let me know when you think he's in your range," Dorman called, having to raise his voice to be heard over the drumming hoofbeats.

"Now!" Falcon shouted.

Both Falcon and Dorman fired, and Cut Nose went down. The others, seeing that, brought their horses to an abrubt halt, then turned and galloped back to the shelter of the rocks and trees.

"By damn, I don't reckon Cut Nose is goin' to be leadin' 'em on any more charges," Dorman said as the two of them looked out at the Indian's body, lying no more than fifty yards away. The rest of the Indians were at least fifty yards beyond Cut Nose's body, and were still riding hard to get out of range.

"How much ammunition you got left?" Falcon asked.

"I don't know—maybe twenty or so shells. What about you?"

"Just what's in my pistol," Falcon said. "You may as well take the ammunition that's in my saddlebag. It's for the Henry, and the one I've got is worthless."

"We aren't going to be able to hold off many more charges like that one we just faced," Dorman said.

One of the Indians started yelling something.

"Damn, so much for the idea that killing Cut Nose would send them home," Dorman said.

"What did he say?"

"He said they are comin' after us. We're goin' to have to get out of here."

"Yeah, well, we aren't going to go far on these horses," Falcon said. "Both of them are pretty badly wounded."

"You're right," Dorman replied. "But we still have to get out of here. You got 'ny suggestions?"

Falcon looked at the steep mountain behind them. "Have you ever been on the other side of this mountain?"

"Yeah."

"What's on the other side?"

"Another mountain."

"And then?"

"Another mountain."

"All right, after we get over all the mountains, what is there?"

"The Little Missouri River."

"Isn't that where Custer is supposed to be?"

Dorman smiled. "Yeah," he says. "Yeah, he is. Hell, if we could get over these mountains, we could join back up with him."

"Then what are we waiting for?"

"How are we goin' to go?" Dorman asked. "There is no pass here. There is no way the horses could make it over these mountains, even if they was both healthy, which they ain't. Hell, my horse is barely standin' as it is."

"Yeah, I know," Falcon replied. "But if our horses couldn't make it, even they were healthy, then that means the Indians' horses can't make it either. And if we get a head start on them, we'll have the advantage over them. We'll go by shanks mare."

"It's goin' to be one hell of a walk, Falcon, my friend, but I'm game if you are," Dorman said. "But what do you mean head start? They aren't more than three or four hundred yards behind us. That sure as hell ain't much of a head start."

"We'll fire a few shots before we leave. The Indians don't know our horses are wounded. If we leave the horses here, that might convince the Indians that we're still here, just waitin' under cover till we get a good shot, the way we did with Cut Nose."

"Yeah," Dorman agreed. "Yeah, your idea just might work at that."

"Fire a couple of shots at them, and let's go."

Both Dorman and Falcon fired a couple of shots each. Then they moved through the back of the little copse of trees where they had taken their stand, rushed through the bushes, ran over pebbles and past rocks and boulders, until they started climbing. Below them, they heard the Indians firing at long range. Then they heard shouts and a furious fusillade of shots as the Indians made their final rush.

"Those are going to be some mad Injuns," Dorman said, puffing with the exertion of climbing.

Falcon laughed. "Damn, Dorman, you mean they weren't already mad?"

The two men climbed for the rest of the day, reaching the highest peak in the entire range. Once there, they looked back. From this vantage point, they could see for miles.

"Holy shit! Look at that!" Dorman said, pointing.

Falcon didn't need it pointed out to him. He saw exactly what Dorman was pointing at. He could see hundreds, perhaps thousands of Indians. These weren't the Indians who were chasing them; these were other Indians, not only warriors, but Indian ponies pulling lodge poles, accompanied by women and children, moving along several different trails, separated from each other, but all going in the same general direction.

"Have you ever seen that many Indians at one time?" Falcon asked.

"No, sir, I have not," Dorman said. "Two Bears was right. These Injuns is comin' from ever'where."

"We have to tell Custer about this. I don't think he has any idea what he's letting himself in for."

"You don't really know the gen'rul all that well, do you?" Dorman asked.

"I haven't known him very long. Why do you ask?"

"'Cause it ain't goin' to make no never mind what we tell him. He has his mind made up to go after the Injuns, and that's exactly what he's goin' to do, no matter how many of 'em there is."

"Well, we'll just have to convince him," Falcon said.

For the next three days, Falcon and Dorman climbed mountains, reaching the top of one, only to see another to be negotiated, and another after that. They had taken their canteens and what rations they could carry with them, but by the third day, they had neither food nor water left, and they were exhausted. To make matters worse, they saw no game at these elevations.

"We're goin' to have to stop here for a while," Dorman said. "I don't think I can go any farther."

Dorman sat down, then pulled off his shoes and socks. His feet were covered with blisters.

"Look at that," he said. He lay back. "You go on if you can," he said. "I reckon I'm just goin' to lay here till I die."

"Isaiah, we've come this far," Falcon said. "We can't give up now. We don't have any food, we don't have any water, we've got to go on."

"It's comin' on nightfall," Dorman said. "I reckon if we'll just spend the night here—maybe get a little rest, I'll be ready to go on come mornin'."

"All right," Falcon agreed. "The truth is, I could use a little rest myself. We'll spend the night here."

They bivouacked under some overhanging rocks on the top of one of the highest peaks in the Bighorn range. During the night, the temperature fell very near to the freezing point. The conditions for Falcon and Dorman were miserable, because neither of them had anything more than the clothes on their back. A cold, heavy rain fell, whipped by a roaring wind that uprooted trees by the hundred. The two men spent a miserable, sleepless night.

June 1, 1876

On the morning of June 1, they found a trail that made walking a little easier than what they had been used to, so they were able to make better time on this day. Dorman estimated that they only had about twenty miles to go now, and because the trail was not as steep, it would not be as hard as the first part of their journey. However, as they were much weaker than they had been when they started the ordeal, they were not able to take as much advantage of the easier trail as they thought.

When they reached the bottom of this hill, though, they found a stream and they drank thirstily.

"Look there," Falcon said, pointing to a large fish that

was floating just under the surface. Falcon leaned over the bank, studied the fish for a moment, then stabbed his hand down into the water and flipped the fish up onto the bank. The fish began flopping around, trying to work its way back to the water, but Dorman was able to stop it.

A moment later, Falcon pulled another one out, and soon, Dorman had both fish speared on a couple of sticks and stuck down into the ground, close enough to a fire to roast.

They had just finished their meal when they saw two soldiers on horseback.

"Hold on there!" Falcon shouted to them.

The two soldiers were startled and they swung toward Falcon and Dorman with their pistols in their hands.

"Ease up there," Falcon said. "We're scouting for the Seventh, and we've lost our horses."

"How do we know who you are?" one of the soldiers asked.

"I think they're tellin' the truth, Russell, I've seen the colored man before," the other soldier said. "I know he's with the Seventh."

"All right," Russell said. "What are you two doing out here?"

"We're trying to get back to the regiment," Falcon said. "We ran into some Indians and lost our horses. And we'd appreciate it if you would ride back, then return with a couple of mounts for us."

"We're bivouacked only about five miles back," Russell said. "You could walk it in under an hour."

"Sonny, we've walked and clumb, and clumb and walked, for nigh on to fifty miles now," Dorman said. "And we ain't in the mood to walk another fifty yards. Just go back there an get us them horses like the man said."

"All right. You two wait right here."

"How long will it take you?"

"I figure we'll be back in about an hour," Russell said. "Maybe a little less."

As the two young troopers rode off, Falcon and Dorman found a place under a tree where they could sit and wait.

"You know what I'm goin' to do when this here scout is over?" Dorman asked.

"What's that?"

"I'm goin' to go back to Louisiana and look up my mammy. That is, if she's still alive. I reckon the fact that I run away as a slave won't be held ag'in me now."

"No, I don't think it will," Falcon said.

"I've got me some money, too," Dorman said. "Don't hardly nobody know this, 'cause I ain't never told no one about it before. But the truth is, I got me near 'bout five thousand dollars of money I've saved up over the years. I figure, if I can go back to Louisiana and find my mammy, I can more'n likely get me and her a place to live and just spend the rest of my days down there."

"That sounds like a good idea," Falcon said.

"I tell you what, Falcon. When I get me a place down there, you'll have to come to Louisiana and pay me a visit some time."

"I may just do that," Falcon said.

"One thing about Louisiana. There ain't no Injuns down there wantin' to lift my scalp. And another thing good is, it don't never snow. And if I don't never see me no snow no more, why, I wouldn't miss it none at all."

"If you do find your mother, I'm sure she will be very

proud of you," Falcon said. "To start out as you did, you have made a good life for yourself."

"I have at that, haven't I?" Dorman agreed. He sat up and stretched. "I wonder how much longer before them soldier boys get back."

"He said they'd be back inside an hour," Falcon said. "It hasn't been an hour yet."

About five minutes later, they heard a whistle.

"There they are!" Dorman said. "Never thought I'd feel this good about seein' a bunch of soldier boys, but I'm right proud to see these troopers."

True to his word, Russell had returned in less than an hour. Lieutenant Weir was with him, along with ten other troopers. There were also two extra horses, as well as some roasted elk and biscuits.

"The gen'rul's girl, Mary, made these biscuits this mornin', and she said she thought you might like them," Lieutenant Weir said. He smiled at Dorman. "I think she's got her cap set for you, Dorman. When she heard you were out here, she made certain I brought some of her biscuits."

Dorman ate one of the biscuits ravenously. "Lieutenant, you tell Mary if we can find us a preacher, I'll marry her before we even get back to the fort."

Weir laughed. "I wouldn't make any promises to her of that nature, Dorman. I think she would take you up on it. Then you would have the general upset with you for taking his cook away from him."

Chapter Sixteen

June 3, 1876
Beaver Creek

It snowed on June 2, and because the snow made trailing harder, General Terry halted the expedition, permitting them to camp the entire day on Beaver Creek. It was a good place to camp because there was water and wood in abundance here. That allowed the troopers to fill their canteens and gather wood, not only for the current fires, but to take with them for future encampments when wood would be scarcer.

Beaver Creek was not fordable for the wagons here, so a bridge had to be built. That meant that while the main body of the expedition rested, to the engineers it was just another day. They had already built several bridges since leaving Ft. Lincoln, so building another one here was nothing new to them.

Many of the troopers found things to do to keep them busy, but most played card games to while away the time, while others just slept in order to catch up on a commodity that had been in short supply from the moment they had left

Ft. Lincoln. Hunting had been fruitful for the last few days and, for the time being, there was enough fresh game to provide every soldier in the expedition with plenty to eat, and a few expressed the opinion that as far as they were concerned, they could just stay here for a week or two, then go back to the post.

"Hell, let the Indians wander around out here if they want to," one of the soldiers said. "What difference does it make anyway?"

While most of the men appreciated the chance to rest, Custer fumed over it, considering it a waste of valuable time. He also thought that letting the men stop and rest would actually have a deleterious effect on their military readiness. Not one to rest personally, Custer spent a lot of time with the scouts, sometimes even riding out with them. And because he had been on several scouting expeditions without locating any significant Indian sign, he tended to downplay the danger of too many Indians when Falcon and Dorman gave him their report.

"What about the Gatling guns?" Custer asked. "Did you find them?"

"Yes, we found them," Falcon answered. "The Indians managed to get away with one of them, but we spiked the one they left behind. We also destroyed their supply of ammunition, which makes the other one useless," Falcon replied.

"Good for you, good for you," Custer said. He stroked his mustache and looked at the two scouts.

"You two men had quite an adventure, didn't you?"

"Yes, sir, if you call walkin' till your feet near 'bout fall off the end of your legs an adventure," Dorman said.

Custer laughed. "Everything in life is an adventure,

Dorman. I'm glad you men managed to get away without getting your scalps lifted. But I wouldn't worry about how many Indians there are out there. The thing to worry about is whether or not we can catch enough of them together to make a fight of it, or if they will just run away the way they normally do."

June 9, 1876

At General Terry's invitation, Falcon accompanied Terry down the Powder River to the Yellowstone, where the riverboat *Far West* was waiting. The boat, with smoke drifting from its high twin chimneys, made a majestic appearance here in the wilds of Montana, so far away from civilization. Captain Grant Marsh was standing at the head of the gangplank as General Terry and Falcon stepped on board.

"Falcon MacCallister," Marsh said, smiling as he extended his hand in greeting. "I thought you would be back in Colorado by now."

"I thought so as well, but things have a way of taking on a life of their own. Now, I'm acting as a scout for Custer."

"Good for you. Custer can always use another good man."

"Do you have mail for us, Captain Marsh?" General Terry asked.

"Yes, sir, I do," Marsh replied.

Marsh held up his finger as if telling them to wait one moment. "Jerry!"

"Yes, sir, Cap'n," one of his crew answered.

"Get the mailbag for the Seventh."

"Yes, sir."

"I'll have the mail brought right here to you."

"Good, I'll have someone pick it up and take it back

upstream to the troops," Terry replied. "Is General Gibbon here?"

"Yes, sir, he arrived about an hour ago," Marsh said.

"Have him meet me in the master cabin, if you would. Colonel MacCallister, with me, please."

Falcon followed Terry into the master cabin, which was located on the Texas deck of the boat. There, Terry took out a map and spread it out on a table, holding it down at the corners with whatever he could find to use. After a moment, Gibbon came in. Gibbon was thin-faced, with a hawklike nose and dark, piercing eyes. A native of North Carolina and a graduate of West Point, he had fought, and was twice wounded, for the North, though three of his brothers had fought for the South. A colonel now, he retained the brevet of major general.

"General," Gibbon said.

"Gibbon," Terry replied. Falcon knew that Terry was upset with Gibbon for not moving quickly enough. This meeting was one week later than he had proposed, but calling his subordinate by his last name, without use of rank, was the only way the soft-spoken Terry expressed his displeasure.

"I understand that your scouts have discovered a village on the Rosebud," Terry said.

"We have, yes, sir."

"How large is the village?"

"I don't believe it is very large," Gibbon replied. "Maybe one hundred lodges or so."

"You don't believe? Can't you be more specific?" Terry asked. "Excuse me, General, but isn't the purpose of your scouting to be able to provide me with such information?"

"Yes, sir, I suppose it is. It's just that I have no real way of telling how large the village is. My scouts suggested that it wasn't a very large village, but their information was—well—let us say, inconclusive."

"Inconclusive."

"Yes, sir."

"General, this is Colonel Falcon MacCallister."

"Colonel MacCallister? Have we met, sir?" Gibbon asked.

"No," Falcon replied. "I'm not a colonel in the regular army, I'm a colonel in the Colorado Guard."

Gibbon looked confused. "If you are in the Colorado guard, what—"

"He is accompanying Custer," Terry said, interrupting Gibbon's question. "He is out here to look for Gatling guns that fell into the Indians possession."

"Good Lord," Gibbon said. "Gatling guns in the hands of the Indians?"

"Don't worry about it, the situation has been dealt with. Colonel MacCallister found one of the guns and disabled it. He also destroyed the ammunition so, though the Indians have the other gun, they won't be able to use it."

"Uh, that may not be true, General," Gibbon said with a rather rueful tone to his voice.

"What do you mean?"

"One of our wagons broke down and we had to abandon it. At first, we thought the only thing on it was canvas and tent stakes. Later, we discovered that there were three cases of ammunition on board. One of the cases was fifty-caliber rounds for the Gatling gun."

"And you didn't go back for them?"

"By the time we discovered we had lost them, it was too late. They were too far back."

"All right, there's no sense in crying over spilt milk," Terry said. "This is what I want you to do."

Terry pointed to the map, indicating where Custer was at the moment, and where he thought Crook was—though as he had had no contact with Crook, he could only guess.

"I'm going to send Custer up the Tongue River, then have him come down the Rosebud. I'll augment your column with three companies from the Seventh, and have you move up the Rosebud. If the village you saw is still on the Rosebud, we'll have them trapped in between."

"You won't trap them, General," Falcon said.

Both Terry and Gibbon looked at Falcon in surprise. "What do you mean, we won't trap them?" Terry asked.

"There are far too many Indians out there for them to be concentrated in a village that small. That was either a temporary village on the way to join one that is much larger—or—the other Indians are coming to join it, in which case it will become much larger," Falcon said.

"What makes you think there are that many Indians out there?" Gibbon asked.

"Have you seen no Indians other than this village?" Terry asked.

"Well, I did have some scouts encounter a war party that was big enough to prevent them from getting through to Custer. But I only had two scouts out there, so it didn't require that large of a party. We just haven't seen anything to suggest that there is a significantly large body of Indians operating out here."

"I have seen them," Falcon replied.

"Have you now? And where was that, Colonel?" Gibbon asked.

"Colonel MacCallister and Mr. Dorman recently returned from a very hazardous scout of their own," Terry explained.

"I see. Well, I'm sure that to a colonel from the Colorado Guard, any significant body of Indians is apt to look very large," Gibbon said. "But I wouldn't worry about it." Gibbon turned his attention to General Terry.

"General, how soon do you want me to start up the Rosebud?"

"Not yet," Terry said. "I think perhaps I'll send a scouting party, in strength, to scout the Powder River to its forks, then to the head of Mizpah Creek down to its mouth, then by Pumpkin Creek to the Tongue River." Terry pointed out his plan on the map. "It just doesn't seem likely to me that there can be that many Indians operating out there, but I am not going to totally disregard the information given me by Colonel MacCallister. I want to find out just what is in front of us. Obviously, any Indians out here are going to be by one of the rivers in order to take advantage of the water."

"General, you know what will happen if you send Custer at the head of that scout, don't you?" Gibbon asked. "If he does find any Indians, he'll turn the scout into an opportunity to attack on his own."

Terry stroked his long, luxurious beard for a moment, then nodded. "You may be right," he said. "All right, I'll send Reno."

June 10, 1876

"I don't understand why Terry sent Reno instead of me," Custer complained as he watched Reno leave at the head of six companies. "There is no way Reno is going to find something, and if he does, he won't have the slightest idea what to do about it. This whole scout is a waste of effort and a waste of time."

"Why worry about time?" Benteen asked. "We aren't on any kind of schedule out here."

"Oh, but we are, Colonel," Custer replied, using Benteen's brevet rank. "We are most definitely on a schedule. The twenty-seventh is fast approaching."

"The twenty-seventh is approaching? I don't understand, General. What is significant about the twenty-seventh?" Benteen asked.

"There is no particular significance about that date, Colonel Benteen. It would just be ten days over a month since we took to the field, is all."

Falcon knew that Benteen was aware of the Democratic convention being held on the twenty-seventh of June, because he had heard him talking about it in relation to Custer's ego.

Custer turned toward Falcon. "Thank you for bringing the mail to me. I had a letter from Libbie."

"I thought you might appreciate that," Falcon said, appreciating the change of subject.

Custer pulled the letter from his jacket.

"Listen to this," he said, as he began reading:

"The servants are doing very well. We are raising chickens. We have forty-three. So many cats about the garrison keep the rats away. The weather is very hot, but the nights are cool. The lights about the hills and valleys are exquisite. The river now is too high for sandbars to be seen.

"About a hundred men with John Stevenson in

*command have gone to the Black Hills. Nearly
twenty-five teams have passed by.*

*"Carter has returned and is chief trumpeter. He
really sounds the calls beautifully. But his long-
drawn notes make me heartsick. I do not wish to be
reminded of the Cavalry."**

Custer lowered the letter.

"Doesn't Libbie write well?"

"Yes, she does."

"Did you know there are actually people who believe
that she writes my articles for *Galaxy* Magazine?

Falcon had heard such rumors, but he didn't respond.

"You aren't the only one who got mail," Tom Custer
said with a broad smile. "Listen to this one, from Lorena.

*"I watch Libbie go about her day-to-day business,
facing the world so bravely, knowing that her
husband is now in the field and could, at any day,
be engaged in the most terrible battle.*

*"I don't know how she maintains such courage.
She is married to the general—you and I are but
recent acquaintances, and yet, I can't help but feel
that there is something deeper and more promising
yet to be discovered between us. And it is that
feeling that causes me to feel such anxiety about
your well-being that, I fear, I cannot hide it as well
as does your sister-in-law. I can but only pray for
your safe return."*

*Actual letter from Libbie to Custer, May 1876. *The Custer
Story*, edited by Marguerite Merrington, 1950.

"That's a very nice letter," Falcon said.

"Did you get one from her?" Tom asked.

"No," Falcon replied. "I didn't."

"Yes, well, it wouldn't have bothered me if you had gotten one," Tom said. He held the letter up and smiled broadly. "I mean, it's pretty obvious which one of us she has chosen, don't you think?"

"Captain, I wouldn't have it any other way," Falcon replied.

The next day General Terry sent Custer out—not on a lengthy scout such as the one Reno was taking, but a shorter, more specific scout to find a trail that would enable the wagons to pass. Custer did so, and wrote of it to Libbie that night.

June 11
Mouth of the Powder River

This morning we left camp, I again acting as guide. General Terry had been in great anxiety for the wagons. He had ridden to the mouth of the Powder and he and those with him had expressed a fear that the wagons would not make it in a month, on account of the intervening Bad Lands. He came to my tent early this morning and asked if I would try to find a road.

The men had only rations for one day left. One company had been sent out the day before, but had not returned. Sure enough, we found them. We have all arrived here safely, and the wagons besides.*

*Ibid.

Chapter Seventeen

June 21, 1876
Mouth of the Rosebud

With Reno absent on his scout, General Terry moved the rest of the column to the Yellowstone, where they were able to set up their bivouac alongside the *Far West*. Custer was getting more and more anxious, and he started agitating Terry to let him go on his own to try and join up with Reno, then to strike at the Indians wherever they might be found.

Terry held him back, but on the afternoon of the nineteenth, he finally received a dispatch, by courier, from Reno.

We have advanced to the mouth of the Rosebud. We have found no Indians, but have found a very large trail with many hoofprints and lodge pole tracks leading to the valley of the Little Bighorn.

"What is Reno doing at the mouth of the Rosebud?" Custer asked. "I thought his orders were to examine only the Tongue and the Powder Rivers."

"They were," Terry said. "He has exceeded his orders."

"And put the entire operation into jeopardy," Custer said angrily. "I told you, you should have sent me."

"Custer, are you trying to tell me that if you hadn't found Indians on the Tongue or the Powder, you wouldn't have gone on to the Rosebud?"

"I may have," Custer agreed. "But it's different for me."

"How is it different?"

"I have experience with the Indians," Custer said. "If I had encountered them, I would have known what to do. I think we should all be very thankful that Reno did not find them, for if he had, the courier might have been bearing the message that his entire command was wiped out to the last man."

"Oh, come now, that's a rather harsh appraisal, isn't it?" Terry replied.

"Are you saying that you don't think it possible for an entire command to be massacred?" Custer asked.

"No, one only has to recall the Fetterman experience to know that it is possible. But Reno's command is much larger and more mobile. And there are three columns out here in pursuit of the Indians. So I think any talk of the loss of an entire command is a bit too much."

"So, what do we do now?" Custer asked.

"We now know where the Indians aren't," Terry replied. "We just aren't that certain where they are. They aren't on the Tongue or the Powder, so they have to be on the Rose-bud, the Little Bighorn, or the Bighorn. I want you to cross the Tongue, find Reno, then come back to the *Far West*."

"I'll go find Reno and bring him back," Custer said. "But you should have sent me after him three or four days ago. We've lost a week with Reno's blundering. In fact, you should have sent me in the first place."

"Yes, Custer, I am well aware of your opinion on the matter," Terry replied wearily.

At three o'clock in the afternoon of Wednesday, June 21, General Terry held a conference in the master cabin of the *Far West*. Present were Terry, Gibbon, Custer, Major Brisbin—who was the commander of Gibbon's cavalry—and by special invitation, Falcon MacCallister.

Custer took the first seat at the table, as if it were his due, even though Gibbon outranked him. Gibbon and Brisbin also had seats at the table, and though Terry offered to have a chair brought in for Falcon, he declined, and chose to lean against the wall with his arms folded across his chest as he looked on.

Again, Terry had the map laid out on the table, held down at the corners with an ink bottle, a paperweight, a canteen, and a pistol.

"Gentlemen, we know that General Crook is in the field, but we don't know exactly where he is. I wish we could coordinate our efforts with him, but that is impossible. In fact, it is going to be difficult to even coordinate our own efforts, but let us hope that our timing is good enough that we can converge in such a way as to prevent the Indians from fleeing, and to convince them to return to the reservation."

"They aren't going to be talked back onto the reservation," Custer said.

"Then we will convince them by force," Terry said.

Custer nodded. "I'm glad we see eye to eye on that, General. A decisive victory over the hostiles now will, in all probability, end the Indian wars out here once and for all. And I intend to have that decisive victory."

"General Custer, may I remind you that my men have been in the field much longer than you have?" Gibbon said. "Brisbin's cavalry has been here since February twenty-second, and the infantry has been here since early March. We have monitored and corralled the Indians for five months, waiting for this operation to begin. I do not understand what you mean by saying that 'you' intend to have that decisive victory."

"Why, General Gibbon, of course when I say 'I,' I am talking about all of us," Custer replied.

"General Gibbon, while I understand what you are saying, I do intend to give the initial attack to Custer," said Terry.

"But, General, I—"

Terry interrupted Gibbon's protest with a raised hand.

"Hear me out," Terry said. "The Seventh Cavalry is numerically stronger. Also, whereas your command is mixed infantry and cavalry, Custer's is all cavalry, which means if the Indians do attempt to escape, Custer will be able to run them down. Your column is half infantry and, no doubt as you move quickly, you will become separated, thus weakening your force."

"I understand," Gibbon said.

"You will not be left out," Terry said. "My idea is to have Custer move quickly and strongly against the Indians, forcing them against you as a blocking force.

"Here is how I propose the operation to be." Terry put his finger on the map to illustrate his strategy. "Custer, I want you and the Seventh to push up the Rosebud on the Indians' trail. Gibbon, you will march up the Yellowstone and Bighorn, to a blocking position at the mouth of the Little Bighorn. If the Indians turn out to be on the Little Bighorn, Custer, you will attack from the south, and Gibbon, you will intercept any who try to get away to the north. Gibbon, how long will you need to get into position?"

"We should be there by the twenty-sixth," Gibbon replied.

Terry looked at Custer. "I assume you will have no problem getting there by the twenty-sixth?"

"I will have no trouble," Custer replied. "General, what if we get there and don't find the Indians?"

"General Custer, once our columns are separated, then you will be essentially on your own," Terry said. "I will give you written orders before you leave."

"Very good, sir."

"In order to give you every advantage, I want you to take four troops of Brisbin's cavalry with you."

Custer shook his head. "No, sir," he said. "No disrespect meant for Brisbin's cavalry, but I feel that the introduction of troops outside the Seventh will just complicate matters. There will be the problem of command and control. I'm convinced that the Seventh will be able to handle any situation that might arise. Besides, you said yourself that the Seventh was already numerically stronger. Taking four troops of Brisbin's cavalry would only serve to weaken Gibbon's column."

"All right, I'll accede to your wishes on that," Terry said. "Now, what about Gatling guns?"

Again, Custer shook his head. "The Gatling guns with caisson weigh over two thousand pounds. I think they would so greatly impede our progress as to take away the very advantage of rapid mobility you pointed out just a moment or two ago."

"All right," Terry said reluctantly. "It is just that we brought them this far, I hate not to see them used. But you know the situation better than I, so I'll go along with you on that as well."

"Do we have any idea of the strength of the Indians?" Gibbon asked.

"My estimate, from what both Reno and Gibbon have found, would be from eight hundred to a thousand," Terry said.

Falcon cleared his throat, and Terry looked up at him. "You have something to add, Colonel MacCallister?"

"I think you are greatly underestimating the number of Indians you are going to face," Falcon said.

"How do you know how many Indians are out there?" Brisbin asked.

"I was on a rather lengthy scout with Mr. Dorman," Falcon said. "We encountered Indians in great numbers, and they all seemed to be moving toward one general gathering place."

"Custer, given that, are you sure you don't want to reconsider taking four troops from Brisbin's cavalry?" Terry asked.

"No need, General," Custer said, refusing the offer a second time. "As we have discussed here, our biggest problem will be in catching them before they discover us and scatter all across the plains."

"Oh, I'm quite sure they have already discovered us," Terry said.

"All the more reason we should move quickly," Custer replied.

"All right, gentlemen, you can return to your commands and get ready. Custer, I'll have written orders for you in the morning."

"Very good, sir."

Falcon left the stateroom when the others did, but Custer remained behind to have a few more words with Terry. Falcon stepped up to the rail and looked out over the bank at the soldiers who had come almost one thousand miles from Ft. Lincoln. Even the greenest and rawest recruits were now seasoned veterans of the march. How they would behave in battle was another question.

"Ah, Falcon, here you are," Custer said, stepping out of the stateroom then. "Come, we must get ready." Seeing Captain Marsh, Custer called to him.

"Captain Marsh, I'm disappointed that you didn't bring my wife up with you. I would have enjoyed seeing her again."

"She wanted to come, and to bring your houseguest with her," Marsh replied. "But I thought it would be too dangerous. Though the Indians have never made a major attack against us, they have taken potshots at us from time to time."

"Yes, I see what you mean," Custer said. He nodded his head. "I'm sure you were correct in not bringing her."

"I'll tell you what, General," Marsh said. "When the expedition is over and I return to Bismarck, I'll send word to Mrs. Custer and if she would care to, I'll bring her back with me when we meet you at your resupply point on the way back."

"Wonderful!" Custer said. "I'll be counting on that, Captain. And I thank you for it."

At dinner that evening, the civilian reporter accompanying the expedition, Mark Kellogg, sought out Falcon.

"It has been an exciting journey, hasn't it?" Kellogg asked.

"It has been interesting," Falcon replied, choosing that word over "exciting."

"I wonder, sir, if I could prevail upon you to read the latest dispatch I am sending with the next mail," Kellogg asked.

"Why me?" Falcon replied.

"Because, like me, you are not a member of the Seventh.

Therefore I feel that your appraisal of the article will be free of any tint of partisanship."

"All right," Falcon agreed. "If you think my opinion is worth anything."

"Oh, I do, sir. I do indeed," the young reporter said. He handed a tablet to Falcon.

"I know that it is a bit overembellished, but I want the readers to get the feel of it, to know what it is like to be with the army on the march. Here, you may use my folding chair as a place to sit while you read."

"Thanks," Falcon said, sitting on the proffered chair and turning his attention to the pages Kellogg handed him.

At Mouth of Rosebud, on Yellowstone River, June 21, 1876*

From June 12, the date of my last communication, until June 19, the only occurrences of General Terry's command were the establishment of a supply depot at the mouth of the Powder River and making the steamer Far West a moving base of supplies, having on board thirty days' rations and forage; the movement of the steamer to the mouth of the Tongue River with the headquarters command on board; and the march of General Custer from the mouth of the Powder River to the mouth of the Tongue River, an estimated distance of forty miles, moving up the valley of the Yellowstone River. During the trip no incident occurred except the display of sharp rifle shooting on the part of General Custer, who brought down an antelope at 400 yards and nearly shot off

*Actual article by Mark Kellogg, the last one he filed.

the heads of several sage hens. The country north of the Powder River, for a distance of twelve to fifteen miles, is very poor, low, and causing hard marching, with a soil producing no grasses, only sagebrush and cactus. En route, on the 15th, the column passed through an abandoned Indian camp, apparently less than a year old. It had been a large camp, being two miles or more in length, and must have contained 1,200 or 1,500 lodges. Game was very scarce, and no buffalo at all were seen.

The Yellowstone is looming high, and its current is so swift, eddying and whirling as to create a seething sound like that of a soft wind rustling in the tall grass. Its color resembles yellowish clay at this point. It is cool and pleasant to the taste, and is a larger body of water than that of the Missouri River above its mouth, but very much superior for purposes of steamboat navigation. The waters of the Tongue River are of a deepish red color, running swiftly, and not very palatable to the taste.

On the 19th of June, General Custer, with six companies of cavalry, crossed the Tongue River, about three miles from its mouth, by fording, and marching to a point about nine miles from where Major Reno with six companies of the Seventh Cavalry were encamped, having returned from the scout he was ordered upon; but, for some cause unknown to your correspondent, Major Reno was unfortunate enough not only to exceed but to disobey the instructions of General Terry. Major Reno made an error in that he crossed, going a due south course, from the forks of the Powder to the Rosebud River, where he found a fresh hostile trail. General Terry *had planned to have Major Reno return to the column, marching down the valley of the Tongue River; and after he had formed the junction, General Custer was to organize his regiment for a scout up the Tongue, thence across to the Rosebud, striking it near its head; thence down that valley towards General Terry, who in the meantime would move by steamer to the mouth of the Rosebud, join General Gibbon's command, march up that valley until he met and joined General Custer. The plan was an excellent one, and but for the unfortunate movement of Major Reno, the main force of the Indians, numbering 1,500, would have been bagged. As it is, a new campaign is organized, and tomorrow, June 22, General Custer with twelve cavalry companies, will scout from its mouth up the valley of the Rosebud until he reaches the fresh trail discovered by Major Reno, and move on that trail with all rapidity possible in order to overhaul the Indians, who it has been ascertained are hunting buffalo and making daily and leisurely short marches. In the meantime, General Terry will move on the steamer to the mouth of the Bighorn River, scouting Pumpkin Creek en route, with General Gibbon's cavalry as well as infantry, which are marching toward the Bighorn on the north side of the Yellowstone. This part of the command marched up the Bighorn Valley in order to intercept the Indians if they should attempt to escape from General Custer down that avenue. The hope is now strong and, I believe, well founded that this band of ugly customers, known as Sitting Bull's band, will be "gobbled" and dealt with as they deserve.*

Chapter Eighteen

June 21, 1876
*Alongside the **Far West***

Custer issued an officers' call to bring, not just the commanders, but every officer of the Seventh to his tent.

"Gentlemen, I am allocating twelve pack mules to each troop. Prepare yourselves for a long, hard march. Take fifteen days rations of hard bread,* coffee, and sugar, and twelve days rations of bacon. Choose your strongest animals to carry reserve ammunition—I want a minimum of twenty-four thousand additional rounds carried with the regiment. In addition, each man will be issued one hundred rounds of carbine and twenty-four rounds of pistol ammunition."

"What about sabers?" Reno asked.

"No sabers. We'll leave them here with the steamer."

"The cavalry without sabers?" Reno said. "That doesn't seem right."

"The sabers will just take up more weight and space.

---

*Called hardtack during the Civil War, but hard bread by the Army of the West.

Also, when a cavalry troop is on the march, the loudest thing you can hear are the rattling sabers. Besides, they are more ornamental than practical. Leave them here."

"Yes, sir."

"I hope you all understand that it isn't just probable that we are going to engage the enemy. It is an absolute certainty that we will."

There was no response.

"You do know what that means, don't you?"

"I think so," Lieutenant Weir replied.

"Look around," Custer said. "Look at the man who is standing next to you. There is a very good chance that one or both of you may not make it back alive. So when you return to your encampment, I want you to write your wills, have your men make certain that they either make out their own wills, or leave verbal instructions as to the disposition of their personal effects."

"Yes, sir," Reno said.

Custer held up his finger. "Mind you don't overly frighten them, just make certain that these necessary details are taken care of."

Falcon studied the faces of all the officers as they listened to Custer. Earlier, the expressions had been of confidence, even a bit of arrogance. Now, even the most confident and arrogant among them was wearing a somewhat anxious expression.

"That's all, gentlemen. You are dismissed."

Just as the officers broke up and started to leave, Custer called out to them.

"Gentlemen, we are going to follow this trail until we find the Indians, no matter how long it takes. That means we may not see the steamer again, so my advice to you is to take along several extra rations of salt. It could be we are going to wind up living on horse meat before this scout is through."

Returning to the individual troop encampments, the officers informed the men that they would be moving out the next day.

General Terry gave permission for any soldier who wanted it to draw one cup of whiskey from the kegs. Most, but not all, of the troopers availed themselves of that offer; then, many gathered for all-night card games. Many others took the opportunity to write one last letter home, and several, Falcon noticed, seemed to have a sense of foreboding.

Tom Custer invited Falcon to join him, Boston, Calhoun, Autie Reed, Keogh, Cooke, and Weir. They were all gathered around a campfire, drinking, joking, and laughing, though Falcon had the idea that a lot of the laughter was forced.

"Jimmi, my boy," Tom Custer said. "Do you think there will be any women in Fiddler's Green?"

"Now, why would I want to be worrying about women in Fiddler's Green?" Calhoun answered. "I'm married to your sister, remember?"

"Ah, yes," Tom said. He held up his finger. "But once you get to Fiddler's Green, that won't matter. Do you think Maggie will never get married again?"

"First thing I'm going to do when I get to Fiddler's Green is look up Major Elliot and ask him just what the hell he was thinking by running off by himself like that back there at Washita," Cooke said.

"I thought Major Elliot was dead," Boston said.

"He is."

"Then what do you mean you are going to look him up when you get to Fiddler's Green?"

The other officers looked at Boston and laughed.

"What's so funny?" Boston asked.

"Yeah," Autie Reed asked. "What is so funny about that question?"

"You boys will find out in a few days," Keogh said.

"No, they won't," Tom said, taking a drink of whiskey from his tin cup. He wiped the back of his hand across his mouth. "If they have any sense, they'll be back with the trains."

"I don't intend to stay with the wagons once the fighting starts," Boston said.

"Me neither," Autie Reed added. "Uncle Autie has said that when we go into battle, I will have the honor of holding the flag."

"You are staying with the trains," Tom said resolutely. "It's bad enough that Autie is going to get himself and me killed. There's no sense in killing you, too."

The little group of men, who had been singing and laughing earlier, now grew quiet.

"Tom, that's a little morbid, isn't it?" Cooke asked.

"You're right, Cooke," Tom said. He smiled broadly, then reached over and slapped his friend on the back. "A few days from now, we'll both be laughing about this— either back in garrison or at Fiddler's Green. No sense in getting all morbid over it now."

"Where is Fiddler's Green?" Autie Reed asked.

"It is more of a what than a where," Keogh answered.

"I don't know what you mean."

"Here's a poem for you, lad," Keogh said. Standing up, he stuck his left hand inside his tunic, held his right arm out in front of him, then stepped forward with his right foot and in a deep and booming voice, delivered his poem:

> *And so when man and horse go down*
> *Beneath a saber keen,*
> *Or in a roaring charge of fierce melee*
> *You stop a bullet clean,*
> *And the hostiles come to get your scalp,*
> *Just empty your canteen,*
> *And put your pistol to your head*
> *And go to Fiddlers' Green.*

The others applauded.

"That still doesn't tell me what Fiddler's Green is," Autie Reed complained.

"Perhaps Colonel MacCallister can explain," Tom Custer suggested, though it was obvious from the tone of his voice that he didn't actually believe Falcon could explain it.

"Fiddler's Green is a place where the fiddler never stops playing, and the glass never runs dry. It's a place where all cavalrymen go after they die, there to await the final resurrection," Falcon said.

"Just cavalrymen?" Boston asked.

"Just cavalrymen," Falcon replied.

"What about people who aren't actually in the cavalry, but who ride with them?"

Tom laughed. "All right, little brother, if you are that set on getting into Fiddler's Green, I reckon I can put in a good word for you. For the two of you," he added, looking over at Autie Reed. "Though you," he said, pointing to Autie Reed, "will have to stand over in the corner until you get a little older. It wouldn't do to have you drinking with the likes of us, as young as you are."

"But, if Fiddler's Green is a place you go after you die, I'll never get any older," Autie Reed complained. "I'll have to stand in the corner forever."

Everyone laughed at that, and this time, the laughter was genuine.

"Colonel MacCallister?" a voice called from the darkness outside the bubble of golden light put out by the campfire.

"Who's out there?" Tom Custer called.

"It's me, sir, Private Burkman."

"Well, John, don't stand out there in the dark, come join us."

Custer's orderly stepped far enough forward that he could be seen.

"What can we do for you?" Tom asked.

"General Custer sent me to find Colonel MacCallister."

"You found him," Tom said. He pointed to Falcon. "He's the only man among us who isn't drunk."

"I'm not drunk," Boston said. "And neither is Autie Reed."

"I said the only 'man' among us who isn't drunk," Tom said, and again, the others laughed.

"What do you need, Burkman?"

"The general's compliments, sir, and he asks if you will join him in his tent?"

"I'll be glad to," Falcon said.

"Colonel MacCallister!" Tom called as Falcon started after Burkman. Falcon turned back toward him.

"We'll be gettin' up a card game in Fiddler's Green. Will you be sittin' in?"

"Not if I can help it," Falcon called back, and again, all around the campfire laughed.

As Falcon followed Burkman through the encampment, they passed a group of soldiers who were singing. The singing was surprisingly good, with the voices blending in perfect harmony.

> *We are ambushed and surrounded*
> *Sergeant Flynn.*
> *But recall has not sounded*
> *Sergeant Flynn.*
> *Our blades run red and gory,*
> *And we'll die for the Glory,*
> *Of the Seventh Cavalry and Garryowen.*
>
> *Garryowen, Garryowen, Garryowen.*
> *In the valley of Montana all alone,*
> *There are better days to be*
> *In the Seventh Cavalry,*
> *And we'll die for the glory of Garryowen*

When Falcon reached Custer's tent, Custer was writing a letter while drinking coffee and eating cookies. Pushing the letter aside, he picked up a tray and offered a cookie to Falcon.

"This is the last batch of cookies Mary made before I sent her back on *The Josephine*," he said. Like the *Far West*, *The Josephine* was a riverboat that had been carrying supplies and mail to and from the expedition.

"Thanks," Falcon said, accepting a cookie. He took a bite. "They are very good."

"Libbie and I have had a lot of people cook for us over

the years we have been married, but I do think Mary is the best yet."

"It is a good cookie, General, but I get the idea you didn't call me here just to enjoy the cookies."

"Huhmp," Custer chuckled. He pulled a cookie crumb from his mustache, held it on the end of his finger for a moment to examine it, then licked it off. "You are a pretty perceptive man."

"You have something on your mind?"

"Are you going with us, or, are you going to stay here with the steamer?" Custer asked.

"I have come this far," Falcon said. "It is my intention to go the rest of the way with you."

"I wish you wouldn't. I wish you would stay here with the boat."

"May I ask why?"

"I just think it would be better that way," Custer said.

"General, if you are concerned about my rank getting in the way, I will tender my resignation to General Terry tonight and accompany you as a civilian scout."

"No, no, it's nothing like that," Custer replied with a dismissive wave of his hand. "It's just that—well—if anything happens—I don't want to be responsible for you."

"General, I'm a grown man," Falcon replied. "And I have been in more than a few tight spots in my life."

"I know, I know," Custer said. "I just want you to understand that you have a choice in this. You are not a member of the Seventh Cavalry. You are not even an active member of the army."

"General, you are in charge of this expedition," Falcon said. "If you order me to stay on the boat, I will do so. But I very much want to go."

Custer paused for a moment, then reached over to his
field desk and picked up a piece of paper and handed it to
Falcon.

"Here are my written orders from General Terry," he
said. "Read them. If after you read them, you still want to
go, I won't stand in your way."

Falcon took the paper from Custer and began to read:

Lieutenant Colonel Custer, 7th Cavalry
Colonel:

The Brigadier General Commanding directs that, as
soon as your regiment can be made ready for the
march, you will proceed up the Rosebud in pursuit of
the Indians whose trail was discovered by Major
Reno a few days since. It is, of course, impossible
to give you any definite instructions in regard to this
movement, and were it not impossible to do so, the
Department Commander places too much confidence
in your zeal, energy, and ability to wish to impose
upon you precise orders which might hamper your
action when nearly in contact with the enemy. He
will, however, indicate to you his own views of what
your action should be, and he desires that you should
conform to them unless you shall see sufficient reason
for departing from them. He thinks that you should
proceed up the Rosebud until you ascertain definitely
the direction in which the trail above spoken of leads.
Should it be found (as it appears almost certain that
it will be found) to turn towards the Little Bighorn,
he thinks that you should still proceed southward,
perhaps as far as the headwaters of the Tongue,
and then turn towards the Little Bighorn, feeling

constantly, however, to your left, so as to preclude the possibility of the escape of the Indians to the south or southeast by passing around your left flank. The column of Colonel Gibbon is now in motion for the mouth of the Bighorn. As soon as it reaches that point, it will cross the Yellowstone and move up at least as far as the forks of the Big and Little Bighorns. Of course its future movement must be controlled by circumstances as they arise, but it is hoped that the Indians, if upon the Little Bighorn, may be so nearly enclosed by the two columns that their escape will be impossible.

The Department Commander desires that on your way up the Rosebud you should thoroughly examine the upper part of Tullcoch's Creek, and that you should endeavor to send a scout through to Colonel Gibbon's column, with information of the result of your examination. The lower part of this creek will be examined by a detachment from Colonel Gibbon's command. The supply steamer will be pushed up the Bighorn as far as the forks if the river is found to be navigable for that distance, and the Department Commander, who will accompany the column of Colonel Gibbon, desires you to report to him there not later than the expiration of the time for which your troops are rationed, unless in the meantime you receive further orders.

> Very respectfully
> Your obedient servant,
> E.W. Smith, Captain, 18th Infantry
> Acting Assistant Adjutant General

Falcon finished reading the orders, then handed the paper back to Custer.

"You read that, Colonel MacCallister. Do you still want to go?"

"Yes," Falcon replied.

Custer nodded. "All right, you can go as a scout."

"Thank you, General."

Chapter Nineteen

At noon, after a full morning of preparation, the Seventh Cavalry was ready to depart on its scout. Always the show-man, Custer arranged for the Seventh Cavalry to pass in review.

The soldiers, even the newest and greenest of the lot, now looked like grizzled veterans with their beards and suntanned faces. They were wearing a variety of uniforms, light blue trousers with dark blue, or gray, or in some cases, small print flannel shirts. Like Custer, Captains Tom Custer, Calhoun, and Keogh, along with Lieutenant Cooke and Boston Custer, were wearing fringed buckskin jackets. The trousers of most officers and men were reinforced in the seat with canvas.

Reno and Benteen were wearing regulation army blouses, but even they, like most of the other men in the regiment, had eschewed the army-issue kepi cap, in favor of hats that would offer better protection from the sun. Many of the men were wearing straw hats they had bought from the sutler for from twenty-five to fifty cents each.

Custer was completely outfitted in buckskin. He was wearing two English self-cocking pistols, ivory grips facing forward, and with a ring in each for use with a lanyard. He was also wearing a hunting knife in a beaded, fringed scabbard, all three weapons attached to a canvas cartridge belt. His horse, Vic, was nearby, and in Vic's saddle scabbard was a Remington sporting rifle, octagon barrel, calibrated for the 50-70 centerfire cartridge.

The Seventh was formed and ready, but the order to move out had not yet been given and Custer stood alongside Terry and Gibbon. The sky was gray and threatening. A rather strong northwest wind whipped the regimental flag, as well as the swallow-tailed red and blue banner with white crossed sabers that was Custer's personal standard. The leaves on the balsam poplar trees fluttered in the breeze, causing the leaves to flash green and white, green and white, green and white. The flashing leaves could almost create the illusion that the forest itself was on the march. Because Custer would be taking the review, Reno was temporarily at the head of the column.

"Major Reno, pass in review!" Custer shouted his order.

Reno stood in his stirrups, then turned to look back at the formation.

"Forward!" he called.

"Forward!" The supplementary commands rippled down through the column as the troop commanders gave their own response.

"Ho!" Reno shouted, and the regiment started forward in columns of fours.

Custer had massed the trumpeters from every troop, and

it was they, not the band, that played "Garyowen" as the Seventh passed by rank and file.

Falcon rode with Varnum, Dorman, the white scouts—Lonesome Charley Reynolds, George Herenden, and Fred Gerard—as well as the Indian scouts—Bloody Knife, Mitch Boyer, White Man Runs Him, Hairy Moccasin, and Curly. They rode at the rear of the mounted troopers, but ahead of the wagons. Shortly after they passed by, Custer mounted Vic, then galloped to the front of the column.

"Now, Custer, don't be greedy!" Gibbon called as Custer rode by. "Wait for us!"

"No, I won't," Custer called back.

"Lieutenant Varnum, what do you think Custer meant by that answer?" Falcon asked. "Did he mean, no, he wouldn't be greedy? Or, no, he wouldn't wait?"

Varnum laughed. "General Custer is a man of precise words. I think he knows exactly what he said, and he knows exactly how confusing his response was. Look over there."

Varnum indicated Gibbon and Terry. The two men were engaged in an animated discussion, and though he was too far away to hear what they were saying, there was no doubt in his mind but that they were discussing Custer's ambiguous response.

The column moved up the Yellowstone for two miles to the mouth of the Rosebud. There, the Rosebud was from thirty to forty feet wide and about three feet deep, with a gravely bottom. The water was also slightly alkaline, and because of that some of the soldiers, who had intended to fill their canteens, decided not to.

Proceeding along the Rosebud, and riding in the choking

dust kicked up by so many horses, the column made camp that evening. Once they were encamped, Custer called for a meeting of all his officers.

"How many of your men have filled their canteens?" Custer asked.

"General, have you tasted that water?" Lieutenant Hodgson asked. "It tastes like shit."

"Why, Benny," Lieutenant Weir said, "how do you know what shit tastes like?"

The others laughed.

"Come on, Tom, you know what I'm talking about," Hodgson replied. "The water is alkaline."

"Colonel MacCallister, did you fill your canteen?" Custer asked.

"Yes," Falcon replied.

"Why? I mean, you heard Lieutenant Hodgson. The water is brackish."

"Now, General, that isn't exactly what Benny said," Tom Custer said, and again, there was laughter. "He said it tastes like—"

"Yes, I know what he said it tastes like," Custer replied, cutting his brother off. "But I am making a point here. Colonel MacCallister, why did you fill your canteen, knowing that the water was brackish?"

"I always take advantage of water when I find it," Falcon answered. "You never know when you are going to need it, and even brackish water is better than dying of thirst."

Custer smiled broadly, and clapped his hands quietly. "Good, sir, good for you." He turned to look at the other officers. "Listen to Colonel MacCallister, gentlemen," Custer said pointedly. "There could well come a time during this scout where you would give a month's pay for one canteen of brackish water.

"Tom, how is the pack train doing?" Custer asked.

"Why are you asking me?" Tom Custer asked.

"I beg your pardon, sir?" Tom Weir responded.

"I mean Captain Tom McDougal," Custer said.

"It's clear to me that we have just too damn many Toms around here," Keogh said, and again, the officers laughed.

"The mules are carrying just about the maximum they can carry, General," Captain McDougal said. "It's all we can do to keep up."

"Do the best you can."

"Yes, sir."

"As of now," Custer said, continuing his briefing, "we are to do all that we can to prevent the Indians from discovering us. From now on, all orders will be given by hand signals, verbally, or with couriers. No more trumpet calls. Tomorrow morning, have the stable guards awake the troops at three a.m. We will move out at five a.m. sharp. Captain McDougal, will you be able to handle that?"

"Yes, sir," McDougal replied.

Custer took a deep breath and looked at all the officers for a moment before he spoke again.

"Now, gentlemen, I'm going to discuss something that no commanding officer should ever have to discuss with his officers, but I think it needs to be discussed."

The expression on Custer's face was grim and the smiles left the faces of the other officers as they paid attention to him.

"I think that every one of you know that I'm willing to accept recommendations from the most junior second lieutenant in the regiment, provided that recommendation comes to me in the proper form.

"But it has come to my attention that, during the march out from Ft. Lincoln, my official actions have been talked about, and criticized, by officers of this regiment in contact with officers of General Terry's staff.

"I don't like that, gentlemen. I don't like that one bit." Custer held up his finger. "And I'm telling you now that all such criticisms must stop at once. If you have something to say to me, be man enough to say it to my face. Because know this. Anyone I find guilty of such behavior will be dealt with to the fullest extent that army regulations will allow."

"General," Benteen said. "Will you not be kind enough to inform us of the names of those officers who are guilty of this? I mean, it seems to me as if you are lashing at the shoulders of all to get to a few."

"Colonel Benteen," Custer replied, using Benteen's brevet rank. "I am not here to be chastised by you. And even though the relationship you and I have isn't of the warmest personal nature, I can tell you, for your own gratification, I will state that none of my remarks have been directed toward you."

"Thank you, sir, for clearing that up."

"Gentlemen, return to your commands. We came only twelve miles today. I intend, by an early start and hard marching, to make up for that tomorrow."

As the officers left, Custer called out to Falcon. "Colonel MacCallister, will you remain for a moment, sir?"

Falcon nodded, then stood by as the regimental officers disappeared into the dark.

"Falcon," Custer said. "While I refused the offer of

Gatling guns, I do not relish the prospect of a Gatling gun being used against us. At first, I wasn't worried, but the fact that Gibbon lost a box of fifty-caliber Gatling gun ammunition has reawakened my concern. I would like for you to take one of the Indian scouts with you and range out some distance from the column to see if you can locate that gun."

"All right," Custer replied.

"You can take White Swan, Curly, Bloody Knife, or anyone you choose. Or, if you wish, you can even take one of the white scouts."

"I would like to take Dorman," Falcon said.

Custer chuckled. "So, you choose to take the black white scout."

"Yes. As you know, we scouted together before and we worked well together. I trust him in dangerous situations."

"I understand your reasoning," Custer said. "If you want Dorman, then by all means, take him."

"Then, with your permission, General, I'll get Dorman and we'll leave now," Falcon said. He started away from Custer's tent, but Custer called out to him.

"Falcon?"

"Yes, General?"

"This is the twenty-second. If at all possible, I would like for you to rejoin the column by dark on the twenty-fourth."

"It might take a little longer than that," Falcon replied. "What about evening of the twenty-fifth?"

"That might be too late," Custer replied without further amplification.

* * *

Falcon found Dorman checking a skewered rabbit that was suspended over a campfire.

"Damn, you do have good timing," Dorman teased. "Here, I thought I was going to have this rabbit all to myself, and you show up. I guess I'll have to share it with you."

Dorman pulled the rabbit off the skewer, then tossed it back and forth from hand to hand for a few moments.

"Is it hot?" Falcon asked with a chuckle.

"No, I'm just playing a little game of pitch and catch," Dorman replied, laughing.

Finally, the rabbit cooled enough for him to hold it, and he tore into two pieces, giving one piece to Falcon.

"You may not want to share that when you hear what I have to ask," Falcon said.

"If that's the case, maybe I'd better share it with you before you tell me what you have in mind," he said.

Falcon took a bite of the rabbit. "Oh, this is good," he said. "What did you do to it?"

"I rubbed in cayenne and salt," Dorman said.

For a moment, the two men ate in silence, enjoying the food.

"Are you goin' to tell me, or not?"

"It isn't what I'm going to tell you. It's what I'm going to ask you," Falcon said. "I'm going out on a scout, away from the regiment. I want you to go with me."

"We're goin' to look for that other gun, aren't we?" Dorman asked.

"Yes, we are."

"Yeah, I heard that Gibbon lost a case of ammunition. You think the Indians got it?"

"I think we have to assume they did. If they didn't, we haven't lost anything by looking for them. If they did and we don't look for them, we could well ride into an ambush, and I don't have to tell you how much damage that gun could do on a column of men."

"I can imagine."

"Custer said I could take any scout I wanted, and I chose you."

"Well, now, ain't I the lucky one?" Dorman said. He sucked the meat off a bone, then tossed it aside.

"You don't have to go if you don't want to. I can find someone else if I have to."

"Now here, just a week or so ago, you said you wanted to marry me for my cookin', but now you are willin' to run off with someone else," Dorman said. "You really know how to hurt a fella's feelin's."

Custer laughed. "What do you say? Will you go with me?"

"I'll go," Dorman agreed. "I 'spect we'd better tell Varnum about it, though."

Chapter Twenty

Falcon and Dorman were about five miles away from the camp. There was no moon and it was very dark, but they were able to find their way by following along the bank of the Rosebud. Because the stream meandered back and forth, they crossed it about five times in the first five miles. When they reached a broken bluff, about ten miles ahead of the camp, Falcon called out to Dorman.

"Hold up here," Falcon said. He tried to look at his watch, but it was too dark. Taking a match from his shirt pocket, he struck it by snapping his thumbnail across the head. In the light of the flame, he checked the time, then, extinguishing the flame, he put the watch back in his pocket.

"What time is it?" Dorman asked.

"Two fifteen. I wanted to leave last night, because I think we need to put some distance between us and the column if we're going to have any possibility of moving around without being seen."

"I agree," Dorman said.

"But, we could be one hundred yards away from the gun

now, and not even see it in the dark. So, I suggest we stay here until daylight."

"I ain't goin' to argue with you about that," Dorman said. "No, sir, I ain't goin' to argue one little bit."

June 23, 1876
Along the Rosebud

Shortly after Falcon and Dorman got under way the next morning, they came across the Indian trail Reno had found. The trail was at least one hundred yards wide, and the very ground had been plowed up by horses' hooves and lodge poles. It was easy to follow. The trail was a wide, brown road that stood out vividly against the lush, green grass.

"Lord in heaven," Dorman said when they cut across the trail. "How many Indians does it take to make a trail this wide and this deep?"

"Thousands," Falcon replied. "Maybe fifteen to twenty thousand."

"I don't think the gen'rul has any idee of this, does he?" Dorman asked.

"I think he believes the number will be somewhere between eight hundred and a thousand."

"If there's twenty thousand injuns, that means five thousand or more warriors."

June 24, 1876

It was early the next morning when they spotted the gun. There were about six Indians with it, pulling it down the center of the road that had been carved by so many before them.

"Ha!" Dorman said. "Pullin' that gun, they couldn't keep up."

"Let's get after them," Falcon said, slapping his legs against the side of his horse.

The horse was an army horse, and was neither as responsive nor as fast as Hell. Nevertheless, within a minute, it was obvious that he and Dorman were closing the distance with the Indians.

When they were within a hundred yards of the gun, one of the Indians looked around. Seeing Falcon and Dorman galloping up behind them, the Indian let out a shout.

Responding to the shout, the other Indians turned, and seeing that they had the advantage in numbers, started galloping toward Falcon and Dorman. By now, they were within pistol range, and Falcon brought two of them down with two quick shots. The Indians, armed with rifles and war clubs, suddenly decided that the better part of valor would be a quick retreat, and they broke away, two going to the right and two off to the left. Dorman started after those two.

"Let them go!" Falcon shouted. "We need to get the gun!"

Reaching the gun, Falcon reined his horse to a stop, then leaped from the saddle. The first thing he saw was a broken axle that had been jury-rigged. That the gun was heavy and had a busted axle, coupled with the fact that the Indians weren't used to working with wheeled vehicles, made it easy to understand why they had not been able to keep up.

"Look there," Falcon said, pointing to a box that was tied to the caisson. "It looks like they did find the ammunition Gibbon lost."

"That's interesting all right, but maybe you had better look there," Dorman said.

Looking in the direction Dorman indicated, Falcon saw not the ones they had just encountered, but a new, substantial body of Indians coming toward them.

"We need to skedaddle," Dorman said.

"Too late. As slow as these horses are they would run us down. We're going to have to fight."

"Ain't goin' to be much of a fight," Dorman said. "This ain't like it was last time where we had somethin' to be behind. This time we're goin' to be standin' out here naked as a jaybird."

Falcon broke open the box of ammunition.

"Well, now, what do you know?" Falcon said with a broad smile. "Sometimes, you just get dealt the right cards."

"The right cards? What are you talkin' about? They's got to be at least twenty of them heathens," Dorman said nervously.

"There are ten magazines, preloaded with forty rounds each," Falcon said. He removed one of the magazines and put it into the breach. "Hold the horses," he said.

Dorman took the reins of the two horses, then waited as the Indians continued to gallop toward them. A few began firing, but the range was still fairly significant, and they were shooting from the back of galloping horses, so the bullets passed harmlessly over the heads of Falcon and Dorman.

Falcon waited until they were considerably closer. Then he started turning the crank.

Within seconds, the Gatling gun had spit out forty rounds. Four of the charging Indians went down with the first fusillade. Falcon's reaction had been totally unexpected, and the rest of the Indians, surprised by the sudden firepower, stopped their charge. For a moment of confusion, they just milled around. Then, seeing the gun was apparently empty, they renewed their charge.

Falcon jerked the first magazine out and slapped another one in. Once more, he started twisting the crank, and again the gun started spitting out bullets in rapid fashion. Three more Indians went down.

By now, the Indians had lost almost half their number. Realizing that continuing the charge would be foolish, the remaining Indians turned and, with whoops and shouts, galloped away.

"Whoooeee!" Dorman said. Laughing, he took off his hat and slapped it against his knee. "Yes, sirree, that gun is pure somethin'."

"Let's destroy it and get out of here," Falcon said.

"Destroy it? Don't you think we ought to take it back to the gen'rul?"

"No. In the first place, busted up like it is, I'm not sure we could even get it back to him. And in the second place, he wouldn't take it if we could. Remember, he was offered a battery of the guns and he turned them down. And those were newer models than this one. This is an older model, because it was going to a state militia."

"How are we going to destroy it?"

"We'll fill the chamber and barrels with dirt, then we'll smash the magazines," Falcon said.

For the next few minutes, the two men worked quickly, Falcon filling the gun with dirt while Dorman used the war club of one of the dead Indians to destroy the ammunition magazines.

With the gun destroyed, they remounted and left the

trail they had been following, then went back to the Rose-bud to rejoin Custer.

There were no signs along the bank of the creek that Custer had yet passed, so they knew they were ahead of him. Going back up the Rosebud, they reconnected with Custer at about one o'clock, where the column had stopped alongside one of the tributaries of the Rosebud, called Mud Creek. There, the men had made coffee, though the water was even more brackish here than it had been in the Rose-bud and the coffee was almost too bitter to drink.

When Falcon and Dorman first raised the camp, Custer was gone, having ridden off with Varnum. The two officers returned at about three o'clock and, seeing Falcon, Custer smiled.

"Hello, Colonel," Custer said, swinging down from his saddle and handing the reins to his orderly. "Did you find the gun?"

"Found it and destroyed it," Falcon replied.

"But not before he kilt about twenty Injuns with it," Dorman put in.

"Really?" Custer replied.

"I think Mr. Dorman is exaggerating a bit," Falcon said with a chuckle.

"A bit maybe, but not much. When we found the gun, we was jumped by a bunch of heathens, but Falcon here turned that gun on 'em and just cut 'em down like a scythe through wheat."

Custer frowned. "I thought there was no ammunition for the gun."

"You were right to be concerned about the ammunition Gibbon lost," Custer said. "The Indians had found it."

"Well, I'm thankful you found it as well," Custer said. "I'd hate to think of having to go against that."

"To be honest, we probably wouldn't have had to worry about it," Falcon said. "The axle was broken; I don't think they could have ever put the gun in position to give us any trouble."

"Nevertheless, you accomplished your mission and should be congratulated. Did you see anything else?"

"You mighty right we seen somethin' else, Gen'rul," Dorman said. "You got 'ny idea how many Injuns is out there?"

"All the signs indicate that the village might be quite large," Custer said.

"Quite large?" Dorman replied. "The village might be quite large? Forget a village, Gen'rul, I believe them Injuns is puttin' 'em together a city. Goin' up ag'in 'em's goin' to be a lot like tryin' to attack Denver."

"Oh, I think not," Custer said easily. "Think about it. How would that many Indians sustain themselves in one place? They would run out of wood and game very quickly, and they would either have to separate, or move on. And if there are as many as you say, that's ideal for us. Indians don't organize into a cohesive military unit. If they have six hundred warriors, that means they have six hundred individuals, unled and uncoordinated. And you do remember what Euripides said, don't you?"

"Euripides?" Dorman shook his head, then spit out a wad of tobacco. "I don't rightly remember ever meetin' the fella."

Custer laughed out loud. "It's unlikely that you would have met him, since he died a long time ago. But he said, and I quote; 'Ten men wisely led are worth one hundred without a head.' No, my friend, regardless of how many Indians we may meet, the advantage is ours."

After the break, Custer ordered the column to get under way once more and at seven forty-five that evening, they camped again on the right bank of the Rosebud, having come twenty-eight miles that day.

Dinner that evening consisted of hard bread fried in bacon grease, called skillgilly by the soldiers. As Falcon was finishing his meal, Keogh called over to him.

"Colonel MacCallister, m' boyo, come and join us. I've saved a snug nook with beautiful grass just for you."

"Thank you, Myles," Falcon replied, carrying his saddle and saddle blanket with him. There he found Captain Keogh, Captain Benteen, Captain Godfrey, Lieutenant Porter, and Lieutenant DeRudio.

Though the other horses were kept together in a roped-in "stable", Keogh's horse, Comanche, was tethered to a nearby tree. As Falcon walked by the horse, it whickered and ducked its head. Falcon rubbed Comanche's ears.

"Comanche, you old rake," Keogh said. "Sure'n you're tryin' to make me jealous now, are you, by cavortin' so with the colonel and here himself bein' an outsider?"

"Comanche is a good horse," Falcon said.

"Aye, that he is," Keogh replied. "'Twas in a fight against the Comanche on the Cimarron River at Beaver Fork, back in sixty-eight it was, that he showed his true mettle. Two wounds he had, either one of which would have stopped the ordinary horse. But Comanche never lost a step, carried me through till the end. Saved my life, he did. That's why I bought him from the army, and made him my own personal horse. Yes, sir, I went from Ireland to Italy, where I fought with Papal forces at the Battle of

Castelfidardo, served as a Vatican Guard, then came to America to fight in the Civil War. I was at Shenandoah Valley, Fredericksburg, Chancellorsville, Brandy Station, Battle of Five Forks, and Gettysburg, but never once did I come across a horse the equal of Comanche. I named him Comanche after the heathens we did battle with that day.

"Comanche, that's a fitting name," Falcon replied.

"Say, there's Reno over there," Godfrey said. Reno had found a tree and was sitting under it all alone. "Myles, didn't you invite him to join us?"

"Aye, lad, that I did," Keogh replied. "But the major declined. He is a bit of a loner, methinks."

"Maybe he thinks he is too good for us," DeRudio said.

"Lieutenant, I'll not have junior officers speak disparagingly of senior officers in my presence," Benteen said rather sharply.

"Sorry, sir, I meant no disrespect," DeRudio replied contritely.

"We're sharin' some personal stories here, Colonel MacCallister," Porter said to break the pregnant pause. "That is, all of us but DeRudio. DeRudio is spinnin' yarns, expectin' us to believe them."

"Hey, what do you mean, spinning yarns?" DeRudio complained as the other officers laughed.

"I didn't say we weren't enjoyin' them, Charley," Porter said. "I just said we didn't believe them."

The others laughed again.

"Colonel MacCallister, I have a question," Benteen said. "The couple who came to entertain us, Andrew and Rosanna MacCallister, they are you brother and sister-in-law?"

"No, they are my brother and sister," Falcon replied. "They are twins."

"Sure'n didn't I say as much, Fred?" Keogh asked.

"You did," Benteen admitted. "It's just that if they are your brother and sister, your blood kin, does that mean you also have talent?"

Falcon laughed. "I'm afraid not," he said. "When it came to our family, I'm afraid they got all the talent."

"Well, they certainly are entertaining," Benteen said. "I think when this campaign is over, I shall take a leave, then take my family to New York to see them."

"Don't just go see them in a play," Falcon said. "Please call upon them socially. I know they will appreciate it."

"I will, and thanks." Benteen stretched, then looked at the others. "If you boys think we are going to camp here all night, you have another think coming. If I were you, I'd quit all the palavering and try to get some sleep."

"Do you know something we don't?" Keogh asked.

"No, but I know Custer," Benteen said. "And there's not a doubt in my little military mind but that we'll be pulling out of here in the middle of the night."

Chapter Twenty-one

June 24, 1876
Bivouac on Mud Creek

Because it was a moonless night, it was pitch dark when the camp was awakened at eleven o'clock and told to move out. To Custer's frustration, however, it was taking some time to get the pack train across the creek.

Custer kept the column waiting while he went back to check.

"McDougal, what is the problem here?"

"The mules won't take to the water," Boston said. Both Boston and Autie Reed were with the pack train.

"Colonel Keogh!" Custer called, using Keogh's brevet rank. "Are you within the sound of my voice?"

"Aye, General," Keogh called from the darkness.

"Get these mules across the creek."

Keogh, astride Comanche, materialized from the dark. Swinging down from the saddle, he looked over at McDougal. "Come on, lad, if you, a Scotsman, and I, a son of Ireland, work together, I'm sure we'll be to convince these recalcitrant English mules to cross a wee bit of a stream."

It took an hour and a half to get the train across the stream; then the column resumed its march. It was so dark, however, that the only way they could maintain unit integrity was for the rearmost man in each troop to pound his cup against his saddle.

Falcon was riding with Benteen when Keogh came up beside him.

"I've not an idea in Sheol where we are, I can't tell head nor tail from this miserable pack of mules that make up the train, and I can't see two feet in front of my face."

All the time Keogh was complaining about the mule train, the banging of the cups rang throughout the valley.

"I wouldn't worry about the mules," Benteen said. "Nothing but an Indian could run one of them off. One of the packs might slip off and be left behind, but we could always recover it in the morning when it's light enough to see."

At that moment, the banging of tin cups on the saddles stopped, and the column came to a halt. Then word was passed down from the front.

"Dismount, but don't unsaddle. Rest in place."

"Dismount, but don't unsaddle. Rest in place."

The command continued to be passed down the ranks, though with slight variations so that, by the time it reached the last troop, it was:

"Dismount, leave the saddles on. Rest where you are."

Shortly after the column halted, Lieutenant Varnum rode back to find Falcon.

"Colonel MacCallister, it'll be light soon. I wonder if you would like to ride out on a scout with me."

"Only if you quit calling me colonel," Falcon replied. "That makes it a little awkward, don't you think?"

Varnum chuckled. "Yes, sir, I guess you are right."

"And I'd be honored to go on a scout with you."

"Here, you might need a little breakfast," Keogh said, handing Falcon a couple of pieces of hard bread and a strip of dried meat. "The jerky is from the last elk we cooked," he said.

"Thanks.

"Say, Captain Keogh, how about switching horses with me?" Falcon teased. "Mine is a little tired."

"Colonel, m'lad, you can have Comanche when you pry his reins from my cold, dead hands."

"So, is that a no?" Falcon asked. Those near enough to hear the banter between the two laughed.

Falcon and Varnum rode off on their scout. They had gone only about five miles ahead when Falcon called out. "Lieutenant, look ahead. Do you see the smoke?"

"Yes," Varnum said. "That's not just a few lodges, is it?"

"No, I think not," Falcon replied. "The way the smoke is spread out, I'd say that village is three, maybe four miles from side to side."

They started forward again when Falcon saw someone coming.

"There's Bloody Knife," he said.

"Good. I sent him, Mitch Bouyer, and Charley Reynolds out last night."

Seeing Falcon and Varnum, the Crow scout rode toward them.

"What did you see?" Varnum asked.

"Many Sioux camped on Little Bighorn," Bloody Knife said.

"Where are the others?"

"They wait, make sure Sioux not leave." Bloody Knife twisted around and pointed to an escarpment. "From there, you can see camp."

"Good, good. MacCallister, you can wait here with Bloody Knife and the others if you like. I'll go back and get Custer."

Falcon climbed to the top of the ridge, then looked out toward the Little Bighorn River, which was twisting in a series of U shapes as it ran through the broad valley. On the east, from which side Falcon was looking, the river ran alongside steep bluffs, ranging from eighty to one hundred feet high. On the opposite side of the river was a wide, flat plain. There, in the distance, Falcon saw something that looked like a low-lying brown carpet.

"What is that?" Falcon asked, pointing.

"You can see?" Mitch Bouyer asked.

"Yes."

"Ponies," Bouyer replied. "Many, many ponies. Maybe twenty thousand ponies."

It took about an hour for Varnum to go back for Custer, and when they returned, Reno, Benteen, and Cooke had come along as well. The little group rode to the top of the ridge, where Falcon, Bloody Knife, Bouyer, and Reynolds were waiting.

"Now, what do you see?" Custer asked.

"Many ponies," Bouyer said. "Big village, there." He pointed. "It is the biggest village I have ever seen."

Custer pulled a pair of field glasses from his saddle pouch, then looked in the direction Bouyer pointed. He looked through the glasses for a long moment, then lowered them.

"I don't see anything," he said.

"They are there."

"How many?" Custer asked.

"We will find enough Sioux to keep us fighting two or three days."

Custer smiled. "Oh, I guess we'll get through them in one day." He lifted the binoculars and looked again. "You are sure they are there?"

Bloody Knife turned his hand over and wiggled his fingers. "From here, the ponies look like worms, crawling in the grass."

"Gen'rul, I think you ought to know that we've also seen at least three war parties returnin' to the camp," Charley Reynolds said. Charley Reynolds was carrying his arm in a sling.

"What's wrong with your arm?"

"I got a cut in my ring finger, and it's up and festered on me," Reynolds said.

"Did you do anything for it?"

"I put me a poultice of a strip of bacon and some axle grease on it," Reynolds replied. "That ain't helped none, and I have to tell you it's hurtin' somethin' fierce."

"I'm sorry to hear that," Custer said.

"Gen'rul, I think you got to figure that the Injuns has done seen us by now."

"Yes, I'm afraid you might be right," Custer said. "All right, let's return to the camp. We don't have a minute to lose."

When they returned to the column, Tom Custer was waiting for them, and he asked to speak with Custer for a moment. Falcon watched the two brothers engage in an animated discussion, but they were too far away for him to be able to hear what they were saying. When he saw Dorman a moment or two later, the black scout filled him in.

"One of the pack mules lost a case of hard bread during the night march up here," Dorman said. "Keogh sent a sergeant and some men back to retrieve it, and they seen a bunch o' Sioux openin' the box. They shot at each other a couple times. Then the Sioux run off."

Once again, Custer called a meeting of all his officers. As usual, his orderly had stuck his command pennant in the ground to mark the place as headquarters, but a freshening southerly breeze caught the banner, causing it to flap briskly, then blow down. As Falcon was nearest the flag, he picked it up and stuck into the ground again, this time using a bit of sagebrush to help support it.

Because of the heat of the day, Custer had taken off his buckskin jacket, and was now wearing a dark blue army shirt, buckskin pants tucked into his boots, and a gray, broad-brimmed hat. There was no insignia of rank on his shirt, but no rank was needed to establish his position of command.

"Gentlemen," he began. "It is beginning to appear as if we have been discovered and my biggest fear is that the Indian camp will break up, scattering in all directions. So, from this moment forward, we will have no advance elements. Instead, we will advance in force, find the village, and strike as soon as possible."

June 25, 1927
MacCallister, Colorado

"We advanced to the head of what is now called Reno Creek," Falcon said as he continued telling his story to Zane Grey, Libbie, and his great-granddaughter. "There, Custer formed the regiment into battalions. Major Reno was given command of one of the battalions, Captain Benteen was given command of another, and Custer took command of the largest single battalion. Captain McDougal and his company guarded the pack train and brought up the rear."

"Who did you go with?" Zane Grey asked.

"Well, I had been with Dorman for most of the time and when they divided up, Dorman was with Reno, so that's where I went as well."

"Falcon, do you recall about what time of day that was?" Libbie asked.

"It was about nine o'clock in the morning," Falcon answered.

"The reason I asked is, you may recall that June twenty-fifth was a Sunday, and several of the wives of the post had come to my house for a Sunday prayer service.

"Our little group of saddened women, borne down with one common weight of anxiety, sought solace in gathering together in our house. We tried to find some slight surcease from trouble in the old hymns: some of them dating back to our childhood days when our mothers rocked us to sleep to their soothing strains. I remember the grief with which one fair young wife threw herself on the carpet and pillowed her head in the lap of a tender friend. Maggie sat dejected at the piano, and struck soft chords that melted into the sounds of the voices. All were absorbed in the same thoughts, and their eyes were filled with faraway visions and longings. Indescribable yearning for the absent men, and untold terror for their safety, engrossed each heart."

June 25, 1876
Ft. Lincoln, Dakota Territory

"Lorena, would you be a dear and stand on the porch just outside the front door, telling our guests that they don't have to knock? They can just come right on in."

"Yes, I would be glad to," Lorena said.

"What about the chaplain?" Margaret asked.

"I'm afraid we are going to be on our own, Maggie," Libbie replied. "The chaplain must conduct Sunday services for the troops who have remained in garrison. But I will read from the prayer book. We won't be able to celebrate the Eucharist, but that certainly doesn't mean that we won't be in communion with one another."

"And with our husbands," one of the other ladies said.

"Yes," Libbie answered. "And with our husbands."

One by one, the wives of those who were on the scout with Custer arrived at the commandant's house. It was not only the officers' wives who came, but the wives of the NCOs as well, including some who were post laundresses and to whom clung the sharp smell of lye soap.

Libbie read a few lines from the Book of Common Prayer; then someone suggested that they share some of the letters from their husbands. Libbie started it by reading her latest letter from Custer; then Maggie read one from her husband, Jimmi Calhoun.

"Lorena got a letter from Tom, but I won't embarrass her by asking her to read it," Libbie said.

"Oh, read it, please do," one of the other ladies said, and blushing, Lorena agreed to read but one paragraph. Retrieving the letter, she cleared her throat and began to read:

"The days are hot with the rigors of the trail, but the spirits of all the men are high. The nights are cold and lonely, and I asked myself, how can I be lonely as I am surrounded by the entire regiment? Then I think of you back there and myself here, and I know why I am lonely."

Lorena looked up and saw the smiles on the faces of all the wives.

"Miss Wood, I can only say that, if you marry a soldier, be prepared to be lonely, for that is the lot of a soldier's wife," one of the others said.

"Maggie, if you will play the piano, we can sing a hymn, then all return to our homes and think of, and pray for, our husbands who are so far away from us now."

Maggie sat at the piano and began to play the hymn "Nearer My God to Thee." The ladies sang:

> *Nearer, my God to Thee,*
> *Nearer to Thee.*
> *E'en though it be a cross*
> *That raiseth me,*
> *Still all my song shall be.*
> *Nearer, my God, to Thee,*
> *Nearer, my God, to Thee,*
> *Nearer to Thee.*

June 25, 1927
MacCallister, Colorado

Libbie finished her story by actually singing some of the hymn. Rosie joined with her then. Smiling through her tears, Libbie finished singing.

"You have a very sweet voice, my dear," she said to Rosie. "Remembering your namesake, I am not surprised. You come by it honestly."

"Thank you, Mrs. Custer," Rosie said.

"Falcon, I interrupted your story. Please continue."

"Where did I leave off?" Falcon asked.

"General Custer had just divided his regiment into three battalions," Zane Grey answered.

"Oh, yes. Shortly after he divided the regiment into three battalions, they reached the creek that was known then as Ash Creek, but is now known as Reno Creek. Custer ordered Benteen to take his D, H, and K troops and head south to a line of bluffs about two miles off, at an angle of forty five degrees; to send a well-mounted officer and ten men in advance; and to pitch into any Indians he might find. He was also told to notify Custer at once if he saw anything.

June 25, 1876
Ash Creek

Falcon watched as Benteen and his battalion started off toward the south toward the line of bluffs that blocked any view of Indians who might be there.

A rider approached Major Reno.

"Major, General Custer requests that you ride down the left side of the creek, while he rides down the right side," the rider said.

"All right," Reno replied. Then, standing in his stirrups, he gave a hand signal indicating his battalion should cross the creek. At this point, the water was easily forded and the hooves of so many horses kept a sustained splash of bubbles sparkling in the sunlight, until finally all were across.

The regiment, minus Benteen's battalion, now proceeded down the creek, with Reno on one side and Custer on the other.

"I hope we ain't goin' to need the pack train," Dorman said, twisting around in his saddle. Falcon also tried to look behind him, but the pack mules were so far back that they couldn't be seen.

They continued on for about three more miles, then came to a fork where the creek they were following joined the Little Bighorn. Here, Reno led his battalion back across the creek so that the two columns were joined. They saw a lone teepee, inside of which was a dead warrior, ceremonially laid out with his life possessions to include a bow and arrows and a shield.

"I've got the bow!" Boston said excitedly, coming out of the teepee and holding to bow over his head.

"The shield is mine!" Autie Reed claimed, displaying it with enthusiasm equal to Boston's.

"Burn the teepee," Custer ordered, and a couple of troopers set fire to it.

They heard a yell from the top of the hill that was just north of the teepee. It was Fred Gerard, waving his hat and shouting.

"Here are your Indians, General, running like devils!" Gerard called.

Some distance ahead, Falcon saw what Gerard was talking about. A party of warriors were galloping at full speed toward the river.

"We haven't come this far to let them get away!" Custer said. "Reno, take the scouts with you and push ahead at a trot!"

"Scouts!" Reno shouted, and Falcon joined Varnum, Dorman, and the other scouts as they moved out ahead of the column at a brisk trot.

Falcon could tell by the gait of his mount that the horse was on the verge of physical collapse. Man and animal had been pushed hard for over a month now, long hard days, short, often sleepless nights, and with little food or forage.

But the horse gave Falcon all it had, and for that, Falcon was grateful. To Falcon's right front, he could see a huge cloud of dust boiling up from behind the high bluffs that hid the Little Bighorn Valley.

When they reached Medicine Tail Coulee, which led down to the river at the central ford, Reno halted, and they looked across the creek.

"Major," Falcon said, pointing. Here, for the very first time, they could see the village clearly. It was large—so large they it was impossible to see just how large it was because the other end of the village just disappeared in the distance.

"Damn," Reno said.

"When's the last time you seen somethin' that big, Falcon?" Dorman asked.

"Last time I was in New York," Falcon replied. He was exaggerating, and he knew that Dorman knew he was exaggerating, but even in the exaggeration, there was some truth.

Custer and Cooke came riding up quickly.

"What do you see?" Custer asked.

Falcon pointed to the village across the river. This time, Custer needed no binoculars. He could see the village quite clearly.

Custer took off his hat and waved it over his head as his horse, Vic, made a couple of high-stepping circles.

"We've got them this time! We've got, 'em boys!"

When the rest of the regiment rode up, Custer held up his hand to halt them.

"Trumpter Martin!" he called.

The Italian trooper rode quickly to the general.

"Orderly, I want you to take a message to Colonel

Benteen. Ride as fast as you can and tell him to hurry. Tell him it is a big village and I want him to be quick and to bring the ammunition packs."

"Yes, sir," Martin replied.

"Orderly, wait!" Cooke, the adjutant, called. "I'll give you a written message."

Cooke wrote something on a page from a small book; then he tore the page out and handed it to Martin.

"Now, Orderly, ride as fast as you can to Colonel Benteen. Take the same trail we came down. If you have time, and there is no danger, come back, but otherwise, stay with your company."

"Yes, sir!" Martin shouted and, taking the message, he whirled his horse about and started galloping back along the column.*

"Major Reno, I want you to cross the river here and attack the south end of the village. I will support you," said Custer.

"Yes, sir," Reno replied.

"Colonel MacCallister!" Custer called. "You come with me."

Falcon, who had been riding with Dorman and Reno, left Reno's battalion and joined Custer. Just as he joined, Boston and Autie Reed came riding up. Tom Custer was sitting his horse, very close to his brother. He frowned when he saw Boston and Autie.

"What are you two doing here?" Tom asked. "You are supposed to be back with the train."

---

*Actually, Martin did not leave until after the Reno and Custer columns had already separated.

"If there is going to be any action, we want to be a part of it," Boston said.

"Yeah," Autie said. "I'm not going to miss out on this."

Falcon saw the expression in Tom's eyes. Oddly, it was one of resignation and sadness.

"General," Tom said. "Shouldn't we leave Colonel Mac-Callister with Reno?"

"Why?" Custer asked.

"Reno has never fought the Indians before. I have a feeling MacCallister has."

Custer looked at Falcon for a moment; then he nodded. "Tom's right," he said. "You'll probably be more helpful with Reno. Do you mind?"

"You are in command, General," Falcon said. "I go where you send me."

Falcon started to turn away, but Tom called out to him.

"Wait a moment, will you?"

Falcon stopped until Tom caught up with him.

"Tell Lorena," Tom started. "Tell her I think it would have worked."

"Tom, if you don't want this situation to get any more serious, shouldn't you tell her that yourself?"

Tom's response was a rather melancholy smile. He stuck his hand out in offer of a handshake. Falcon took it.

"When you see me at Fiddler's Green, the first drink is on me," Tom said.

Chapter Twenty-two

Reno's total force consisted of 134 officers and men and sixteen scouts. His battalion was just crossing the river when Falcon rejoined him. As the horses crossed, they stuck their muzzles down into the water, drinking briefly. Seeing the horses drink this water with obvious enjoyment, after having refused to drink the water back at Ash Creek, Falcon poured his brackish water out and refilled his canteen, dragging it through the water as he came across.

Once Reno reached the other side, he formed his troops in a battalion-front formation, then sat there for a long, silent moment.

"Custer did say he would support me, didn't he?" Reno asked Falcon.

"Yes," Falcon replied.

Reno looked down the long line of his soldiers. Not more than one in three had ever heard a shot fired in anger.

And though Reno had a sterling Civil War record, this would be his first engagement against the Indians.

The expressions on the faces of the men ranged from eagerness to determined to apprehensive to the verge of panic, but all sat their saddles, waiting for the order to be given.

Reno raised his right hand high, held it for a moment, then brought it down sharply.

"Charge!" he yelled.

They galloped, in battalion-front, galloping down the valley at a pace that was faster than many of the younger soldiers had ever ridden a horse. Ahead of each company within the battalion front, rode the commanding officer of that company, along with the trumpeter and guidon bearer.

The trumpeters had been forced to be quiet for the last two days. But now they blared out the clarion call of charge, each call louder than the other as they competed, not only against each other, but also against the drumming sound of the hoofbeats of well over one hundred galloping horses.

Ahead of them, Falcon saw warriors coming out of the village, afoot and on horseback, preparing to meet the charge. But instead of closing the distance toward the charging soldiers, they began riding back and forth, raising a great cloud of dust. As Falcon saw this, he realized the dust wasn't incidental. They were raising the dust cloud on purpose. They were trying to mask something.

Squinting his eyes, Falcon peered through the dust and as he did so, he saw a small ravine in which hundreds of warriors were waiting for them.

"Reno!" Falcon shouted, pointing. "Look there!"

"Battalion, halt!" Reno shouted, holding his hand up.

"Major, no, we can't halt here!" Falcon said. "We have to carry through the attack!"

One soldier, unable to control his horse, shouted in fear as his mount dashed ahead of the others, heading straight for the Indians.

"George! George, get back here!" some of the other soldiers called, but try though he did, the cavalryman couldn't bring his horse around.

As he came even with the Indians, several leaped out of the ravine and ran toward him. He was knocked off the horse. Then the Indians gathered around him, then began clubbing him. His panicked cries ended instantly.

"Dismount!" Reno said. "Horse holders, retire to the timber over there. The rest of you, form a skirmish line!" By doing that, Reno had immediately reduced the strength of his force by one fourth. And the soldiers remaining, no more than about eighty, could stand no closer than about ten feet apart.

Falcon dismounted with the others, and stood alongside Dorman as they waited.

"I don't think we should'a stopped," Dorman said.

"No, we shouldn't have," Falcon agreed. "We're on the defensive now. A cavalry unit should never be on the defensive."

Some of the soldiers began firing, even though the Indians were too far out of range for the shooting to be effective.

"Stop shooting!" some of the sergeants yelled. "You're just wasting ammunition!"

Hundreds of Indians started rushing toward the little thin line of defenders, the roar of their weapons interspersed with their war whoops and shouts. The soldiers were returning fire as rapidly as possible, but as they were using single-shot weapons, they had to extract the empty shell casings and replace them with new cartridges between each shot. To facilitate this, most were holding extra rounds in their hands, and sometimes as they tried to load, they would drop the shells, then have to bend over to search frantically for them on the ground. A few were clawing desperately to extract the empty shell casings from the chambers.

Reno shouted over to Falcon. "What do you think of this?"

"I suggest we get into those trees," Falcon said, pointing to a thicket about sixty feet to their left.

"I agree," Reno called back. He was about to give the order to mount, when a bullet hit Bloody Knife right between the eyes. Blood, and a bit of Bloody Knife's brain detritus, flew into Reno's face, and because his mouth was open preparatory to giving the command, some of it went into his mouth.

"Ahhh!" Reno shouted in revulsion. He began spitting. "Mount!" he shouted.

The order to mount was spread down the line, and the horse holders brought up the horses.

"Dismount!" Reno ordered, even as he was mounting his own horse.

Some of the soldiers were mounting in response to his first order; then some began to dismount in response to his second order.

"Reno is panicked," Dorman said. "He needs to—uhnn!"

Dorman was hit in the stomach and he fell to the ground. Falcon knelt beside him.

"Get out of here, Falcon!" Dorman said.

"I'm not going to leave you here," Falcon said.

"Retreat!" Reno shouted, spurring his horse back toward the river. The others galloped after him.

"Go!" Dorman said. "Get out of here!"

"If I get you on your horse, do you think you can hold on?" Falcon asked.

By now the bullets were whistling by as the Indians continued to advance. They were now within one hundred yards.

"I can try," Dorman said.

There was only one horse left, but Falcon managed to grab its reins, and he lifted Dorman into the saddle, then slapped the horse on its rump. The horse started toward the river, but got no more than about ten feet when Dorman was hit a second time. Dorman stayed in the saddle for another fifty feet or so, then fell. The horse, riderless now, continued to gallop away, leaving Dorman on the ground and Falcon afoot.

As the Indians swooped down on Falcon, he pulled his pistol and shot two of them. The others swerved around him and continued on toward the retreating soldiers.

Falcon's first thought was to run toward the river, but he knew that in order to do so, he would have to run right through the middle of the attacking Indians. That left him no choice but to run into the little thicket that had anchored the left side of Reno's original skirmish line.

"MacCallister, over here!" someone called, and running to the sound of the voice, Falcon jumped down into a shallow depression. There, he saw Lieutenant DeRudio and one of the sergeants.

"Is Dorman dead?" DeRudio asked.

"I don't know," MacCallister admitted. "But right now it's too hot out there to check it out."

"Colonel MacCallister, I've never met you, I'm Sergeant Tom O'Neil," the sergeant said, sticking out his hand.

Falcon chuckled as he took the sergeant's hand.

"What's so funny?" DeRudio asked.

"I don't know. Here we are, the sergeant and I, shaking hands like we were just meeting on a downtown street in Denver," Falcon replied. "It just strikes me as funny."

O'Neil laughed as well. "Yeah," he said. "I see what you mean."

The sound of gunfire continued to come from the river, rolling back across the half mile or so of flat ground between Falcon and the river.

Falcon could see the Indians riding back and forth on the bank, pouring fire into the retreating soldiers. Benny Hodgson's horse was shot from under him, and the young lieutenant leaped into the water. One of the soldiers came back and extended the stirrup of his horse to Hodgson and, by holding onto the stirrup, Hodgson was pulled quickly across the stream.

"Good man," Falcon said, talking about the trooper who had come back for Hodgson. But when they reached the other side and Hodgson let go of the stirrup and tried to climb up out of the creek, he was shot.

"Damn," DeRudio said. "They got Benny."

The Indians continued to ride up and down the bank of the river, but at that precise moment, Benteen arrived with his troops and they immediately joined into the battle, providing enough additional firepower to keep the Indians from crossing the river.

The warriors, frustrated because they were unable to cross the river, rode back and forth on this side, sometimes firing across at Reno's troops, and sometimes just galloping up and down shouting and screaming. With the Indians keeping Reno, Benteen, and their men penned down, several Indian women began streaming out of the village. As they came across their own dead, and Falcon was surprise at how many of the Indians had been killed, they knelt beside them, screaming and crying.

Then, they turned their fury toward the dead soldiers, stripping them and mutilating them. They seemed to have a particular hatred for Dorman and they stripped him, bashed in his head, carved out his heart, and cut off his privates.

"I hope he was dead when they started in on him," O'Neil said.

"He must have been," DeRudio said. "He didn't make a sound."

"He wouldn't have anyway," Falcon said.

Falcon lay in the little ravine with the others for the rest of the day.

"What if they come after us?" O'Neil asked. "We sure can't hold them off."

"No, but if they do, we will kill as many of the heathen devils as we can," DeRudio said.

"Find a couple more positions," Falcon suggested. "If they come toward us, fire, then move, and fire, then move, and fire again. Maybe we can make them think there are more of us here."

"Good idea," DeRudio said. "Let's look around, pick out second and third positions."

The carefully conceived plan wasn't needed, becaise darkness moved in and the river could no longer be seen.

"If we are ever going to get out of here, now is the time," Falcon said.

"I agree, "DeRudio said.

It was slightly overcast, and the moon was but a thin crescent, so when they moved out of the thicket, they were able to use the darkness to cover their movement. They couldn't see the river from there, but they were able to find their way easily by following the trail left by dead bodies: Indians, soldiers, and horses.

"DeRudio, there's a party of Indians coming toward us," Falcon whispered.

"Get down," DeRudio ordered.

"No, wait," Falcon said. "There are only eight of them, and if they do come toward us, we'll have the advantage, because I don't think they see us. Stop moving, pull your pistols, and wait."

Following Falcon's suggestion, the three men held their pistols at ready, but they weren't needed. The Indians veered away before they reached them.

Once the Indians disappeared into the night, the three men continued their approach to the river.

"O'Neil, climb into the water," DeRudio said. "See how deep it is."

"Give me your hand and hang on to me as you go in," Falcon said.

O'Neil got into the water, but it was neck deep there, and the current was so swift that it nearly swept the sergeant off his feet. Falcon pulled him out.

"It wasn't this deep where we rode across," DeRudio said. "We can't cross here."

"Wait," O'Neil said. "Lieutenant, I've got to have a drink of water. My throat is so dry I'm dying."

"Good idea," DeRudio said, and he and O'Neil lay down to drink from the water. Falcon, who had a full canteen, drank from it, and kept watch while the others slaked their own thirst.

Moving downstream, they found a place where they could cross and, plunging into the water, they worked their way to the other side. But when they came ashore, they discovered they were on an island, and, in the dim glow of moonlight, saw that the other side was a high, steep bluff that would be impossible to climb.

"Now what?" DeRudio asked in frustration.

"We're on an island," Falcon said. "I think that means we'll be safe for the night. Let's wait until it lightens up enough to see what we are doing. And to let the troops see us," he added. "I wouldn't want to escape the Indians, only to be shot by our own men."

"Good point," DeRudio said.

The three men waited through the night. Then, in the lighter gray of predawn, they saw a body of men riding down the bank on the opposite side. They were in uniform and the one in front was wearing a buckskin jacket.

"That's our men!" O'Neil shouted.

"Yes, that's Tom Custer," DeRudio said. "Tom!" he called. "Tom Custer! Over here!"

The riders stopped and looked toward O'Neil's voice. Then, suddenly they all began shooting, the bullets frying the air and cutting through the bushes. They were Sioux, wearing uniforms they had stripped from dead soldiers.

Falcon knew, at that moment, that Tom Custer was dead, and the fact that some Indian was wearing his tunic probably meant that General Custer was dead as well, for he would never have abandoned his brother.

None of the bullets fired by the Indians hit either Falcon, O'Neil, or DeRudio, and fortunately, none of the Indians came into the water after them.

The three men ran to the other side of the island, stooping over so low that they were concealed by the grass. But just as they reached the other side, they ran into a party of six mounted Indians. The sudden appearance of Falcon and the other two startled the Indian ponies, and they reared and bucked, causing two of the Indians to fall off. Those Indians ran toward the river. The other Indians fired, but because their horses were milling about, their shooting was inaccurate. Falcon, DeRudio, and O'Neil opened up on them. Falcon got two, DeRudio and O'Neil got one each.

"If we're going to go, we need to go now!" Falcon shouted, and leading the way, he plunged into the river and worked his way to the far bank with O'Neil and DeRudio behind him.

"Who goes there?" a voice called, when they reached the other side.

"Lieutenant DeRudio, Sergeant O'Neil, and Colonel MacCallister," DeRudio called.

"MacCallister, it's me, Varnum. This way," another voice called.

Going toward Varnum, the three were once again reunited with the rest of the battalion.*

---

*DeRudio and O'Neil were not actually reunited with Reno until the second night.

June 26, 1876
Reno's redoubt

Until noon, the Sioux tried to take Reno's position, but they were beaten back with heavy losses every time. During the fighting, Falcon and Benteen moved back and forth along the line, exposing themselves to Indian fire while inspiring the troops and, when necessary, supplying a little addition firepower on their own.

Reno had taken up a position behind a breastwork constructed from some of the packs. Once, he called out to Falcon.

"I'm convinced that Custer has gone on to effect his juncture with Terry," Reno said when Falcon joined him. "He has abandoned us to our fate."

"I'm not so sure of that," Falcon said. "It could be that he is like us, surrounded and unable to break out."

Falcon didn't share with Benteen his suspicion that, not only was Custer's battalion surrounded, but that Custer himself might be dead.

"You saw what happened when Weir tried to go to him. He was pushed back," Falcon said.

"Yes, I saw. But I do think Custer has joined with Terry."

"If so, that would be a good thing," Falcon said. "The combined troops could come to our relief."

"Why didn't Custer support me as he said he would?"

"Only he can answer that."

"I think we should leave," Reno said.

"Leave? We can't leave. For one thing, we have too many wounded. They would slow us down."

"We can leave our wounded," Reno said. "I don't want to do it, but we may have to sacrifice the few to save the many."

"Reno, you don't mean that," Falcon said.

Reno took off his hat and ran his hand through his hair, then sighing, he pinched his nose.

"No," he said. "I don't mean that. I don't know what got into me for saying that. I'm sorry, please forgive me."

Falcon put his hand on Reno's shoulder. "There is nothing to forgive," he said. "It has been a rough twenty-four hours."

"Major!" someone shouted. "Look!"

Looking in the direction pointed to by the trooper, Falcon saw that the Indians had set fire to the prairie grass.

"God in Heaven, they are going to burn us out!" one of the troopers shouted in fear.

"No they ain't, Johnny," another soldier said. "As long as that fire is on the other side of the river from us, it can't hurt us."

"Oh, yeah, I guess you are right," Johnny said, his voice showing his relief. "But what the hell are they doing?"

It soon became evident what the Indians were doing, because, in addition to the smoke, they also started the women and children milling about, dragging limbs behind them to stir up a large cloud of dust to mingle with the smoke. Within half an hour, the village, which had been easily seen before, was so obscured by smoke that the soldiers could see virtually nothing on the other side of the river.

"Be on the alert, men!" Benteen called out. "They may launch an attack from all the smoke and dust!"

For the next hour, the men were tense as they waited apprehensively for the upcoming attack.

By seven o'clock that evening, though, their worries eased somewhat when they saw thousands of Indians— warriors, squaws, and children—on horseback, being pulled by travois, and walking, along with many more ponies and dogs. The village was no more and the giant procession was leaving the site, winding its way up the slope on the far side of the valley, headed for the Bighorn Mountains.

"Major, the Indians are gone," Weir said. "We need to get through to Custer."

"No," Reno replied. "It is Custer's responsibility to get through to us. I have no orders suggesting I join him."

"Maybe not, but *you* do," Weir said to Benteen.

"What do you mean by that?" Benteen said.

"Trumpeter Martin said that he brought you a note from Custer. May I see it?"

"The note was for me, not you," Benteen said.

"May I see it?" Weir asked again.

With a sigh, Benteen pulled the note from his shirt pocket and handed it to Weir.

Benteen: Come on. Big Village. Be quick. Bring Packs.
W.W. Cooke.
   P.S. Bring Packs

Weir read the note aloud, then handed it back.

"We will wait here for Custer," Benteen said.

Reno stayed in position throughout the night, just to make certain the Indians were gone. The next morning, with good water now available and the packs brought up, the men had a decent breakfast of bacon, hard bread, and coffee. Not having heard from Custer throughout the day and the previous night, Benteen and Reno had now come around to Weir's idea, and were making plans to send at least one troop forward to make contact with Custer. Since Weir had tried unsuccessfully two days earlier, they agreed that his troop would be the one that would push forward.

"Major Reno, troops are coming!" one of the troopers shouted, pointing to a column of blue approaching from some distance.

"It has to be Custer," Reno said.

"Major, you might want to check this out," DeRudio said. "When we were on the island, we saw what we thought were soldiers, but it turned out to be Indians wearing uniforms they had taken off the dead."

"Yes," Reno replied. "Yes, you might be right. I need a couple of volunteers to ride out and see."

"I'll go," Falcon offered.

"So will I," Varnum added.

Falcon and Varnum mounted horses, then galloped out to meet the advancing party. It turned out to be General Terry.

"Where's Custer?" Terry asked.

"General, that's the same question we were about to ask you," Varnum replied.

Chapter Twenty-three

June 28, 1876
Custer battlefield

Approaching the battlefield, the first things Falcon saw were a lot of white objects lying on the ground. At first, he was confused as to what they were. Then he realized he was looking at bodies. Almost to a man, the soldiers had been stripped naked, and their bodies now lay bloating in the sun.

There was an eerie quiet among the men as they moved, thunderstruck, across the battlefield.

Jimmi Calhoun was found exactly where he should have been, in position behind his men, who were arrayed in proper skirmish formation.

Tom Custer was lying on his face. Tom Custer was the most mutilated of all. He had been scalped, his skull had been crushed by war clubs, his body bristled with dozens of arrows, and his heart had been cut out. Keogh had not been mutilated, nor had his crucifix been taken.

General Custer was found on the highest point of the

field, sitting, not lying, between two dead soldiers, his arm resting on top of one of the corpses. Other than the fact that he had been stripped naked, Custer's body was undisturbed.

Custer's command was dead—to the last man.

"I've found all the officers, but one," Weir said. "General Custer, Tom Custer, Keogh, Cooke, Calhoun, Reily, Crittenden, Smith, Porter, and Sturgis. Also young Boston Custer and Autie Reed."

"Who's missing?" Reno asked.

"Harrington. We haven't found him."

"Keep looking, he has to be here somewhere."

"There are a few horses still alive," Weir said. "But all are wounded."

"Shoot them," Reno ordered.

Weir relayed the orders to a couple of troopers, and they wandered around the battlefield, shooting the wounded horses. Then Falcon saw one of the horses wandering aimlessly around the battlefield. The horse was weak, his halter was hanging under his chin, and it was apparent he had been wounded several times.

"Wait!" Falcon called out. "Isn't that Comanche?"

"Yes, it is," Lieutenant Nowlan said. "Major, I ask you to spare Comanche."

"Don't be silly," Reno replied. "Why let the creature suffer?"

"Let me look at him."

Nowlan was the field quartermaster and he and Falcon went over to examine the horse. The horse, recognizing them, began to nuzzle them.

"Seven," Nowlan said to Falcon. "He has seven bullet wounds, but none of them are fatal."

"Do you think he can survive?" Falcon asked.

"Yes, I think he can."

"I think he can, too."

"I know I would certainly like to give him a chance," Nowlan said.

"Major Reno," Falcon called. "Let us bring the horse back. I think he can survive."

"For what purpose, MacCallister?" Reno replied, a little irritated by the request. "It's going to be all we can do to get the wounded troopers back. We have no time nor room for a horse."

"Major, think about it," Nowlan said. "If we can save Comanche, he will be the living representative of what happened here."

"Bring the horse back," General Terry said, speaking before Reno could answer.

"Thank you, sir," Nowlan said. He reached up and patted the horse on its face, then spoke soothingly into its ear. Comanche nodded his head, then followed Nowlan off the battlefield.

"Get them buried, and draw a map so we know where they are," General Terry ordered.

As the burial detail went about its sad and grisly task, Falcon returned to the site of Reno's Redoubt. There, he saw the men busily constructing litters for the wounded. Fifty-two men had been wounded in the two-day fight and there was but one doctor left alive to treat them. Dr. H.R. Porter was a civilian and Dr. De Wolf had remained with Reno's battalion when Custer divided his command. Dr. De Wolf had been killed trying to climb the bank when the battalion retreated from its first position, leaving Porter alone to deal with the wounded.

"We have quite a few miles to cover," Reno said. "I think we should construct travois. It would be faster and easier than having to carry them."

"Have you ever ridden on a travois, Major?" Falcon asked.

"No, I haven't. But I have certainly seen the Indians use them."

"A travois is fine if you are going over smooth, level ground," Falcon explained. "But if you are traveling over rough and rocky ground, like the ground we passed over on the way to this point—it can be a very rough ride. And for a wounded man, it can be extremely painful."

"All right," Reno said. "I see no need to subject these men to any further discomfort. We will use stretchers."

June 29, 1876
Far West *at the mouth of the Little Bighorn*

After a long, slow, and difficult march, the remnants of the Seventh Cavalry, carrying their wounded on stretchers, finally reached the steamboat *Far West*. But because General Terry had sent a dispatch rider ahead, by the time they arrived, preparations were already under way to receive the wounded.

Long grass had been pulled from the banks of the river and laid to a thickness of several inches on the deck of the boat. Heavy tarpaulins were spread over the grass to create one large mattress, and on that mattress, the wounded soldiers were carefully and gently laid in rows, leaving enough separation to allow Dr. Porter to move through them. Comanche was placed in the stern of the boat, and a couple of troopers were detailed to look after him.

As preparations were being made to get under way,

Major Reno and Captain Benteen asked Falcon to come to Reno's tent. Reno had already established himself as the new commander, having marked his tent with the regimental flag. He had also reissued sabers, and both he and Benteen were wearing them when Falcon answered the summons.

"Mr. MacCallister," Reno began.

It did not escape Falcon's notice that Reno had called him mister, instead of colonel.

"Captain Benteen and I have talked it over, and we think it would be better if you returned to Ft. Lincoln on the steamer."

"You are in command, Major," Falcon replied. "I'll do whatever you want."

Because Falcon had agreed so readily, no further explanation was necessary, but Reno felt that it was.

"It's just that—well, Custer always referred to you as a colonel, and while you are a lieutenant colonel in the Colorado Guard, you have no authority or military standing within the Seventh Cavalry," Reno said.

"Nor have I ever assumed as much," Falcon replied.

"I'm not saying you have," Reno said. "But many of the men heard Custer referring to you as a colonel and they might not understand the nuances. We have been through a very difficult campaign. I cannot afford to have the troopers confused as to who is in command."

"What the major is saying is, he feels his authority would be threatened by your presence," Benteen said. "If you are on the boat, that won't be a problem."

"I understand," Falcon said. "Of course, I will be more than pleased to return on the steamer."

"And perhaps you could do something else for me," Benteen said. He took an envelope from his pocket. "In going through the mail, I found this letter from General Custer to Mrs. Custer. It is going to be very difficult for her to receive this letter after her husband is already dead. You know her—perhaps it would be easier for her to get it from you."

"Yes, I think it might be easier for her," Falcon agreed. "That is very thoughtful of you, Captain."

"I think it is well known that I did not like Custer," Benteen said. "But I hold no animosity toward his widow."

Falcon accepted the letter; then, with a nod toward the two officers, he left the headquarters tent to look up Lieutenant Varnum. He found Varnum overseeing the reshoeing of one of the horses.

"I'm going back on the boat," Falcon said.

"I'm not surprised," Varnum replied. "I overheard Reno and Benteen talking about it." He chuckled. "I wish they felt as threatened by me. I wouldn't mind an easy ride back on the boat."

June 30, 1876
On board the Far West

Dawn had just broken when Captain Grant Marsh gave the order to cast off the lines. Falcon overheard General Terry tell Marsh to use every skill at his command to make the trip back to Ft. Lincoln as fast as was humanly possible.

The boat was draped in black, and the flag was at half-staff as Captain Grant Marsh blew the whistle and started downstream. With steam pressure at the maximum, he pushed the boat over growths of water willows, around sandbars, and through dangerous rapids for fifty-three miles to the mouth of the Bighorn, where it emptied into the Yellowstone.

Late that afternoon, the boat reached the Yellowstone, where it had to lay over until late in the afternoon of July 3 in order to ferry Gibbon's command over to the opposite bank of the river. By this time, fourteen of the wounded men had recovered enough to be able to leave the boat and finish the journey with Gibbon's command.

At five o'clock, the ferrying duty was completed, and Marsh gave orders to push away and start downriver.

"Cap'n, seein' as it's soon goin' to be dark and we'll have to put in anyway, don't you think we'd be about as well off waitin' till mornin' to start out?" Ben Thompson asked. Thompson was Marsh's second in command.

"We aren't going to put in," Marsh replied. "We're going to run all through the night."

"Cap'n, we can't do that. There sandbars, islands, and such, to say nothin' of havin' to follow the channel," Thompson protested.

"The moon will be full tonight," Marsh replied. "It'll be bright enough if we pay attention. We can do it. I mean, look at these poor men we're taking back. We have to do it."

Captain Marsh and his other pilot, Dave Campbell, took turns at the wheel, working in four-hour shifts. Below, in the engine room, firemen disregarded fatigue and soreness as they fed wood until the boat was quivering with steam pressure that was high enough to keep the needle at the red mark in the gauge.

The boat raced downriver at twenty miles per hour, its whistle echoing and reechoing off the cliffs that framed the river. Sometimes, the *Far West* would hit a snag, or some other object, with such force that Falcon would have to grab onto something to keep from being thrown down.

At eleven o'clock on the night of July 4, the *Far West*

tied down at the wharf in Bismark, within sight of Ft. Lincoln. It had made a journey of one thousand miles in just fifty-four hours.

Falcon walked up to the wheelhouse where Marsh and Campbell were both sitting down on a cushioned bench.

"Captain Marsh, Mr. Campbell," Falcon said. "What the two of you have just done will go down in the history books to be remembered forever." He pointed to the deck, where already arrangements were being made to take the men off the boat and get them to a hospital. "These men owe you their lives, and America owes you its respect."

Marsh sighed. "That's all well and good, Falcon, but right now I would trade it all for a bunk and a pillow."

Chapter Twenty-four

Falcon was quiet for a moment, letting the impact of his story sink in.

"If I may," Libbie said, "I would like to take up where you left off and finish the story."

"Yes, please do," Zane Grey said.

"As you remember, the day before had been Independence Day, and we had a gala celebration on the post. The band played patriotic songs, fireworks were set off, and we had a dance, which, as the commander's wife, I attended, even though my heart was not in it, because as you know, I had the most terrible premonition throughout the entire time my dear husband was on the scout.

"As Falcon said, the *Far West* docked at Bismark at eleven o'clock on the night of July fourth. At the time, I was blissfully unaware of the fact, but I know now that at two a.m. on July the fifth, Captain McCaskell, who was then in command of the post, called in Dr. Middleton, the post surgeon, and his executive officer, Lieutenant Gurley, to tell them the terrible news."

July 5, 1876
Ft. Lincoln, Dakota Territory

It was seven a.m. and Libbie, her sister-in-law Maggie, and her houseguest Lorena were having breakfast when the maid told Libbie there was someone in the living room wanting to speak to her.

"Goodness," Libbie said, picking up the napkin and dabbing at her lips. "Who wants to talk to me at this hour?"

"No doubt some soldier's wife with a problem that she thinks only you can solve," Maggie said.

"Don't be that way, dear," Libbie said. "We are all in the same boat out here. Especially now."

"You're right," Maggie said. "I'm sorry."

Libbie smiled. "No need to apologize. I know you didn't mean anything hateful."

The smile was still on Libbie's lips as she stepped into the living room, but when she saw Captain McCaskell, Lieutenant Gurley, and Dr. Middleton, all standing together, the smile disappeared.

Libbie took a gasping breath and put her hand to her heart. She tried to speak, but the words stuck in her throat.

"Mrs. Custer," Captain McCaskell said. He cleared his throat and started again. "Mrs. Custer, I—uh—am sorry to have to tell you this."

"Oh," Libbie said, her face now twisting into an expression of horror. She put her hand over her mouth.

"Libbie, what is it?" Maggie said, coming into the living room then.

Libbie reached out and took Maggie by the hand, squeezing it tightly.

"Please, Captain," Libbie said. "Go on."

"I have a dispatch that I received from General Terry last night. It might be best if I just read the report.Clearing his throat again, he began to read.*

"It is my painful duty to report that on the 25th of June, a great disaster overtook General Custer and the troops under his command. At 12 o'clock of the 22nd he started with his whole regiment and a strong detachment of scouts and guides from the mouth of the Rosebud; proceeding up that river about twenty miles, he struck a very heavy Indian trail, which had previously been discovered, and pursuing it, found that it led, as it was supposed that it would lead, to the Little Bighorn River. Here he found a village of almost unlimited extent, and at once attacked it with that portion of his command which was immediately at hand. Major Reno, with three companies, A, G, and M, of the regiment, was sent into the valley of the stream at the point where the trail struck it. General Custer, with five companies, C, E, F, I, and L, attempted to enter about three miles lower down. Reno forded the river, charged down its left bank, and fought on foot until finally, completely overwhelmed by numbers, he was compelled to mount and recross the river and seek a refuge on the high bluffs which overlook its right bank. Just as he recrossed, Captain Benteen, who, with three companies, D, H, and K, was some two (2) miles to the left of Reno when the action commenced, but who had been ordered by

*Actual dispatch from General Terry.

General Custer to return, came to the river, and rightly concluding that it was useless for his force to attempt to renew the fight in the valley, he joined Reno on the bluffs. Captain McDougall with his company (B) was at first some distance in the rear with a train of pack mules. He also came up to Reno. Soon this united force was nearly surrounded by Indians, many of whom, armed with rifles, occupied positions which commanded the ground held by the cavalry, ground from which there was no escape. Rifle pits were dug, and the fight was maintained, though with heavy loss, from about half past 2 o'clock of the 25th till 6 o'clock of the 26th, when the Indians withdrew from the valley, taking with them their village. Of the movements of General Custer and the five companies under his immediate command, scarcely anything is known from those who witnessed them; for—"

Here, Captain McCaskell stopped reading for a moment and he looked up at Libbie.

"Please, Captain, continue," Libbie said in a small voice.

McCaskell cleared his throat again, then continued.

"No officer or soldier who accompanied him has yet been found alive. His trail from the point where Reno crossed the stream passes along and in the rear of the crest of the bluffs on the right bank for nearly or quite three miles; then it comes down to the bank of the river, but at once diverges from it, as if he had unsuccessfully attempted to cross; then turns upon itself, almost completing a circle, and closes. It is marked by the remains of his officers and men and the bodies of his horses, some of them strewn along

*the path, others heaped where halts appeared to have
been made. There is abundant evidence that a gallant
resistance was offered by the troops, but they were
beset on all sides by overpowering numbers. The
officers known to be killed are"*—again, McCaskell
looked up—*"General Custer; Captains Keogh, Yates,
and Custer; and Lieutenants Cooke, Smith, McIntosh,
Calhoun, Porter, Hodgson, Sturgis, and Reilly, of
the cavalry. Lieutenant Crittenden, of the Twelfth
Infantry, along with Acting Assistant Surgeon
D. E. Wolf, Lieutenant Harrington of the Cavalry, and
Assistant Surgeon Lord are missing. Captain Benteen
and Lieutenant Varnum of the cavalry are slightly
wounded. Mr. B. Custer, a brother, and Mr. Reed, a
nephew, of General Custer, were with him and were
killed. No other officers than those whom I have
named are among the killed, wounded, and missing."*

"Mrs. Custer, is there anything I can do for you?" Dr.
Middleton asked.

"Yes," Libbie said. "Would you hand me my shawl,
please? I have taken a chill."

The three men, all of whom were already sweating, for
the day had dawned quite warm, looked at each other.
Then, Lieutenant Gurley got the shawl and wrapped it
around her shoulders.

"If I can do anything," McCaskell said. Then, turning,
he, Dr. Middleton, and Lieutenant Gurley started to leave.

"Captain McCaskell!" Maggie called. "Is there no message from my husband for me?"

McCaskell looked at Maggie, wondering for a moment
if she did not understand what he had just told them.

"No, Mrs. Calhoun. I'm sorry. There are no messages."

Tears began streaming down Maggie's face. She ha just lost a husband, three brothers, and a nephew.

"Captain, wait," Libbie said. "There are many wive who will have to be informed. Please, let me go with you

Libbie followed Captain McCaskell and his notificatio team, first to the officers' quarters to inform their wives, the down to laundress row to inform the wives of the enliste men. She stood by as, one by one, they were told, offerin what solace she could, even as her own heart was broken.

She knew this was exactly what her husband would wan Or, would have wanted, if he was alive.

It was just after noon when Libbie returned to the con mandant's quarters. Mary had lunch prepared, but neithe Libbie, nor Maggie, nor even Lorena felt like eating.

Libbie looked around the house, at the furniture that sh and Custer had hauled all over the country, at the huntin trophies Custer had bagged, at the table where Custer sa to write his *Galaxy* articles, at the piano, and at the photo hanging from the picture rail: her favorite of Custer, an one of General Sheridan.

The home was large and comfortable, and in no plac she had ever been had she been more comfortable. But thi was the commandant's home, and Brevet General G.A Custer was no longer the commandant. She was no longe the commandant's wife, and, as a matter of fact, she wa no longer an army wife.

How cruel life was, she thought at that moment. Othe wives, upon learning of the untimely death of their hus band, would at least have the comfort of their home unt they recovered. She would not. As of this moment, Libbi Custer was not the resident of this house. She was merel a visitor, someone who would be forced to leave, not onl this house, but the entire army.

As Libbie was contemplating the terrible turn of fate that had befallen her, Falcon was shown in by Mary.

"Oh, Colonel MacCallister," Libbie said, standing and walking over to him. He embraced her, and held her for a long moment as she wept into his shoulder. Looking round, Falcon saw Lorena sitting in a chair near the wall.

"Where is Maggie?" Falcon asked Lorena.

"She has taken to her bed," Lorena answered. "This has been terribly hard on her, too."

"Yes, I imagine it has."

"Did—did you see Tom before—before this all happened?"

"Yes," Falcon said. "And he had a message for you."

"A message? What sort of message?"

"He said for me to tell you that he thought it might have worked."

Tears sprung anew to Lorena's eyes. "He said that?"

"Yes."

"I mean, he said it exactly that way? That he thought it might have worked?"

"Yes. I think Tom had a premonition. That was his way of wanting me to tell you that he loved you."

"Oh," Lorena said, and now the tears were coming harder. "Oh, thank you, Falcon. Thank you for telling me that."

"Libbie," Falcon said, lifting her head and looking at her. "I have the general's last letter for you, when you are up to reading it. Do you want it now?"

"Yes, oh, please, do give it to me now."

June 25, 1927
MacCallister, Colorado

Once more, Libbie lifted the handkerchief to her eyes and dabbed at the tears. By now, though, the handkerchief was soaked, and young Rosie brought a new, clean, and dry one to her.

"Thank you, darling," Libbie said. "Falcon, I have the letter that you brought me that terrible day. Would you like me to read it?"

"Yes, please do," Falcon said.

Libbie removed an envelope from her purse, then pulled out a well-worn and, obviously, often-read letter.

She began to read:

My darling, I have but a few moments to write as we start at twelve, and I have my hands full of preparations for the scout. Do not be anxious about me. You would be surprised how closely I obey your instructions about keeping with the column. I hope to have a good report to send you by the next mail. A success will start us all toward Lincoln.

I send you an extract from General Terry's official order, knowing how keenly you appreciate words of commendation and confidence in your dear Bo: "It is of course impossible to give you any definite instructions in regard to this movement, and, were it not impossible to do so, the Department Commander places too much confidence in your zeal, energy, and ability to impose on you precise orders which might hamper your action when nearly in contact with the enemy."

*Your devoted boy, Autie.**

*Actual letter, as recorded in *The Custer Story*, edited by Marguerite Merington.

Libbie looked up after finishing the letter, and even though it was over fifty years later, her eyes glistened with tears.

"I also have the last letter I wrote to him," she said. "And, as this letter didn't get there until it was too late, he never read it. Would you like to hear it as well?"

Falcon knew that she very much wanted to read it, and he nodded. "Yes," he said. "I would very much like to hear it."

Libbie put the letter from Custer back into her purse. Then, she removed a silk handkerchief and wiped her eyes before she took out the next envelope. Like the first letter she read, this one was well worn and often read. Pulling the letter from the envelope, she cleared her throat and began to read.

"My darling Bo, I feel so badly I was not on board the boat, but I might have found myself so conspicuous on the steamer if you had gone off on a scout.

"I cannot but feel the greatest apprehensions for you on this dangerous scout. Oh, Autie, if you return without bad news, the worst of the summer will be over.

"The papers told last night of a small skirmish between General Crook's Cavalry and the Indians. They called it a fight. The Indians were very bold. They don't seem afraid of anything.

"The Belknap case is again postponed. Of course that worries me. The prosecution is going to call you as a witness. Politicians will try to make something out of you for their own selfish ends. But I hear you say, 'Don't cross bridges till you come to them.'

"I am perfectly delighted with your 'Galaxy' War

article, but I wish you had not spoken for McClellan so freely. Still, I don't see how you could have consistently given your opinions of the War without giving him his just due. It finishes Mr. Chandler as a friend, I fear, and for that I am sorry as he can be a very tenacious enemy, and of late has been only a passive friend. I honestly think you would be better off with some policy, with such powerful enemies. A cautious wife is a great bore, isn't she, Autie?

"You improve every time you write. There is nothing like this McClellan article for smoothness of style. I have this month's Galaxy with the Yellowstone article. How fortunate you had left it with Mr. Sheldon. I am anxious about the one you sent by the Buford mail. The mail was dropped in the Yellowstone and they must have attempted to dry it before the fire, for all our letters are scorched. Maggie's to Jim had been re-enveloped at Buford.

"I think to ride as you do and write is wonderful. Nothing daunts you in your wish to improve. I wish your lines had fallen among literary friends. And yet, Autie, I wouldn't have you anything but a soldier.

"It is the hottest day of the season, yet cold chills are running up and down my back at your description of the Yellowstone fight. I am glad you gave Tom his due. Of course you appreciate his valor as a soldier, yet you do not want to be puffing your own family. Mother will be pleased for 'Tommie.' Your mention of him would satisfy the most exacting of mothers.

"I cannot but commend your commendation of General Stanley. To ignore injury and praise what is

praiseworthy is the highest form of nobility. I could not do it. My soul is too small to forgive.

"I know you have a gift for finding roads, but how nice of General Terry to acknowledge your skill and perseverance that way.

Maggie and Lorena are entertaining Dr. X and Mr. G in the parlor. I went in, for manners, but was too heavyhearted to stay. Mr. B called. He told me of Buttons' resignation because Grant treated him unfairly, but it was withheld till after the convention.

"The wildflowers are a revelation, almost the first sweet-scented I have ever known. The house is full of bouquets.

"With your bright future and the knowledge that you are positive use to your day and generation, do you not see that your life is precious on that account, and not only because an idolizing wife could not live without you?

"I shall go to bed and dream of my dear Bo. Libbie."

"As I said, he never got to read this letter," Libbie ex-lained as she was putting the letter back into the enve-ope. "It was returned to me unopened by"—she paused or a moment, then glanced over at Falcon—"you. You rought it back to me, didn't you? You brought this one to e the same time you brought Autie's letter to me."

Falcon nodded. "Yes," he said quietly.

Wiping her tears again, Libbie tried to smile. "I know it s foolish to cry after all these years."

"It isn't foolish at all," Falcon said.

Ibid.

"What did you do next, Mrs. Custer?" Rosie asked.

"May I answer that, Libbie?" Zane Grey asked.

Libbie smiled through her tears. "Yes, if you wish."

"Libbie Custer has become a very successful writer, writing not only about General Custer, but other books, as well as articles for newspapers and magazines. She writes about public affairs, is considered expert on art, the opera, and ballet. And she is a lecturer, too. She talks about her husband, also about the social and economic status of women.

"For someone who was left only with a widow's pension of thirty dollars per month, Libbie has overcome great odds because she is forceful and strong. She is also a very shrewd investor, who has become quite prosperous, and has traveled in England, Germany, Egypt, Turkey, China, and Japan.

"And," Zane Grey said, smiling, "I am proud to say that she is not only a fellow writer. She is my friend."

"Oh!" Rosie said, clapping her hands gleefully. "Oh, that is wonderful. But—"

"But what, dear?" Zane Grey asked.

"Whatever happened to the other lady? To Lorena?"

"I'm afraid I don't know," Zane Grey said.

"Oh, we kept in touch for a while," Libbie said. "Lorena returned to Washington and married an English diplomat. When his assignment to Washington was over, they moved to England."

"Does she live there now?"

"No, dear. She and her husband were coming to America for a visit. They were on the *Titanic*. Lorena survived, but her husband went down with the ship."

"Oh," Rosie said. "That's awful. She was in love with two men, and both of them died. I wonder where she is now?"

"She's in St. Louis, Missouri," Falcon said, without any further explanation.

Zane Grey saw that Rosie was about to ask Falcon about Lorena, and sensing that Falcon didn't want to talk about her, he asked a question of his own.

"Falcon, whatever happened to Clete Harris, Jim Garon, and Jay Bryans, the men who stole the Gatling guns? Did you ever run across them again?"

"Oh, yes," Falcon said. "I ran across them again."

Chapter Twenty-five

It had been a year since Clete Harris, Jim Garon, and Jay Bryans made good their escape from Montana, leaving just before the climactic battle. They had been able to take advantage of the fact that the Indians were preparing to meet Custer, and that the army was preparing to meet the Indians. They were unmolested as they left the territory.

After Potter escaped from the post stockade, he left Colorado and met with Harris and the others in Cheyenne, Wyoming. There, they divided the money, which turned out to be over five thousand dollars, then each went their own way.

High living during the year just past, to include gambling, liquor, and women, had taken all money. It had been Harris who'd gotten three of them together, with a plan that would, in his words, "make us rich again."

That was one week ago. Now the three were gathered in a thicket of willow trees, just outside the town of Green River, Wyoming. It was still early in the morning and from

there, they could not only see the town, they could hear th
sounds of a beginning day of commerce.

They watched some men as they hitched up a team o
mules to a freight wagon; they listened to the ring of
blacksmith's hammer as he worked a piece of steel, stil
red hot from the forge. They heard a couple of cows bray
ing to be milked, and from the Chinese laundry came th
singsong voices of the "Celestials" as they went abou
their daily labor.

"All right," Harris said. "Do both of you know exactl
what to do?"

"What's there to know?" Garon asked. "We ride into t
town, stop in front of the bank, go in, get the money, the
ride out."

"There's a little more to it than that," Harris said
"Garon, you stay outside with the horses. I want then
there when we come out—and I mean I want them there
If we have to leave fast and I see you ridin' off, I swear
will shoot you myself."

"I'll be there," Garon promised.

"Bryans, you go in with me. We won't shoot anyon
unless we have to, but if we have to, don't stand there wit
your thumb up your ass. If you hesitate, even for
moment, more'n likely you're the one that's goin' to win
up gettin' shot. Do you follow me?"

"Don't worry. I know what to do."

"All right, let's ride on into town, but let's not all go i
together. I'll go first. Garon, you wait five or ten minutes
then you come in. Bryans, you come in after that. We'
sort of meet in front of the bank. That way, nobody will se
us all together until it's too late for anyone to do anythin
about it. You boys ready?"

"I'm ready," Bryans said.

"Yeah," Garon said.

Harris swung up into the saddle, then looked down at the two. "All right, let's do it," he said.

Harris rode in first. He saw the proprietor of the meat market sweeping his front porch. A dog lay in the sun on the porch, so secure in his position that, even as the sweeper came toward him, he didn't move. Several kids were gathered in the yard of the school building while a teacher stood out front, watching over them. Two old men sat in rocking chairs on the porch in front of the general store.

Harris stopped in front of the apothecary, just across the street from the bank, dismounted, then lifted his horse's left forepaw, pretending to examine the shoe.

Looking up, he saw Bryans and Garon riding into town as well and, though they weren't exactly together, they were close enough that Harris thought they should be further separated. All three waited at various places up and down the street until the bank opened. As soon as someone inside the bank turned around the sign reading OPEN, the three men came together. Garon remained in his saddle. Harris and Bryans handed him their reins; then both men went inside the bank.

There were no customers yet, and the teller, who had just posted the OPEN sign, was walking around to the teller cage. He smiled at Harris and Bryans.

"Good morning, gentlemen, you are early this morning," he said.

"Yeah, well, you know what they say," Harris said. "The

early bird gets the worm." He pulled his pistol and pointed it at the teller. "Or in this case, the early bird gets the money."

"Oh, my!"

"Empty the safe," Harris said, waving his pistol.

Bryans went back to the door and turned the sign around so that, once again, it indicated the bank was closed.

The teller was so frightened that his hands were shaking visibly as he opened the safe. He took out a stack of bills and held them out toward Harris.

"Here, Harris, have him put the money in this bag," Bryans said, handing Harris a cloth bag.

"Bryans, you dumb bastard, you said my name," Harris replied irritably.

The teller had just finished filling the sack when a new customer came into the bank.

"Hey, Johnny, you forgot to turn the sign around," the customer said. "It says you are still closed. I turned it back for—" The customer stopped in mid-sentence when he realized what was going on.

"Bank robbery!" he shouted at the top of his voice. He turned to go back outside, but before he could get through the door, Bryans shot him in the back. He fell through the door, lying half inside the bank and half outside.

"Let's get out of here!" Harris growled.

With Harris clutching the now-filled sack of money, the two men ran out of the bank, stepping over the customer's body. The horses had been startled by the sound of the gunshot, and they were milling around in the street, making it difficult for Garon to control them.

"Garon, you get those horses under control now!" Harris shouted angrily.

After one more turn, Garon managed to quiet the horses. Then he held out the reins so Harris and Bryans could swing into the saddle. Once mounted, they slapped their legs against the sides of their animals, and the horses bolted down the street toward the edge of town.

By now, several of the townspeople had heard the gun-shot, and had seen the three men leave the bank at a gallop. Some of them were calling out: "Bank robbery! The bank is being robbed!"

"Shoot up the town!" Harris shouted to the others. "Keep their damn heads down!"

Without even looking, the three bank robbers began shooting. It had the desired effect, as those who had come out of the stores and buildings to see what was going on now rushed back inside.

Unharmed, the three men galloped out of town.

Nobody chased them, because everyone's attention had been drawn to the schoolyard.

There, two children and the schoolmarm lay dead.

When Falcon took the train to Green River, Wyoming, he carried with him a copy of the newspaper he had read two days earlier. The newspaper had the story of a bank robbery that had taken place in Green River a week earlier. Three men had robbed the bank, and the teller had heard all three names called. The names were Harris, Bryans, and Garon.

Falcon had not been specifically looking for the three men in the year since the Custer massacre; there had been other things to keep him occupied. But he hadn't forgotten about them, and when he heard the three names together, he knew this was them.

When he stepped down from the train, he saw a wanted poster attached to the front wall of the depot.

WANTED!
For Bank Robbery and Murder
Dead or Alive.
Harrison – Garon – Bryans

$500 for each man.

See Sheriff Mickey Dancer,
Green River, Wyoming Territory.

When Falcon pushed the door open to the sheriff's office a short time later, he saw two men playing checkers: one player inside a jail cell, the other sitting on a stool just outside the cell bars.

"Is Sheriff Dancer here?" Falcon asked.

"I'm Sheriff Dancer," the man on the stool outside the bars said.

"Ha! I got you!" the prisoner said. "Crown me."

"I'd like to crown you," the sheriff grumbled as he stacked a second checker on top of the prisoner's piece. After that, he turned to Falcon.

"What can I do for you?" he asked.

"I'm here to talk to you about Clete Harris, Jim Garon, and Jay Bryans," Falcon said.

"Clete, Jim, and Jay, huh? Those are their first names, are they?" Sheriff Dancer asked.

"Yes."

"Well, we never knew their first names. Nobody in town had ever seen any of 'em before. Only way we got their last names is because they were dumb enough to use them. How do you know them?"

"I've been looking for them for over a year."

"Are you a lawman?"

"No."

"A bounty hunter then?"

"No. This is personal."

"Personal, is it?"

"Yes."

"How personal?"

"These three men stole some guns that I was responsible for," Falcon said. "They sold those guns to the Sioux. The Sioux used those guns against Custer."

"You say you were responsible for the guns?"

"Yes," Falcon said, without going into further detail.

"How do you know they were used against Custer?"

"Because I was with Custer at his last fight."

"What?" Sheriff Dancer asked, surprised by Falcon's announcement.

"Actually, I was with Reno."

"Oh, yeah, forgot about the ones with Reno." The sheriff stroked his chin and studied Falcon for a moment; then he shrugged.

"Well, I can see how you might take somethin' like that just real personal. And when you get right down to it, I don't reckon it makes no never mind who finds 'em or why—long as the sons of bitches get what's comin' to 'em," Dancer said.

"Do you have any leads on them?" Falcon asked.

"I thought I did, but it didn't pan out. One of the freight wagon drivers said he thought he saw one of the men over in Bitter Creek. But when I wired the city marshal over there, he checked on it and came up empty. I figured maybe Harley did see him, but the fella had passed on through. Only, Harley has been back to Bitter Creek twice, and he claims to have seen him both times. Then, the other day, the stagecoach driver said he seen one of the men over there also."

"Did you get in touch with the marshal again?"

"Yeah, I did, and he said he would keep an eye out for them."

"You said the freight wagon driver's name was Harley?"

"Yeah, Harley Barnes. The stagecoach driver is Norman Case."

"Do you think they would talk to me?"

"I expect they would, though Case is more'n likely out on a run right now. But you can probably find Harley down at the freight office. Tell 'im I sent you."

"All right, thanks. And thanks for the information," Falcon said, starting for the door.

"Hold on a second," the sheriff called.

Falcon stopped, then turned back toward the marshal.

"I could make you a deputy, but that wouldn't give you any jurisdiction over there. What I can do, though, is give you this here warrant that Judge Feeler wrote out for me. I don't have any authority over there, but the judge does, so I reckon you could serve it as an officer of the court, so to speak."

The sheriff opened a drawer on his desk, pulled out a piece of paper, and handed it to Falcon. "Truth is, I don't know how legal that is, but it might give you some cover."

"I appreciate that, Sheriff," Falcon said.

"If you can bring the galoots back alive, I'd love to hang 'em," Sheriff Dancer said. "But if they are belly-down over their saddles, why, that won't bother me none at all either."

Falcon nodded, then went back outside and walked down to the freight office that was at the far end of the street.

"Harley Barnes? He's out back packing a wheel hub. He's a big fella and, more'n likely, he'll have grease up to his elbows," someone inside the office said.

There was a wagon out back, blocked up with the right front wheel removed. A rather large man was sitting on an upturned barrel, packing grease into the hub of the removed wheel.

"Would you be Harley Barnes?" Falcon asked.

"Yes, sir. Who might you be?"

"Falcon MacCallister."

A broad smile spread across Harley Barnes's face. "The Falcon MacCallister?" he asked. "I've heard of you, mister." Barnes extended his right hand, but when he saw it was filled with grease, he pulled it back, then rather sheepishly wiped it on his trousers. "What can I do for you?"

"I understand you saw one of the men who robbed the bank, over in Bitter Creek."

"Hell, I've seen all three of 'em over there," Harley said. "A couple of times."

"How do you know it was them?"

"Because I was sittin' in this very wagon, right out front, when they come gallopin' down the street, shootin' an' yellin' like fiends from hell. They passed right in front of me, no more'n ten, twelve feet away."

"Sheriff Dancer said the city marshal over in Bitter Creek says he hasn't seen them," Falcon said.

"Yeah, well, the marshal over in Bitter Creek is lyin', 'cause I seen him standin' right next to one of 'em in the saloon."

"Did you point it out to the marshal?"

"No," Barnes said. "They was takin' on like they was just real good friends. I figured he not only wouldn't believe me, it could be dangerous to even mention it."

"You may be right," Falcon said. "Mr. Barnes, I thank you for your information. I'm going to go over there and have a look around myself."

"What are you going to do if you find them?" Barnes asked.

"I'm going to kill them," Falcon said flatly. He turned to walk away, but Barnes called after him.

"Mr. MacCallister?"

"Yes?"

"Try the Yellow Dog Saloon."

Falcon touched the brim of his hat, then walked down to the depot to catch the next train to Bitter Creek.

Falcon was carrying a small grip with him when he stepped into the Yellow Dog Saloon after detraining in Bitter Creek. It was late enough in the day that the wagon wheel that hung over the saloon to support a dozen kerosene lanterns had been lowered. One of the employees of the saloon was busy lighting all the lanterns and, with the firing of each new lantern, some of the gloom was pushed away.

The saloon was doing a brisk business, and there were more people coming into the place even as Falcon stepped over to put his back to the wall while he surveyed the room. He stayed against the wall until all the lanterns were lit and the wagon wheel pulled back up and tied off. There was enough light now for him to scan the entire saloon, and looking around, he satisfied himself that none of the three men he was looking for were in there.

Feeling a little grubby from a couple of days on the train, he stepped up to the bar.

"Where can a man get a bath?" he asked the bartender.

"We got us a jim-dandy tub in a room in the back," the bartender answered. "It come all the way from St. Louis. It'll cost you twenty-five cents for water, ten cents if you want it heated, and fifteen cents more for a soap and towel."

"I've got my own soap and towel," Falcon said, holding up his grip. "But I'll take the water heated." He slapped a fifty-cent piece onto the bar. "And I'll have a beer while I'm waiting for the bath."

"All right," the bartender said. He took the money, drew a beer from the keg, then set it and the ten cents change down in front of Falcon. "I'll get someone to heat the water and fill the tub for you," he said.

"Thanks."

Falcon picked up the beer, then turned his back to the bar to look out over the clientele. He didn't see any of the men he was looking for, so he started looking for a card game—one that was honest and had a congenial attitude about it. Falcon enjoyed playing poker, but he didn't like playing if some of the players were too intense, or were gambling with money they couldn't afford to lose.

Also, he had learned that in a friendly game, players tended to talk more, and it was always a lot easier to get information from sociable conversation than it was by asking questions. There were three games going on, but only one of the three seemed to fill the bill, and at that game, every seat was taken.

"Your water is ready," the bartender said a few moments later."

"Thanks." Falcon drained the rest of his beer, then went into the back room, where he saw a large tub filled with water. Sticking his hand into the water, he ascertained that, while it wasn't hot, it was warm enough. And truth to tell, he was so in need of a bath that it didn't really make that much difference to him whether the water was hot or cold.

Half an hour later, feeling human again, he went back to the main room of the saloon and ordered a supper of ham and fried potatoes. Just as he was finishing his supper, a chair opened up at the game he wanted and he walked over to see if he could join them.

"You're welcome, mister," one of the players said, and the others seconded the invitation. He stuck his hand across the table. "The name is Charley Knox. I own the hardware store here. This is Beckworth, he owns the livery, and this is Zell. He runs the newspaper."

Falcon played three hands with them, winning one and losing two. It was always good to ease into the conversation, so he hadn't asked any questions and he hadn't picked up on any specific information. He was just trying to formulate how to get the information he needed when he overheard something from one of the other tables that caught his attention.

"I told Custer to take them Gatling guns," the man said. "I stood right there and told him that, just afore he took that last ride. But he didn't listen to me. No, sir, he didn't listen at all."

Falcon turned in his seat to get a look at the man who was talking.

"Don't pay no attention to him," one of the cardplayers at Falcon's table said. "He's told that story more'n a dozen times, and he changes it most ever' time."

"Yeah," one of the other players said. "It's surprisin' Stevens can even find anyone to listen to his stories anymore."

"What did you say his name was?" Falcon asked.

"Stevens."

Falcon shook his head. "It isn't Stevens."

"It isn't?"

"No, sir. His name is Clete Harris. He and two other men, Jim Garon and Jay Bryans, are wanted back in Green River for murder and robbery."

"Damn, I heard about that," Zell said. "I ran the story about it in my newspaper. I never put that with Stevens, though."

"I don't know, he may be right," Beckworth said. "You say there was three of them?"

"Yes," Falcon said.

"That sort of fits. Stevens, or whatever his real name is, runs with a couple other galoots, and they all three got to town at about the same time."

"Now that I think on it, they don't none of them work, far as I can tell. But they always seem to have money," Knox said. "And the thing is, they are great friends with Clayton."

"Who is Clayton?"

"He's the city marshal. That's funny. If these here galoots

are the ones you say they are, wonder why Clayton is so friendly with them?"

"Excuse me, gents," Falcon said. He stood up from the table, then walked over to the table where Harris was continuing with his story.

"I was right there with Custer when all the fightin' commenced. I seen him go down, last one to go down he was, 'cept for me."

"How'd you get away, Stevens?" one of the others at the table asked. "From what I heard, the Injuns kilt ever'one."

"Yeah, well, the Injuns didn't see me. What I done was, I rolled over into some real tall grass and I stayed there real quiet 'till them heathens was finished with their scalpin' and all."

"You are lying," Falcon said.

"What did you say to me, mister?"

"I said you are lying. And while I don't normally care whether a man lies or not, your lies are stealing honor from good men. And I won't allow that."

"You won't allow it?" Harris stood up so quickly that his chair fell over with a loud pop. He backed away from the table, staring menacingly at Falcon.

The others who had been sitting at the table with Harris got up and moved away quickly. The sound of the falling chair, plus their sudden action, alerted all the other customers in the saloon so that all conversation stopped, and everyone who perceived that they might find themselves in the line of fire moved away quickly. That caused other chairs to fall over and tables to squeal as they were pushed out of the way all around the room.

"That's right, I won't allow it. You're Clete Harris, aren't you?"

"What? No, my name is Bart Stevens."

"I know who you are, Harris, and you know who I am. You were the foreman of the jury that let Garon off. Later, you, Garon, Bryans, and Richland sold Gatling guns to the Indians."

"I don't know what you are talking about."

"What the hell, Stevens, or Harris, or whoever you are," one of the other men who had been sitting at Harris's table said. "You sold Gatling guns to Injuns? I spent some time in the army, mister. That's about as low as you can get."

"He's crazy," Harris said. "I don't know what he is talking about."

"I have a judge's warrant for your arrest," Falcon said. "Take your gun out, real slow, and drop it. We're going to go see the marshal."

"No need go anywhere to find me," a third voice said. "I'm here."

The town marshal had just come into the saloon, and when Falcon looked toward him, he and the marshal recognized each other at the same time.

"MacCallister!" the marshal shouted.

"Potter," Falcon said.

Graham Potter had been the civilian telegrapher back at Ft. Junction. It was Potter's telegram that set up operation in which Falcon's old friend, Sergeant Major O'Leary, and four others had been killed.

"I'm the law here, MacCallister. If there's any arrestin' to be done, I'll be doin' it. Boys, if you want to know the truth, this here is Falcon MacCallister," Potter said. "He was the commanding officer of the Colorado Home Guard, only he stole rifles and Gatling guns from his own regiment and sold them to the Indians. If there is arrestin' to be done, I'll be doin' it," he added.

"Not today, not ever," Falcon said. "You are the one who set it up so Harris could take the guns, so as far as I'm concerned, you are as guilty as Harris, Garon, and Bryans are. I intend to put you into your own jail until we can get the sheriff here."

"There's two of us, there's only one of you," Potter said

"That's all right. I've got enough bullets for both of you," Falcon's pistol was still in its holster.

"You're crazy if you think you can come into my town and start making wild claims like that."

"I would appreciate it, Potter, if you and Harris would both just take your guns out real slow."

Falcon was studying the expressions on the two men's faces. At the first confrontation, both Potter and Harris were tense, even frightened. But then a strange thing happened. Simultaneously, the tenseness left both their faces, and on Potter's face, the beginning of a small grin appeared.

"Well now, I don't plan to do that, MacCallister," Potter said.

Falcon cut a quick glance toward the bar and when he did, he saw in the mirror why Potter was grinning. Standing at the railing of the upstairs landing were Bryans and Garon. Both were pointing their pistols at Falcon.

Suddenly, Falcon launched himself to his left, pulling his pistol and diving to the floor as he did so. Turning onto his back, he slid for a few feet across the floor, even as the two fired at him. One of the bullets hit a glass on the table where Harris had been sitting, sending out shards of glass and a shower of whiskey. The other bullet dug into the floor where Falcon had been standing but a second earlier.

Falcon fired back two quick shots. He hit Bryans between the eyes, and the man fell back. Garon caught a bullet in his stomach and he fell forward, crashing through the railing, then doing a half flip as he fell on his back onto the piano below. The piano gave off a loud, discordant sound.

At that moment, Falcon felt the sting of a bullet nicking his left arm and, rolling back over, he shot Harris, who had just shot him. In the meantime, Potter ran around behind the bar and shot the bartender. Then, he grabbed the double-barrel shotgun behind the bar.

"You go to hell, MacCallister!" he shouted as he aimed the gun at Falcon.

Before he could pull the trigger, though, there was another shotgun blast from the far end of the bar and Potter spun around with blood and brain matter spewing from his head and splashing onto the mirror. Looking toward the second shotgun, Falcon saw the bartender, bleeding from the shoulder, holding a smoking double-barrel shotgun exactly like the one Potter had grabbed.

"You go to hell, you bastard! You didn't think I kept just one gun back here, did you?" the bartender muttered angrily.

June 25, 1927
MacCallister, Colorado

Falcon had walked back out to the front of his house with Zane Grey and Libbie Custer. He was standing alongside Zane Grey's Packard automobile.

"My friend," Zane Grey said. "That was quite a story. I do wish you would let me write it."

"I'd rather you not," Falcon said.

Zane Grey smiled. "Don't worry, I gave you my word that I wouldn't, and I won't." He chuckled. "Besides, even at your age now, I don't think I would want to cross you."

Falcon smiled as well. "At my age, I just depend upon the integrity of men who give me their word."

"Among men of good faith, that is all that is needed," Zane Grey said. "Well, Libbie, you were a little concerned about your schedule. It looks like we will have plenty of time to get you to the train."

"Yes," Libbie said. "And I'm so glad I came." Libbie smiled at Falcon, then embraced him. "You know, Falcon, after my Autie, there never was another man for me. But if there had been." She let the sentence hang. "Good-bye, my dear, old friend."

"Good-bye, Libbie," Falcon said.

Falcon walked back up onto the porch and stood there as the Packard drove away.

"Big Grandpa, what did Mrs. Custer mean when she said there had never been another man for her, but if there had been?" Rosie asked.

"She didn't mean anything by it, darlin'," Falcon said, putting his arm around his great-granddaughter's shoulder.

Rosie laughed. "You know what I think? I think she was flirting with you."

"Do you now?" Falcon asked, laughing as the two of them started back into the house.

Falcon began whistling "Garryowen."

AUTHOR'S NOTE

Listed below are the known names of the officers, surgeons, civilians, and soldiers who died with Lieutenant Colonel (Brevet Major General) George Armstrong Custer at the Battle of the Little Bighorn.

Those who died with Reno are not listed here.

Bvt. Maj. Gen'l. G. A. Custer

CAPTAINS
M. W. Keogh • G. W. Yates • T. W. Custer

LIEUTENANTS
W. W. Cooke • A. E. Smith •
Donald McIntosh • James Calhoun • J. E. Porter •
B. H. Hodgson • J. C. Sturgis • W. Van W. Reily •
J. J. Crittenden • H. M. Harrington

ASSISTANT SURGEONS
G. E. Lord • J. M. De Wolf

CIVILIANS
Mark Kellogg • Boston Custer • Autie Reed

SOLDIERS
W. H. Sharrow • Geo Eiseman • James Dalious •
Gustave Engle • J. E. Armstrong • James Nathersall •

Rich'd Rollins • Alpheus Stuart • Jnd Sullivan •
Ignatz Stungwitz • T. P. Sweetser • Ludwig St. John •
Rich'd Dorn • Garrett Van Allen • Jere Finley •
D. T. Warner • August Finckle • Henry Wyman •
T. J. Bucknell • Chas Vincent • Wm Kramer •
Pat'k Colden • Geo Howwell • Edw'd Housen •
Jnd Brightfield • Fred'k Hohmeyer • Christopher Criddle
• Rich'd Farrell • Henry Voss • Nathan Short •
Wm Moodie • John Thadus • G. B. Mask • W. B. Right •
Edwin Bobo • J. S. Ogden • H. E. French • W. B. James •
Jnd Foley • Thos Hagan • Dan'l Ryan • H. S. Mason •
Jnd King • G. G. Brown • F. E. Allan • A. H. Meyer •
Jnd Lewis • Thos McElroy • August Meyer •
C. A. Moonie • Fred'k Meier • W. H. Baker •
Edgar Phillips • Rob't Barth • Jnd Rauter • Owen Boyle
• Edw'd Rix • James Brogan • J. H. Russell •
Edw'd Conner • S. S. Shade • Jnd Darris • Jere Shea •
Wm Davis • Syker Henderson • James Garney •
Jnd Henderson • Anton Dohman • Andy Knect •
Timothy Donnally • H. T. Liddiard • Wm Gardiner •
Pat'k O'Connor • C. W. Hammon • Henry Shele •
Gustav Klein • Wm Smallwood • Herman Xnauth •
James Smith 1st • James Smith 2nd • W. L. Liemann •
Christian Madson • Benj Stafford • Joseph Monroe •
Cornelius Vansant • Sebastian Omling • Mich'l Kenney •
Pat'k Rudden • Fred'k Nursey • Rich'd Saunders •
J. N. Wilkinson • F. W. Siglous • Chas Coleman •
Geo Warren • Benj Brandon • Edw'd Botzer •
Benj Brandon • Edw'd Botzer • J. R. Manning •
Martin Considine • Thos Atcheson • James Martin •
Lucien Burnham • Otto Hagemann

THE EAGLES SERIES BY
WILLIAM W. JOHNSTONE